Reviews

"Your style is fast-paced, engrossing and addictive. It reminds me of Liane Moriarty's work, specifically her book, 'The Husbands Secret'. I thought your book was extremely powerful and emotive, I adore your style."
Ana Rodriguez, Author.

"I thought this book was downright brilliant. I was either constantly feeling shocked or heartbroken. The way you write is so powerful - I have never had books that makes me cry the way yours have. Can't wait for more."
Chloe, Bookstagrammer.

"I have just finished the book…oh my…where to start. Another roller coaster read. An absolutely beautiful, heartwarming, emotional book I absolutely loved it. We all have highs and lows in life and this book just captures that fact perfectly. Your books are amazing, and they bring out emotion which I love."
Lyn, Bookstagrammer.

"Wow, wow, wow! That was not what I was expecting at all. I thought I had shed all the tears during Reasonable Lies but clearly, I was mistaken. Beautiful writing as usual, you really are so talented."
Danielle, Bookstagrammer.

"I loved Sarah in Reasonable Lies, and now I love her even more. All in all, this was a beautiful read, and I cannot wait to read it again. Another 5-stars for a super talented author."
Abigail, Bookstagrammer.

"The best thing about your books is that there isn't really a 'traditional' ending and I love that about them."
Claire, Bookstagrammer.

"So, I absolutely loved this book!
I would love to sit here and list all the parts I loved the most, but I'd end up writing the whole book."
Alice, Bookstagrammer.

"Wow, you've done it yet again Traci. Another great book from T.A. Rosewood. Was good to hear Sarah's story after Reasonable Lies and I wasn't expecting that sort of storyline."
Anna, Bookstagrammer.

"I absolutely loved this one. It felt really personal, and the dedication after recent events is beautiful. Well done, you've smashed it again."
Heidi, Bookstagrammer.

"You have a true gift for writing."
Sandra, Bookstagrammer.

Secrets & Lies

T.A. ROSEWOOD

ISBN 978-1-80068-499-7
ASIN 1-80068-499-7

In Memory of Val.
Stepmother & Friend.
Missing you Eleventy-Four.

Secrets & Lies

To Karen,

Thanks for being on the tour!

[signature]

Prologue

Looking straight back into her eyes, Sarah began shaking, not with fear but with shock at the impending situation that was now upon her. She just wanted to get her caffeine fix with her usual double shot Americano coffee and get back to her man in the salon where he was patiently awaiting his flat white and millionaire shortbread.

Married just six months ago, this wasn't how things were meant to start for them as newly-weds. They'd had their fantastic honeymoon in Jamaica, bought their new home together and now, this normal daily trip to her favorite coffee shop, meant things were about to change, her life was about to get even more complex than she had ever imagined.

"You are Sarah Roberts, aren't you?" said the timid voice from behind the counter, leaning forward as she passed the takeaway containers and brown paper bag containing Sarah's usual large chocolate chip cookie and Tom's biscuit.

Spluttering back, "well, I was Roberts…" she paused, "I mean, yes I am but, I'm married now so no, but erm…"

"I knew it was you. Hi, I'm Kate...well, Katie," the girl shyly replied, seeing the confusion in Sarah's eyes as she glanced around the room, "I've been looking for you for months, can we talk?"

Sarah's heart began thumping hard in her chest, '*Katie? Shit, it can't be? It couldn't be Katie standing right here in front of her. Surely not. But it was, it was Katie,*' she thought to herself as she swiftly plucked up the courage to finally answer, "erm, no sorry, I…well, I have to get going, I've got to get back to work, my husband, he's waiting for me, sorry, I can't stop right now," she flustered all her words, picking up the cups and turning to walk away bumping into the next customer in line in a panic, "I'm so sorry, excuse me," she apologized.

"Sarah," the girl's voice remained strangely calm but slightly raising her tone, she called out, "Sarah, you forgot your biscuits," and waved the brown bag in the air in the hope that Sarah would come back.

Turning around to see the strawberry-blonde haired girl holding up the paper bag, Sarah just stared at her for what seemed like minutes, but she couldn't make her feet do anything. They were frozen on the spot and people were starting to stare at her and began asking if she had finished her turn in the queue, but their words sounded muffled. She had certainly finished, and she didn't want to return in a hurry. She didn't have any interest in returning towards the counter, even for the bag of goodies.

"I'm sorry…," Sarah apologized again as she bumped into another customer as she made her way out of the store, "excuse me, please, sorry, let me through, sorry, sorry," she continued as her feet finally led her to the doorway and out of the coffee shop in a sweat. She was walking as fast as her little kitten-heeled boots would allow, spilling the steaming hot coffee out of the top of the containers, and her mind began to race even more with question upon question, '*what had just happened, did it just happen? How had she found her and why had she found her, why now, what the hell was going on?*'

Nothing seemed to make sense and her head was full of everything but nothing. Dizzy, lightheaded, she felt sick and had a pounding ache in her chest from the panicked state she had got herself into. She needed to sit down before she made a complete fool of herself and fell in the street and what if Katie had followed her out, she couldn't faint in front of her, no, she couldn't do that. So, she quickly made her way to a side alley, slid down the wall, and crouched down breathing heavily, trying to calm down and make sense of what had just occurred.

Chapter One

If Sarah had known that this day would have come along so quickly, before she had expected it to, to be fair, before anyone close to Jane had expected it to, she would've told her best friend the truth. She would have confessed what she had done all those years ago to the one and only person who understood her more than anyone else in the world. But the reality now was that life had been taken away from her friend, and she regretted her hidden secret even more right now and today, she felt even worse and thought how she would never forgive herself for it. Not ever.

Her best friend, her most trusted and loyal pal, Jane, had passed away, taken well before her time, well before anyone her age should have died and from a horrid disease which had affected her wonderful family once before.

Sarah felt so lonely without her, like she'd lost part of

herself on that sad day, just before Christmas, but she had to be strong, she had to be there for the others that were left behind. The others being Jane's husband, the beautiful twins, and Jane's absolute gem of a mother, Janice; the mother Sarah had adopted for herself throughout the years since meeting Jane at primary school. This extremely special family who Sarah adored needed her now more than ever and she wouldn't fail them, especially at this heartbreaking time.

It was the day they had all been dreading since Jane's death. The day of the funeral had finally arrived. When they each had to face saying their last goodbyes to the amazingly brave person that was Jane Walden.

Sarah had helped Karl with every tiny detail, been there for the children, helping them to cope just a little bit more each day, keeping their sad faces smiling with her craziness and loving them. She spent all her spare time with Karl, trying to console him and keep him strong, sometimes sitting up till the small hours together, just to make sure he was okay, but, today, she felt weaker than normal and needed to let some of her own emotions out. She had been the rock for the Walden family and was determined that she was not going to lose it in front of them, so she locked herself in the downstairs toilet and just wept silently, for what seemed like an hour but, was only five minutes or so. She felt so fragile and slightly nauseous at the thought of having to lay her friend to rest but also knew that her best pal was at peace. She didn't have to put up with any more pain and the family didn't have to have the awful sad feelings for that wonderful lady. Sarah had to snap out of it to cope with today. She just had to.

She hated crying as it was, she hadn't cried like this since the day Jane told her the awful news that she was dying of breast cancer and there was nothing more the doctors could do for her. Sarah had not known how to deal with it at first, she had felt angry and confused, then sad and tearful, but had assigned herself as the bestest friend that Jane had needed during the following months and especially during the last few weeks of being alive.

Within six months, she had watched the decline of her best friend's health, her once gorgeous thick hair gradually thinning; having most of it, including her eyebrows, fall out, her tiny frail body which had once been so perfectly hourglass figured, become thin, just skin and bones in the end. Sarah had still loved her with all her heart and Jane knew that all along.

Today though, she felt as though her heart was going to be truly broken for the rest of her life and she didn't know how to cope with these awful heart shattering feelings inside of her. Her partner in crime, her other half, the Ginger to her Fred was gone and it felt so unfair.

She had to give herself a kick up the butt and sort her face out before facing Karl, the twins or anyone else for that matter, '*come on girl,*' she thought to herself as she glanced in the mirror splashing her face with cold water, '*sort it out woman, you've got this now.*'

Just as she wiped her face dry, there was a quiet tapping on the door, "Sarah my darling, it's time to go lovely,"

Janice's calming voice said and then asked, "Are you ok my dear?"

Sarah gave her head a final shake off and unlocked the door to see Janice with a fist full of tissues at the ready, "I'm sorry Janice, yes, I'm alright, I just needed a few quiet moments on my own, you know. I'm ok now though, let's go say goodbye." Sarah bravely put her arm around Janice's frail shoulders. This poor lady had lost her husband and now her daughter and she needed to look after her, not fall apart, especially today, she had to be brave and support this family as they had through all her ordeals in life so far.

They didn't need to say anything else, smiling at each other knowingly, Sarah locked her arm into Janice's and went to find Karl and the children who were watching the hearse arriving outside the house.

~

During the service in the crematorium, Karl had attempted to make a speech, his dedication to his wife, but was unable to finish it. The emotions just got too much for him and his knees suddenly crumbled, his hands trembling with pure heartache, so Sarah had helped him back to his seat and the celebrant had taken over, reading a few of the fondest memories of his wife for the next few minutes with a photo gallery being displayed on a large screen.

Sarah sat beside him, staring at the beautiful wicker coffin just feet away from her, listening to the special tune that had been chosen by Jane before her death. She felt mesmerized by it, and knowing her friend was inside there, soon to be gone forever, hurt like hell. Just as a fat tear trickled down her face, Cassie gently took hold of her hand. Sarah looked down at Jane's gorgeous daughter, her little flushed cheeks bearing small glassy tears that softly fell into her lap. Sarah wondered, in that split second as she gazed into the little girl's pained eyes, what would her own daughter have looked like? Would she have the dark piercing eyes of the father who didn't want anything to do with her or, would she have Sarah's blue eyes and strawberry blonde hair, would it now be dark and curly, like his? She had often thought about those tiny details, but today wasn't the right time to be having these thoughts, surely, she shouldn't. This wasn't the time to think about her own sordid secrets, her hidden life that only her and a few family members had ever known about, (two of whom were not living anymore now), but she just couldn't help it. For some reason today, she felt even more guilty for handing over that beautiful little bundle of pinkness all those years ago. Why had she been talked into it and why hadn't she spoken up and kept her instead? She could've been here to help her through this ordeal, she could have experienced the love and friendship that Jane had given her over all the years, and she knew deep down within her heart that Jane would have loved her so much and ultimately, forgiven Sarah for what she had done.

Shaking the painful thoughts from her mind and squeezing Cassie's cold hand, just a little reassuringly, she looked back up as the deep red, crematorium curtains closed around the white wicker basket coffin and that was it, Jane was gone, Sarah would be forever without her best friend now and it hurt like crazy. Like the hurt she had to undertake when she lost her parents, and she didn't want to feel this agony anymore.

The final tune played as a video image gallery of Jane began playing again on the screens on the walls in front of them. The photographs had everyone feeling even more love for Jane and as the less serious poses came to view, some fond laughter and joy. The fancy dress parties, the memorable hen-do, the crazy faces that Sarah and Karl had drawn on Jane's very large pregnant tummy. Memories flooded back to each person in the room for various reasons and they celebrated the life now lost with heartfelt grief and fondness.

'Goodbye' by The Spice Girls was coming to an end, there wasn't a dry eye in the whole room and Karl looked utterly broken into a billion pieces or more. Sarah reached her arm across to him and rubbed his shoulder, he glanced toward her, ashen white, and tears slowly but silently rolled down his pale cheeks. She watched as Robbie tipped his cap down further to hide his tearful eyes. She hoped so much that she was going to be able to help them all grieve and keep Karl strong. She had to help him, and the kids deal with this ordeal, in honor of Jane. She would do this for her.

The service seemed to be over no sooner than it had begun. The family and Sarah all held hands as the congregation made their way out into the gardens to admire the huge array of flower displays laid down by her small silver name plaque. It was like a bed of red roses; Jane's favorite flower and it was an incredible sight. A few people had also bought red heart-shaped balloons to accompany the bunches of flowers, it was very touching. People gathered and spent time talking about their friendships and relationships with Jane.

Sarah noticed that Karl had sat down on a nearby bench, his legs just weren't feeling strong enough to keep him standing upright now, so she made her way over to him leaving Cassie with Janice.

"Hey, how are you doing?" she asked, holding his trembling hands. He was fiddling and twisting his wedding ring round and round anxiously staring blankly into space.

"Hey...I don't know Sarah. I just don't know how to feel or how to act today, I feel, well...I just feel...empty, you know, just so empty without her," he said quietly.

"I'm here for you Karl, you know that right?" she looked into his glazed and bloodshot, red, eyes as she crouched down in front of him.

He just nodded back, looking over to his two children who were standing beside their grandmother heads down and being comforted in her arms, "How am I going to help those two with this when I don't know how to cope with it myself?" he said.

"You will Karl, you just will and I'm here for as long as you want me to be, for you, the kids, and Janice, I promise, I'm not going anywhere, okay?" Sarah wiped another tear from his face as he stared forward to the children.

This was so difficult to handle, so sad and so unfair but she wouldn't let her friend down, she would look after them no matter what she had to do, even if it meant changing her whole life and her own future.

Sarah watched on as Karl finally stood up and tried to make his way through the crowd, but everyone wanted to speak to him, everyone wanted to let him know how wonderful Jane had been to them and it was very touching. And they weren't wrong. Not by any means. She was, and always would be, the most wonderful person, the bestest friend anyone could have imagined having in their lives and one that would never be forgotten.

With all the formalities over, the day ended with a small gathering back at the house. Sarah and Janice helped to clear up while Karl spent some time with the children upstairs making sure they were okay. Robbie was trying to lose himself in his computer games and Cassie knew only that she needed to paint, draw, express her feelings that way so Karl let them do whatever they needed to do.

"I'm going to get off now Janice, do you want a lift home?" asked Sarah, grabbing her jacket which was hung on the staircase.

"No dear, I'm staying here tonight, just in case, well, you know, in case these darlings want or need anything this evening or tomorrow. Karl has not had a scrap of food all day, he wouldn't even have any breakfast this morning. I do worry about him, you know, so I'm going to make him something, just some pasta or maybe an omelet. He has to keep his strength up, doesn't he now, my dear, he needs to keep strong for those little ones upstairs?"

"Yes, that's a great idea, Janice, do you want me to stay too? I can kip on the sofa so you can have the spare room, it's a bit more comfortable there?"

"No, no my dear, we will be fine. I'll just potter in the kitchen and make sure he eats something, there's a bit of ironing that needs to be done too so I'll set to doing that in a little while, just as soon as the washing up is done and put away," she replied as she started busying herself with some drying up of dishes and plates.

Sarah looked on with great sadness but total respect. She knew that Janice was breaking inside but she was such a resilient and strong woman, just like Jane had been and she loved her so much, "Okay, text me or ring me if you do need me to come back, at any time too, I don't mind alright? I just have a bit of admin work to catch up on for the salon, but it can wait if you need me here. I'll come straight back and do it in the kitchen."

"No dear, go on my darling, you get to your work, we can't have you falling behind with that now, can we? What would Jane say, you know how she loved getting all that admin malarkey organised and in check. I'll call you if needed, my dear," Sarah kissed her cheek before leaving Janice busying herself around the room.

The fresh air hit her face as she stepped out the front door, it was mid-January and bitterly cold now the sun had gone down. Janice was right, Jane loved all things admin and she had to keep it organised but maybe tonight, she could leave it be. She needed to get her head down for a few hours. She was exhausted and after sitting down with a quick glass of wine back at home, she had quickly dozed off on her small couch with the admin staring at her from the coffee table.

Chapter Two

A few days after the funeral, Sarah remembered the important job Jane had asked her to carry out. She had to collect the special letters that had been written and hidden in the shed at the cemetery. Sarah was supposed to give each one out to the rest of the family with the instruction of only doing so after the funeral. Jane had spent so much time there in her last year of life visiting and chatting to her father who was also buried there, knowing that she was dying too. Most days, it was because she was nearing the end of her life and as she wasn't working anymore, she had to go somewhere that Karl wouldn't think to look for her or where she may get spotted. It was one of Jane's last wishes and the shed had seemed the perfect place to hide them until such times that they were needed. It had been her safe haven during the final months especially.

This favour was going to turn out to be a day that would change Sarah's future and shape a whole new chapter in her life.

When she arrived at the cemetery later that morning, she noticed him sitting on the bench, the exact same place where they had briefly met all those weeks ago when Jane was still alive and very excited about finally setting Sarah up with her newfound friend, James.

"Hi...Tom, isn't it?" she asked quietly as she glanced round to see his face. His handsome face at that.

Slightly startled, Tom replied, "Oh. Hi, yes...erm...Sarah, isn't it?" he said nervously, hoping he hadn't got her name wrong.

Their first meeting had been so brief, but something had clicked between them quite unknowingly for Sarah at the time as she had been so preoccupied with her mission of caring and looking after Jane that day. The disappointment of the blind date that Jane had arranged not turning up had been more important than getting another date hooked up. They had made an impact on each other though that's for certain, and today, this was even more clear, as they both seemed to have a slight blush to their cheeks at this new meeting moment.

"Yes, that's right, we met here a few weeks back. I was visiting here with my friend, Jane, she used to spend quite a bit of time here before she died."

"I remember. It was my little brother's birthday, wasn't it?" he nodded and pointed towards another gravestone, "So, hello again, I err..." he continued, his words stumbling awkwardly as he stood up to greet her, taking her hand and landing a gentle kiss on it, "I have been meaning to call you actually."

"Oh, really?" she responded in surprise as they sat down on the bench.

"Yes, I got your number from the graphics on your car that day, but...well, I just haven't yet plucked up the courage to ring or text you," he continued, "Silly really, at my age, hey, feeling nervous about ringing a lady?"

Sarah's cheeks flushed a little again and she chuckled back, "Did you want to book some beauty treatments for yourself or someone else, someone special? We do gift vouchers now. I've got some leaflets in the car that I can sort out for you if you like," she gestured toward the car park, "We have various men's treatments available too actually," she replied, assuming that was the reason for taking down her number.

"Erm, no, it wasn't any of that, I think I'm beyond help in the beauty department if I'm honest," he laughed back, "Look, tell me if this is a bit too forward but, I just wondered if you might like to go for a coffee with me sometime or lunch maybe?" He smiled at her and continued, "I wanted to ask you that day we met, you know, when you came to the car with my photo I left behind with your friend, but, well I got the impression you were both a bit busy with something else and didn't want to intrude or seem rude and annoying, or, oh I don't know, a bit full on?"

Sarah's cheeks became even more reddened,

remembering that she had quite fancied him that day especially after he'd kissed her hand so romantically and when they had chatted very briefly in the car park, but she hadn't wanted to act on it either due to her duties with Jane, "erm, yes, that would be lovely actually, let me just check my diary for this week," she replied nervously as she began to rummage through her bag, finding her phone. She always had to put appointments into her phone calendar as soon as she could, she hated bits of paper with notes on. She was a hundred percent digital girl.

"Awesome. I've just not had the courage to ring or text, as I said, but, hey, look at us meeting by chance today and that means you've saved me finally plucking up the balls to call," he laughed, fidgeting slightly beside her, "are you on your own today?" he asked, looking over to her car, which was parked just outside the grounds, near to the entrance gates.

"Yes, I've just come to collect something out of the shed for Jane. She, well, she passed away the week before Christmas," Sarah's head hung down slightly as she held back tears. It still hurt so much to utter those words out loud to anyone and if she was honest with herself, it still didn't feel real, and she wished she would wake up and have Jane back with her. She so wished for that to happen more than anything.

"Oh, I'm so sorry," he apologized, "She seemed like such a lovely person."

"Thank you. She was lovely, truly amazing. She was the loveliest person I ever knew, my best friend, the bestest friend in the world," she took a deep breath, "I just can't believe she's not here anymore. It still doesn't seem real, you know. Like some kind of nightmare that we will wake up from soon."

He reached over and gently placed his hand onto hers, "It does get easier as the time passes," pausing as she looked down to their hands, "believe me, when my brother left us, my heart felt completely crushed, and I never thought I would be able to cope without him. We were always so close, well I thought we were anyway. He was all the family that me and dad had left after mum died, just us three boys. I just wish he'd have talked to me before..." he paused again to take a breath but as he glanced into her sad eyes, he decided he needed to change the subject, "Sarah, is there anything I can help you with? I'm happy to just be a shoulder to cry on if that's what you need now, someone to talk to and that, but I'll understand if you'd rather tell me to bugger off and do one," he smiled nervously at her hoping to not offend but he hadn't.

Smiling back at his caring face, she replied, "Thank you. That's very kind of you. Look, let me grab this thing out of the shed, and then maybe we could pop into that coffee shop over the road? A nice chat over a hot drink would be great right now to be honest, if you're not busy obviously?"

"Sure. It's my day off today so I'm available all day, it must be your lucky day hey? Do you need any help with fetching anything?"

"Maybe?" she answered as they both got up and made

their way to the shed.

After a bit of resistance with the padlock, they managed to get it open and stepped inside where it all looked very organised and Sarah thought to herself, *'very Jane-like'.*

Sarah noticed the gold tin straight away, exactly where Jane had said it would be and once they had locked the shed again, she took the tin of letters and placed it in the back of her car before they made their way over to the coffee shop.

As Sarah stared thoughtfully out the window, wondering what the letters would say, she caught sight of Tom's reflection, standing at the counter ordering their drinks. How strange that he should be there today at the gravesite. It's like there had been some sort of coincidence to her deciding to go today, like Jane had made it happen. Maybe she'd managed to finally matchmake after all her other failed attempts over their years as friends. She did feel some strange connection to this man, something she hadn't really felt before and she wondered how this would go and why she had these feelings towards him.

Her thoughts were interrupted as he approached the table with a tray, "I hope you don't mind, but I got us a chocolate chip cookie to share. Is it wrong to assume ladies need chocolate at stressful times?"

Chuckling back, a little nervously, she replied, "Haha, that's funny and no, not at all. Jane always gets us a cookie with our coffees..." realising her words were in the present tense instead of being past, she stopped for a moment, "Well, she used to, you know, before she..." stopping herself in her tracks, she sighed, shook her head and took a deep inhale of breath before composing herself again, replying, "Thank you, that's really sweet of you and weirdly strange at the same time," she smiled up at him hoping that she didn't seem like a complete nutjob.

Tom could see she had just gotten flustered, "So, what's in this little gold tin thing then? Do you have any ideas?" he asked as he placed the coffee cups on the table and discarded the tray onto the chair next to them.

Sarah proceeded to tell him that all she knew was that the box contained letters written by Jane before she died and that she had to deliver them to each person over the next few days.

"Oh, I see. That's a thoughtful thing for her to have done. I'm sure she knew you were the right person for the job," he broke the cookie in half and passed it to her.

She grinned back at him, taking her share, "I just don't know the best time to pass them on. Knowing Jane and how good she was with words, they're not going to be an easy read," she took a bite of the cookie and remembered all the times they had shared one together, "God, I miss her so much already. Her gorgeous twins are in bits most of the time, and Karl, her husband, the poor man, he's, well he's just broken. I just wish I could make it easier for him, I really do. He's such a sweetheart and he's trying to be so brave for the children and Jane's mum. She's totally crushed too, losing her daughter like that," she wiped the corner of her mouth of crumbs and then licked her finger enjoying the final taste of the cookie and watching him devour his share.

"It's probably her way of saying goodbye to everyone. I wish we'd had that opportunity, you know, for James to say goodbye to us, although I wish he had asked for help instead of doing what he did, but as they say, everything happens for a reason, I'm a great believer in that," he looked straight into her eyes as she took a careful swig of her drink, blowing it gently beforehand, "look, as I said earlier, it will get easier Sarah. Right now, it's fresh and raw, everyone is sad, in pain mentally and hurting badly, but I'm sure you'll do the right thing and get those letters delivered at exactly the right time for your friend," he reached across and stroked the sides of her hands as she hugged them around her coffee mug, "it will be okay Sarah, trust me."

She sensed such warmth from him and was increasingly more attracted to this friendly stranger today who had seemed to arrive just at the right time for her. It was as though something magical had occurred, like something intense and lovely was happening inside of her and she hadn't felt this type of thing for a very long time, maybe ever.

~

She continued to see Tom as much as possible during that weekend and they began to fall for each other almost immediately, to her surprise more than anyone else. She had always vowed to be 'a single girl' forever and hadn't ever expected to fall for someone who she had met at a cemetery in the strangest of circumstances too.

"I think Jane had something to do with our first meeting that day at the cemetery you know," she commented as they lay beside each other on the grass in the park enjoying some rare late afternoon sunshine.

"What do you mean?" questioned Tom, leaning onto his side, and brushing her hair gently, away from her face.

She paused for a moment as she remembered the day Jane had been so excited to get her to meet someone at the cemetery, that someone being James. It hadn't gone to plan at all, but maybe...just maybe...it was fate playing a hand in both their lives, and as Tom had said, everything happens for a reason. That was why he was in her life right now. He had come into the picture on that strangely, weird day, but now, she was so glad he had, and it felt perfect in every way. More than she had ever imagined she could feel about someone for a very long time. No-one had come close to this feeling, not even the early 'in love' days when she was a teenager thinking she had found the one. This was awesome and she loved this emotion that had stirred up in her heart, warming it just a little bit more each time he spoke or touched her hand.

"Oh, don't worry. I just have a feeling she knew we'd meet somehow, someday," she leaned into his chest as they lay back down, and smiled to herself, thinking of her best friend and how happy she would be if she were here seeing this image. Knowing that her crazy best friend had finally found someone that she really cared for and didn't even mind the thought of having his male things in her house, like she had been worried about before. All those years where Jane had tried to get her matched with someone, and it had happened this way. Her best friend was still with her, in some sort of way, and these heartwarming feelings began to fix her broken heart just a little and she needed to show this man off to her extended family as soon as she could.

"Hey, listen, it's the twin's birthdays in a few weeks' time. I'm planning a little get-together for them with Karl and the family, so he doesn't have the stress and worry about it. Would you come and meet them? If you don't think it's too soon obviously, I don't want to scare you off."

He chuckled back, "I'm not going anywhere if that's cool with you so, sure, I'd love to come, just let me know the date and time etc. and I'll book the day off work if I can, it's always a bit hectic in January/February time but should be fine if I've got enough notice for them."

"Okay, great, I'll text you all the info, so you have it to hand when you're next at work," she continued, "I know Karl is worried about Jane's birthday in a few months too, so I'd like to help him. It's just that it would've been her fortieth. We had such a big party planned before she got diagnosed, we were going to visit Las Vegas and everything. She was really not fazed about hitting forty, I never understood that to be fair," she laughed, "I'm not looking forward to that one."

Tom laughed back, "You'll still be as beautiful and funny as you are now Sarah. It's just a number after all."

He seemed to know the right thing to say all the time, she loved that about him so much and she couldn't wait to introduce him to her extended family.

Chapter Three

The twins were turning fourteen today and Sarah was determined to try and make it a special day for them both.

She had taken them out a few weeks before to spoil them with early birthday gifts, chatting to them about their upcoming celebrations and what they wanted it to be like. A quiet home party was what they had decided on and even though they would now have to celebrate without their mother being there in person, Jane would always be there in spirit, so it was Sarah's job to make it extra perfect for them and less stressful for Karl to have to deal with.

'Damn you Cancer,' Sarah thought to herself as she placed the last few bottles of fizzy pop onto the side in the kitchen. She had organised an intimate gathering at her place to celebrate with only a small number of the twins' close friends from school. Karl's parents had managed to

come over to England for the week too which the twins loved. They hadn't seen them since the funeral, having to get back to Australia just a few days after and it had perked them up just a little bit to have their grandparents around again.

Sarah also wanted today to be a chance for everyone to meet Tom, especially Karl. It was important for her that they liked each other and got on as Sarah had no intention of not being around for Karl and the kids anytime soon. But as the afternoon went on, there was no sign of Tom, he was late, and the day was nearly over already.

She thought back to when she and Jane had gone to meet James at the cemetery, and he hadn't shown up, only to find that that person in question had just been a spirit sent to help Jane through her diagnosis. Surely, she hadn't imagined all this time with Tom. No, that was a stupid thought and she removed it straight away from her crazy mind. He would be here soon enough. She was sure of it, he wouldn't let her down, not today of all days.

"This has been a really lovely day Sarah, thanks for doing all of this," Karl gave her a kiss on the cheek, "the kids needed it too I think, I wasn't sure how to approach the first birthday with Jane not actually being here, you know for them coping with it."

"It was my pleasure babe. Can't let these beauties not enjoy their special day hey," she replied, rubbing his arm as he sat himself down on the little stone wall in the garden, swigging on the cold beer that she'd brought out for him.

Sarah glanced down at her watch, it was nearly half

past five, so, where was he? Where was Tom? *'Maybe he'd chickened out, maybe it was just too soon for him to meet everyone'* she thought to herself. Trying to distract herself, she sat down beside Karl, grabbed a beer for herself and sighed.

Turning to watch the kids kicking a ball to each other, she again began to think about her own deep and dark secret. If only she could tell someone, if only she felt strong enough and not so ashamed of it, she could have confided in Jane before her death. She should have at least told her of all the people in her life. She'd always meant to at some point, but the moment never seemed appropriate, the moment seemed to never be the right time.

Her life was moving in the right direction workwise and her love life even but now she felt that she would never be able to tell a soul for the rest of her days. There wasn't a single person she felt that close to anymore. Not enough to reveal that sort of thing anyway. If only she had owned up earlier on, she may not have to keep playing it out repeatedly in her brain and punishing herself over the years.

Just then, her thoughts were interrupted as she felt a gentle hand rest on her shoulder, it was Tom. Swinging round to see him, she quickly stood up and flung her arms around him, "you came," she cried, feeling his warm body against hers.

"Of course I did," he replied laughing at her sudden embrace, "I'm so sorry I'm late though, there was an emergency at the hospital so I couldn't leave.

Karl looked up at the stranger now in Sarah's tight

grasp. He'd heard so much about her new man, but they'd not had the chance to meet yet.

"Oh, it's fine," Sarah replied with joy and a Cheshire cat smile on her face, "I'm just so glad you are here now," she stood back still holding his arms tightly, "Karl, this is Tom, Tom, this is Karl," she said nervously as she pointed her arm in turn, "Tom is my, erm, new friend?" she stammered awkwardly. Although she had briefly mentioned Tom to them all, he hadn't been formally introduced yet due to all that had been going on over the past few weeks with Jane's funeral and then she had been so busy with the birthday party plans.

Tom leaned forwards and held his hand out to shake Karl's, "it's lovely to finally meet you mate, I've heard so much about you and the children."

Karl smiled back realising who it was and replied, "thanks, great to meet you too, sorry it hasn't been a bit sooner but what with Jane…" he shook his head as if he felt guilty that his life was moving on without her by his side.

"Hey man, it's cool. I'm sorry for your loss too, it's never an easy time after that sort of thing, my thoughts are with you all."

Karl just nodded back as he passed him a canned beer from the bucket which Sarah had filled earlier.

"Sorry," She whispered to Tom.

"What for?" he whispered back, pulling open the can and taking a large swig.

"Well, I didn't quite know how to introduce you, as in,

you know, my friend? I mean, we are friends I guess?" she replied, awkwardly shrugging her shoulders.

"Don't be silly," he began rubbing the small of her back, "it's fine, we are friends, and very good ones at that," he chuckled, winking at her worried face.

She smiled gleefully at him, staring into his eyes, feeling totally immersed in them and getting that fluttery feeling in her stomach yet again, "I'm going to check on the twins, that's them over there, aren't they both gorgeous Tom?" she pointed.

He nodded as he followed the direction of her point, "They are indeed. Hey look, I got them vouchers each, I don't know what teenagers are into these days," he laughed showing her two envelopes, "do you want me to wait over here?"

"Maybe, oh, I don't know…oh that's really lovely of you, I'm sure they'll be happy with them, you didn't have to do that though."

"Take him over to meet the kids Sarah, they'll like to see a new face, you've been going on about the guy to them for weeks now," interrupted Karl as he stood up and started walking to the kitchen, "I'm sure they think you've made him up. We'll have to get off soon so best go over and meet them before we need to leave, they have school tomorrow too, and Robbie probably has a ton of homework still left to do, you know he likes to leave it last minute."

They all laughed, and then Sarah took Tom over and excitedly introduced him to the kids who, exactly like Karl had said, loved meeting someone new.

The kids had taken an instant liking to Tom, much to Sarah's relief. Robbie enjoyed showing him some of his football tricks especially and was quite happy when he found out they supported the same team too. Always a winning combination for the male bonding thing.

She worried about them having a new person coming into their lives after all they'd been through over the past months, but they knew she would never not see them or leave them out, not for anyone or anything. This was crazy aunty Sarah after all.

It was getting late and the temperature outside in the garden had dropped. All the guests had left so Sarah and Tom decided to go for a little stroll after clearing up.

There was a beautiful stretch of greenery five minutes from her place, somewhere she loved to go and relax during the summer. Her and Jane had a special bench they used to sit on after shopping most of the time and usually knocked back their favourite coffees, cookies and put the world to rights most days.

"Are you warm enough?" Tom asked, placing his arm around her shoulders as they walked together.

"A little bit chilly but I'm okay."

"No, you're not, you're shivering, here, take my coat, that jacket isn't going to do anything to keep you warm, I can feel your goosebumps through it."

"I didn't really think about bringing my big coat, it didn't go with the dress either so, well, you know what us women are like, we suffer for fashion," she answered, teeth chattering slightly through a cute giggle.

As he stood in front of her and put his coat over her shoulders, she glanced up at him. His face was chiseled, beautiful and perfect apart from one little scar just under his chin, "how did you do that?" she asked, running her cold finger over it.

"Oh, boys' stuff. Me and my brother James, were having a competition as to who could jump out of the tree in our garden from the highest point. I won of course but landed on my face and cut my chin up. It never really healed that well but, when I see it, it gives me another fond memory of the lad so…I like it."

"That's cute, well, sort of," she linked her arm into his, snuggling up to him with his big coat warming her body a little bit more now, "are you hungry at all?"

"Erm, a little, what are you thinking?"

"Not sure, really. Do you have any suggestions, any favourites?"

"Chinese, Indian? I'm easy, to be fair."

"Oh yes, let's get a little Chinese, I've got a few bottles of wine left over from today too, maybe we could order a takeaway and watch a film or something. Or…"

"Or?" he questioned looking at her now blushing cheeks.

"Or maybe?" she paused, "Jesus, look at me throwing myself at you? Forget it, I best just get a bath and bed, it's been a long day with all the prepping and there's still a bit of washing up to do…"

Tom stopped and held her arms, looking straight into

her eyes, "Sarah, it's ok. You're not throwing yourself at me at all. We are just two friends having a nice evening stroll and a bit of food, yeah?"

Sarah looked down for a moment, but he gently lifted her head back up, where he noticed tears forming in her eyes, "what's the matter? Why so sad?" he asked softly, "did I say something wrong?"

"No. It's just, well these past few weeks, months, have been so hard, what with Jane dying, the funeral, I feel like I'm, well…I feel as though I'm latching on to you somehow, being a bit…desperate, needy?"

"Hey. You latch on all you like. I am loving spending time with you Sarah, you're not being needy at all," he paused as he wiped a single stray tear that had trickled down her cheek, "you shouldn't feel guilty about moving on either, I know it's hard losing someone so special, but, at the end of the day, Jane wouldn't want you to be alone and sad, would she?"

"No, she wouldn't. She certainly wouldn't. You are so right Tom; she would want me to have a glass of wine for her too. Or maybe a bottle or two, ha-ha, she loved her wine. I know she would love us enjoying ourselves, it's just guilt you know. I'm here and she's…"

"Sarah. Look, I know exactly how you feel, but honestly, this is a coping mechanism, and you should go with it, one step at a time. Look, let's get you home, I'll order some food, run you a bath and you can get some rest while I finish clearing up, you've done enough today, let me help."

She just smiled back at him, "what have I done to deserve you, Tom?"

He raised his eyebrows and shrugged his shoulders in jest and then made their way back to her place, arms entwined, and Sarah felt so much love right now from him, all she could think of was the lovely fluttering in her tummy every time he touched her.

~

"Wow, that was delicious, I'm so full up now though, phew, probably ate more than I should have," Sarah said as she slumped back into the sofa rubbing her tummy and resting her feet on the coffee table.

He laughed back at her and poured them both another glass of wine, "here, sip on this while your dinner goes down and I'll go clean up the plates and then run your bath for you."

"Thanks Tom, you're a star," she took the glass and held out her other hand toward his, which he slid back into hers rubbing the tops of her fingers softly, "I'm so glad you came to the party today," she added.

"It was my pleasure and so lovely to meet everyone at last," he leant down and gently kissed her full on the lips.

They hadn't really had that all important kissing moment yet, it had just been kisses on the cheek or just the very memorable, romantic peck he had given her on her hand that day they had met the first time. This kiss though, it felt extra special, and she felt that strange flutter in her tummy again as his head moved away from her.

As he began to stand back up, she stopped him, placed

her feet on the floor and put her glass onto the table. Standing up, not taking her eyes off his face, she pulled him close again, putting his arms around her waist, "kiss me again," she asked quietly.

He said nothing, reaching her lips with his, this moment felt more alive and exciting than ever before. This man was something else and her heart was melting for him to hold her and never let go.

Two hours later, she woke up with the most beautiful image greeting her. There he was lying next to her, Tom. The most beautiful man snuggled up holding her body. With only her thick grey sofa throw covering them, it had been sensual, loving and the best night she had ever had. Maybe, just maybe, this would last more than a few weeks this time. She couldn't take it for granted, she didn't want to. It could be just all the emotions she was going through right now but, something felt different, something felt right, and she was loving every minute of it. She was going to enjoy this moment. She was going to enjoy this man who had come into her life.

Jane's wish had come true, for her best friend to find someone special, it certainly felt like it was a wish that had been granted to her. Maybe her awful secret could be hidden for now and her life would be completed with Tom now by her side to protect her from any more pain and upset. She couldn't lose anyone else in her life and she was determined to hold onto this one for as long as humanly possible.

Chapter Four

As the months flew by, Sarah fell increasingly in love with Tom. He'd been there to help her through the sad time she had been having and never moaned about sharing the time with Karl and the kids. He understood more than anyone about grief and how to deal with it all. They'd even been to the cemetery together to visit their missed loved ones. Sarah felt a closeness to Tom like no man before and she was loving every moment she spent with him.

"It's funny how we met there isn't it?" he'd said as they'd left the cemetery that morning and walked into town looking for somewhere to have a bite to eat.

"Yes, it is, bit weird but sort of in a good, weird way, if that makes sense?" Sarah replied, clinging onto his arm to keep warm.

"James would've loved you; you know that don't you,

he'd have probably tried it on with you too," he laughed, "We used to come on to each other's girlfriends all the time, just as a laugh, you know, brotherly love and all that."

"You would have always won me over babe, don't you worry," Sarah chuckled back, "Oh, here, let's try this place," she said as she let go of his arm and stepped into a small cafe for her birthday. Her fortieth had crept up on her already and they had planned breakfast out, a bit of punting on the river Cam and then dinner in London at the weekend as Tom had to work this evening.

"This was a good choice sweetheart; do you want another coffee before we set off?" Tom said, wiping his last bit of soggy bread across the runny fried egg on the plate.

"No, I'm good. I need to pop to the loo and then get off to see the kids. Karl has been so hectic with work stuff, I said I'd help him by cooking a few freezer friendly meals and doing a bit of cleaning up and that, just while he gets some paperwork done."

"You are a diamond bird; you do know that don't you?" Tom stated as he watched her brush off the toast crumbs as she stood up.

She just smiled back and grabbed her handbag and jacket. All she wanted was to be there for that family, she didn't see it as being a diamond, but she appreciated his funny sayings and the fact that he loved her helping so much.

He paid the bill and waited for her by the door, watching the hustle and bustle of the Cambridge streets.

He lived just outside Cambridge, nearer to Hertfordshire but travelled to work at the hospital so spent most of his time in the town.

As they made their way along the main road, Sarah thought it was about time that they had some special time together and she had the perfect idea, "I was thinking Tom, about going away for a weekend, just the two of us, what do you think? Can you get a long weekend off work anytime soon, like next week?"

"Next weekend? Erm, yes, I'm off for a week actually from Friday, where are you thinking of taking me?"

"Well, not far. Norfolk actually. Jane and I went there for a hen weekend and the little place we stayed at was so quaint, I'd love to go back there with you."

"Sounds great darling, will you be able to book it at such short notice?"

"I'll give them a ring later this afternoon, if you don't ask, you don't get hey?" she giggled, "If not, there's plenty of places to stay otherwise, I'll text you later and let you know," And with that, she kissed him goodbye as she made her way to Karl's.

Tom was booked on a busy shift at the hospital this evening. He worked in the x-ray department at Addenbrooke's Hospital as a radiologist, which was always super busy, but he loved his job. He also helped in the children's ward sometimes in his free time, reading books to them or playing board games. He had taken Sarah in a few times to meet some of the children and she had been taken by how much fun and laughter he brought to their little faces every time. He loved children, she could see that, another great thing about him.

~

"Thanks so much for this Sarah, I've got to get myself some sort of routine with cooking, cleaning and working," Karl said as he grabbed his pile of paperwork off the kitchen table, "It's just been really hard and all I want to do is spend time with the kids as much as I can. When I get home from work, I just wanna be there for them, you know?"

"Karl, it's no problem, you know I don't mind at all, now go on, get on with your work. I'll make up some batches of meals to freeze so you just have to get them out in the mornings before work. Is that ok?" She bent down into the hall cupboard and gave him his coat before ushering him to the front door, waving his car keys in front of him.

"You are a superstar, you really are," he smiled at her, "I'll only be an hour, just gotta pick something up from work and then I'll be straight back," he swiftly kissed her cheek before running onto the driveway to his car.

Sarah watched him drive off, leaning on the doorway, thinking of how her life had changed so much over the past year and how it was now turning out with Tom. After being let down so many times before by men, she never would have thought she could feel this way about someone again, but she did and it felt so real, so right and so nice. Maybe this time, she could put all her trust issues aside and settle down like Jane had always wanted her to. Could he be the one to tame her wild ways? She would always be crazy Sarah but somehow, she felt as though she was settling down a little bit and it was down to him being there for her and making her feel so special. For now, though, she had to concentrate on her duties here, so she closed the door and began preparing the meals and hoovering while they cooked.

Finishing up and loading the dishwasher, she decided to see if she could get something booked for the weekend and after about half an hour of calls, booking and payments, it was all set. A long weekend in Norfolk for her and her Man, Tom, and she was really looking forward to it.

She was excitedly sending a text to Tom with the information as Cassie arrived home from her friend's house. "Hey aunty Sarah," she said, giving her a hug on her way to the fridge.

"Hello little pumpkin," Sarah replied, squeezing her quick hug in return, "hey listen here madam. I'm going away next weekend with Tom, so you are the lady of the house for a few days, unless grandma is round obviously, then you know she is in charge," they laughed as Sarah gave Cassie the grandmother in charge eyebrows, "So, it's going to be up to you to make sure dad gets all your meals out each morning. They are all labeled in the freezer for him," she paused, watching Cassie nodding in agreement to all the instructions, "maybe we should write a reminder on the notice board for him, you know he'll forget, otherwise or set up some alarm on his phone when he gets in?" she said as she nudged Cassie's arm and reached for the chalk, "I'm only away until Monday and you know you can call me anytime don't you darling?"

"Yes, Aunt Sarah," she agreed.

"Ok, right. I better go then, Tom's promised me a Chinese tonight, your dad should be home in about ten minutes…" her words were interrupted by Karl's arrival, "or maybe now," she said with a huge smile as Cassie sniggered, "we're in the kitchen Karl," she called out to the hallway.

"Hey gang, phew, traffic is manic out there today, you all good here?" He placed his bag back on the table and slumped into the chair looking tired.

"Yes dad," replied Cassie as she gave him a quick hug before going upstairs munching on some more carrot sticks which she had got out of the fridge.

"She is okay, isn't she?" asked Karl, nodding over to Sarah.

"She's fine Karl, look, your dinner for tonight is in the oven, just needs dishing up in about fifteen minutes and then Cassie has all the instructions for the other meals and I've put a reminder on the board up there for you too," she busied herself, gathering her jacket and bag, "I'm going away with Tom for a long weekend from Friday but my phone will stay on if you need me. Hoovering is done, the bathroom is cleaned, and a load of washing is on," she smiled as he just watched on, "I've got to get off now, give us a ring if you're unsure of anything and Karl, get yourself a shave mate, you're not seventeen anymore," she ruffled his bristly chin playfully and left before he could reply. She couldn't wait to get back to hers and meet with Tom to tell him more about the weekend and to get ready for their few days away together.

~

"Tom, do you have a second?" asked Sarah as they strolled along the seaside promenade. Sarah had managed to grab the last available room at the same little place that she and Jane had stayed at which made this weekend even more special for her. She felt almost close to her friend again even if the memories of the weekend were hard to think back on. Finding out your best friend had terminal cancer was heartbreaking, but they had still spent some wonderful few days together despite that.

"Sure honey, what's up?" Tom pointed to a nearby picnic bench as they sat opposite each other, "Is everything alright?" he asked looking at her now thoughtful face.

"Yes, everything is fine Tom. It's just that, well, you know what happened to Jane?" she glanced down at her hands as she reached out to touch his across the table and continued, "you see, Jane had always tried to match me up with someone, and I always messed it up or didn't take it seriously enough, but this time, you, and I, well, it's different. I feel like she had something to do with us getting together, like, she knew we would meet eventually. Somehow, she finally made it happen."

"You're not sick, are you?" concerned she was about to tell him something bad, he squeezed her hand.

"No, no. Sorry. I'm not making sense, am I?" she

paused and glanced back into his worried but beautiful brown eyes, "it's just, well, she always wished for me to meet that special someone and settle down, and I never took her advice. I was never one for just being with one person, a free spirit most of my life, but…"

"But what? Are we breaking up?" Tom's face reminded her of other faces she had seen many times before at that pivotal moment of the 'it's not you, it's me' conversations that she'd had plenty of with other men throughout the years.

"No. God no. I just wanted to let you know that, for the first time in my life, I feel...well...I feel really secure with you, and if we hadn't met that day, you know, when Jane took me to the cemetery and you were there, we might never have met at all, and…" her words became flustered again, she was rambling on now so he moved around to sit next to her and stroked her flushed cheek.

"Sarah, honey, it's fine. I know what you mean."

"I just get the feeling Jane knew. She must have. She knew we had to meet because of…" she was about to say, James, but swiftly realizing she couldn't, she continued, "I want to make her proud and grant her one of her wishes, Tom. She wrote about it in her letter to me, you know the letters we collected that day in the gold tin in the shed?" he nodded back, "Anyway, I'm going to need your help to do it."

"Whatever you want my gorgeous lady. Just tell me what you need me to do?" he asked, smiling.

In a split second, everything became clear to Sarah.

The visit to James that eventful day, the fact that Tom was there, that he'd left his photo behind, she'd had to run after him to give it back, he'd taken her number from her car. Jane had made this relationship happen. She felt sure that she was now looking down on the two of them as the sun began gleaming through some white puffy clouds above, and the sky became suddenly brighter than usual. She gazed up, squinting at the luminous sun rays shining down on them, then turned back to face Tom with pure emotion and joy in her voice, "marry me, Tom. Let's do it," excitedly jumping up from her seat, "let's do it for Jane, but most of all, let's do it for us, let's be an us," she gestured using speech marks with her fingers.

After the initial shock, he stood up as fast as he could, nearly tripping on the bench, held both her hands, and embraced her with a long, sumptuous, and electrified kiss, like no other kiss they'd ever felt.

Her heart was thumping like a drum through her chest, so hard, he could feel it on his. She'd never felt like this in her life before and as he whispered softly into her ear, "I tell you what, you marry me," she felt complete.

She peered up at the sky and winked, smiling with utter glee. Jane had finally got her final wish, for Sarah to find that special someone, to be happy and content and settle down at last. It was the most amazing moment she had ever experienced, and she felt sure it was all because of her one and only best friend in the whole world. There would never be another person like Jane Walden in her life and how she wished she could see her and Tom right now. She would have been so happy and proud of Sarah for taking the plunge and falling in love. Her last words written in that all important letter meant so much to Sarah and she wasn't going to let her down. Finally, Jane had her wish for her best friend to be matched with the perfect man and here he was, making her happy once more.

Tom lifted her up and swung her around as they both shrieked with joy, passers-by watched on wondering what they were doing. But they didn't have a care in the world and embraced their special moment for the rest of the day, texting their close friends and family with the amazing news that they were now officially engaged.

Chapter Five

As Sarah slowly made her way down the aisle, all she could think about was her gorgeous man waiting for her at the other end. As she squinted hard to focus on his face, she could see that he was looking straight at her with tears welling up in his eyes. She thought back to how amazing it had been to meet him on that special day just over a year ago. Her best friend, Jane, had certainly proved a point with her match-making skills, even if they'd been slightly delayed and achieved in a strange sort of way. Sarah meeting Tom that day wasn't just a coincidence and they had realised that soon after as they spent more and more time together.

She just so wished that Jane could be here today to see it all happening, to see how her plans had worked in one form or another. Life was becoming even more amazing for Sarah now that she had Tom in her life, and she thanked Jane every day for it. Thanked her for bringing Tom to her in the crazy way that she had. Sarah had now convinced herself that it was all meant to have been, but she still yearned to have Jane by her side today more than anything in the whole world.

Thanks to Karl's thoughtfulness though, he had brought the spirit of Jane to this special moment. His caring brother-like attitude towards Sarah had become even more special. He had given Sarah a wedding gift just moments earlier in the doorway of the church and it really meant so much to her.

"Here, I wondered if you would like to wear this as your 'something borrowed' thing?" He reached into his suit jacket pocket, pulling out a small black velvet box, opened it and said, "It was one of Jane's favourite pieces to wear to weddings and special occasions." He gently unhooked the bracelet from inside the box and showed it to Sarah.

"Karl, that's stunning. Are you sure you are ok about me wearing it though? I mean, it's Jane's." Sarah replied, admiring it. She had remembered seeing it briefly when Jane was getting ready for one of Karl's work mates' weddings. It had worked perfectly with her outfit as everything had done with Jane. Sarah always admired her taste in fashion and accessories.

"Definitely," Karl replied, putting the box back into his pocket, "I'm sure she wouldn't mind at all. And to be honest, it sort of helps with some unfinished business you two had for today. Walking you down the aisle as she had always planned, you know," he looked into her eyes which had now filled with tears, "Yep, she did tell me the things you two had planned since childhood," he smiled back at her as she took some deep breaths to stop the cascade of tears which were fast approaching, fastened the bracelet onto her wrist, then held out his arm, and said jokingly, "now, come on. Let's get you hitched before you change your bloody mind woman. Tom is waiting very patiently there for his new wife."

Sarah giggled, sniffed back the emotion, and linked her arm into his. She felt so much love in her heart for him. This token of affection for her was incredible and she felt blessed and honored to wear it.

As they made their way into the church, she glanced down again to look at the beautiful bracelet sparkling away on her wrist just as the sun rays hit it as they shone through the stained-glass windows. This little thing meant that Jane could be here somehow, she could walk the aisle with her on her wedding day and she would treasure it, and the feeling it gave her for this special moment in her life.

She missed Jane so much, that evil disease took her best friend way too early and her mixed emotions of sadness then anger hit her most days. She tried to let it go so she could just have the happy memories of that beautiful lady, but it kept rearing up the pain that they all still felt a year on.

Before her death, Sarah had spent every day seeing or at least speaking to Jane on the phone since meeting at primary school. With only one year spent apart after Sarah's parents had been tragically killed in a car accident, they had been glued together, inseparable. She had to go and live with her nan and grandad to get over the tragedy but other than that year away at her aunt's house in Oxford, they had been together most days. Even while away, they kept the friendship alive by talking on the phone every day near on.

She missed her best friend's voice so much, that cheeky laugh she had when they were up to mischief. She missed it even more so on this special day knowing how Jane would've been so ecstatic to see this wedding happening. But Sarah was determined to let Jane's memory give her the strength and the ability to get through this without her. She knew that she wanted her to be happy from her last letter that she left and seeing herself getting married was a day she thought would never happen. A day many of them thought wouldn't happen, not to Sarah, the independent, free spirit of a girl who was never going to be tied down to one man forever. The out-going cheeky minx that she had always been and had vowed to be alone and single forever.

But yes, today she was getting married to a beautiful man who had walked into her life at just the right moment. So now she could finally make Jane's final wish for her come true and she couldn't wait to seal the deal.

"Wow," she whispered, as she glanced across at Karl, holding on to his arm tightly giving it a gentle squeeze, "I'm getting bloody married."

Karl smiled sweetly at her, he'd been so good to her

even while coping with his own heartbreak and grief, helping to plan the wedding, and choosing suits with Tom and Robbie. He'd not once moaned or complained about it and had wholeheartedly agreed to take Jane's place with the honor of walking Sarah down the aisle.

Robbie, that super sweet child, Jane's son, lost his mum too soon. He had found it so hard to return to school and spent most of his days just playing his computer games in his room but for the last few months, during the wedding planning, he'd ventured out and slowly started smiling again, spending more time with his sister and Karl as well as coming to stay with Sarah and Tom every other weekend to play with their four dogs that they had quickly acquired during their dating. He felt so much comfort with Sarah because knowing that she had lost both her parents at such a young age, he could talk to her about it, and she helped him understand the grieving process. She had almost become like his second mum.

She turned around and glimpsed a fleeting look behind her to see Robbie and Cassie proudly following them in their wedding outfits. They were two amazingly brave kids and she loved and adored them so much. She gave them both a cheeky wink and squeezed Karl's' arm again as they continued walking that all important aisle wedding walk.

~

The ceremony was beautiful and just as lovely as they had all planned it with a small number of guests attending. Tom wasn't a big fan of being the centre of attention as much as Sarah was, so they had agreed to only have their close friends and family there. Intimate and private, just how they wanted it, with the reception party held in Karl's Garden under a large garden marquee. This was deliberately decided as it meant another way of bringing Jane into the celebrations in some way.

As Tom kissed his new bride, everyone clapped and celebrated in the grounds outside while pictures were being snapped of the happy couple. The sun was beaming down, and Sarah felt amazing.

"Doesn't she look beautiful Janice?" said Karl, as he passed Cassie his camera to take some pictures.

"She really does my dear and so happy too. I don't think I've ever seen her shine so much, she deserves this," wiping another tear from her already emotional face, she held Karl's arm.

"Yeah, she does, she really does," grasping hold of her hand, they stood watching the happy couple posing and laughing together.

"I love you Mrs. Cooper," Tom pulled her in close as they made their way back to Karl's in the vintage wedding car decorated with matching yellow ribbons.

"Haha, that sounds funny but, I love you too Mr. Cooper," Sarah replied, kissing him straight on the lips and then laying her head on his shoulder. Finally, her man was hers and she had found love at last. She was now a wife and although that sounded crazy to her, she also loved the sound of it too.

~

"So, finally, the crazy girl we all know, and love has

been snapped up, that's you sorted," Karl began when it was his turn for to make his speech, "but seriously, myself and the kids couldn't be happier for you Sarah, we really are so pleased for you aren't we kids?" he paused to look over to the table where Robbie and Cassie were sitting, on their phones but sort of listening, as usual, Karl laughed, "Kids hey?" and everyone chuckled as he continued, looking toward the newlyweds, "Listen, Sarah. You have been in our life for what seems like forever, and it's certainly been a fun, and rather interesting journey so far. You were a rock for Jane, the bestest friend she could've had in her life, at the best of times and even at the worst of times," he looked down slightly emotional, taking a deep breath, swallowing hard to avoid losing it, and went on, "Jane loved you unconditionally, as we all do. I'm sure she's looking down on us all today and loving every moment of it too. You've been an absolute star for me over this past year and I will always be here for you to lend an ear or a shoulder to cry on when you need it. You're like my little sister so I'll always be your stand-in big brother. Always," he paused again as he smiled lovingly at her, "To you, Sarah, and to the very brave man that has taken her on, here's to you Tom, now also my very good friend and drinking buddy, and hey, let's not forget, he's now Sarah's husband," he cried, raising his glass to toast the happy couple and leaning down to kiss Sarah on the cheek who was giggling but also slightly blushing at the beautiful words, "Your turn Tommy boy," Karl announced to Tom as he sat back down.

Sarah mouthed a thank-you to Karl and then squeezed Tom's hand as he stood up to make his speech.

"Okay, I'm not so good at this talking in front of people malarkey, not as good as you obviously are. Thanks for that though," he grinned and winked at Karl, "I don't quite know how to follow that to be fair, but I just wanted to say thank you all for coming today and sharing this special day with us. It's been incredible," he continued, "To Sarah. You are amazing, kind and the most loving person and now you are my amazingly beautiful wife…" he cleared his throat and took a deep breath, "I love you and I thank you for coming into my life when you did," there was a collective 'ahh' from the guests, "and, a special thanks for letting me have our dogs here today too," he pointed out to the garden outside another small marquee that had been erected on Karl's lawn especially for the dogs. Everyone laughed as they watched two of the dogs chasing a ball around, one sprawled out fast asleep under his favourite yellow blanket and another sitting bolt upright like a palace guard dog, looking into the main marquee just waiting for a few scraps of food or a little fuss from anyone. They had rescued them all and couldn't have been without them all day. Tom finished up by saying, "And to Karl and his gorgeous family, I have to say a big thank you for all of this and for accepting me into the most welcoming brood I've known. Now enjoy the food, have fun and let's party," and with that he lifted his champagne flute, toasting his glass and everyone chinked theirs together.

The guests began small talk and made their way to the generous finger buffet which consisted of the simple and traditional, non-fancy foods such as sausage rolls, mini sausages, cheese on sticks, and delicate triangle-shaped sandwiches.

"That was just perfect sweetheart, well done," Sarah reassured Tom as she felt his hands still shaking and slightly clammy with sweat, "You did well for someone who doesn't like making speeches."

He kissed her hand and smiled.

Noticing Karl leaving the top table, she gave Tom's leg a gentle squeeze, "I'm just nipping to the loo, won't be long," she said as she pushed her chair back, ensuring that her dress was dusted off from the pastry of the sausage rolls she had just been munching on. Cassie had spent two hours dressing all the chairs the previous evening with yellow sashes and placing a silk daisy flower in the middle of the bow. They looked gorgeous, spring-like and the attention to detail in the tying of the bows had kept Cassie busy indulging in her creative talents once again.

Reaching the kitchen, Sarah poked her head around the doorway to see Karl staring up at the wall, "You ok mate?" she asked as she walked up to him touching his shoulder gently.

"Hey," he replied, slightly startled as he turned around, "sorry, yes I'm all good. I was off in another world for a minute then, but yeah, I'm fine, honestly. Just wanted to see her face for a bit, you know...say hi," he nodded towards the large canvas on the wall of his beloved wife,

Jane. It was one of her laying on the beach in Florida watching the children playing in the sand. He'd taken it while she hadn't been looking, and it had become one of his favourite photos from the holiday after he'd found out about the cancer just a few short weeks later. She was just staring lovingly at their children, with the sun shining onto her skin, knowing what she did but hadn't said anything and being so brave. When he'd taken the photo, he just remembered thinking how beautiful the image was as he hadn't a clue about what was to unfold for them all.

Sarah just rubbed his arm and looked up at it also, "Your speech was lovely Karl, thank you and thank you for all you've done to make this day perfect. I don't think I could've done it without you, the kids and Janice."

"My absolute pleasure. I think it's helped a lot actually. It's given us something to focus on, to look forward to after last year, and Jane would've loved it, she really would."

"Yes, I know. It was exactly how we had planned it out at school together all those years ago, bless her heart."

There were no more words to say right then. They both just took in the beauty that was Jane and felt thankful that they'd done her proud.

Chapter Six

With their glorious Jamaican honeymoon over, the months were zooming by. They had both gone back to work but decided to take a solid week off as it was time to get their house sorted.

The old Victorian townhouse had come up for sale at a superb price at auction and Tom had gone by himself to put in some bidding as a surprise for Sarah. She had fallen in love with it on viewing a few weeks previously and being just ten minutes' walk from her salon and the hospital where he worked, meant it was a perfect little home base for them both.

She loved it so much and felt like the luckiest lady in town right now with her new husband, their cute gang of dogs and her beautiful Walden family still being so close. Now all they had to do was decorate their new little married home which they'd bought together three months before the wedding.

As they painted the main bedroom that afternoon, they discussed the recent news about Tom's dad and his new romance with Janice, "I can't believe it about Janice and your dad, I mean, it's amazing but, how come you never mentioned it?" asked Sarah as she tipped another slosh of gorgeous dapple-grey paint into Tom's painting tray for him.

"I was going to, but dad swore me to secrecy," he replied, stretching up the wall with his paint roller. "Dad said Janice was a bit nervous about telling you all, so they wanted to keep it under wraps for a bit. She's such a sweet lady, I'm so happy for them. Apparently, she's been round to dads a few times for dinner and lunches. Cute really hey?" he continued as he swiped another load of paint onto the roller and swiftly began another layer, "They really are a great match you know, both a little crazy, but both so deserving to have someone at their time of life," he said, laughing as he glanced back at his new wife who was busy finishing off the masking tape along the bottom wall, trying not to get it stuck on her newly manicured nails.

"Aww, that's so lovely. I'm so pleased for her too. Jane would have been so happy to see her mum with someone finally, she never wanted her to be alone for too long after they lost her dad, she kept telling her to find someone, aww it's cool."

"Yeah, it's great that everyone knows now, I'm sure they are going to be the romance of the year. Anyway,

Mrs. Cooper," he said as he carefully ran the roller down the last bit of wall, "enough about the new love birds, I have been doing a little bit of thinking over the past few weeks. About us and our future and this little love nest we have going on right now," he smirked, "do you want a cuppa, have a little break from this messy painting lark for a bit?" Tom placed his roller into the tray, then wiped his paint splattered hands down his shorts much to Sarah's dismay.

"Don't do that," she said, "they'll be ruined by the time we get them in the bloody wash," she couldn't help but love his funny ways, watching his carelessness but smiling also at the grey hand marks now adorning the thigh area on his, already messy, cutoff jeans. He had ripped a massive hole in them a few weeks back when they got caught on some rose bushes in the garden, so he had decided to create a new look and make them into his DIY work shorts.

"They've had it anyway darling, and they are my new sexy man about the house shorts," he said, smiling back his cheeky and now massive grin at her, "It's fine babe, it makes it look like I do this for a living now, just need a little tool belt and we could do some role play even," he winked at her as he patted her bottom as he walked passed her chuckling to himself. "So, do you want a cuppa and a little chat for ten mins or so in the garden, miss bossy boots?"

"Okay, scruffy pants," she turned round to smile at him, "but don't forget the biscuits, I bought a new packet yesterday, they're in the top cupboard above the microwave. They're your favourite chocolate chip ones. Oh, and let the dogs out for a wee too, will you? I'll be down when I've finished this last bit," she carefully dipped the paint brush into the tin, trying her hardest not to get any drips down the side. She was on the last stretch of cutting in now and she thought to herself how it was looking very neatly done.

"Cool," was his reply and he went down the stairs leaving her to it as he called each dog in turn.

About ten minutes later, he called up the stairs that the coffees were ready, "I'll take them into the garden with the dogs, there seems to be a glimpse of that funny yellow thing in the sky."

"Okay darling," she called back and finished her final stroke of paint, taking a step back to admire how her painting skills had gotten better between walls. Always one for detail and perfection, she had to take charge of this part of the decorating, and she knew that he could reach higher than her anyway being on the short side that she often hated about herself. She carefully wiped the excess paint off the brush onto the edge of the tin and balanced it before making her way downstairs to join Tom and their four pups in the garden.

"Mmm, this is nice, isn't it?" she said as she closed her eyes and tilted her head towards the sunshine that was peeking through the clouds. It seemed like they hadn't had a decent day of weather since the wedding, and it felt nice on her skin.

"Yeah, makes a change doesn't it," he replied, "the

weather has been shocking just recently. Anyway, listen," he said as he straightened his back in the chair, "I've been thinking about something," he passed her the mug of coffee and started to unwrap the biscuits. She had brought a double packet and the dogs were at their feet in no time waiting for one of their treats. Tom always had a handful of their doggy bites in his pockets, no matter what he happened to be wearing. "So, our little spare room," he continued, "have you had any thoughts about what you want to use it for?"

"Erm, not really, no, been too focused on our room," Sarah replied, dunking a biscuit into her coffee and quickly munching on it before it melted and sunk into the steaming hot drink, "maybe a little study to do the books in so they don't have to be done on the kitchen table," she mumbled between biscuit mouthfuls, "or I could have a small at-home beauty room or how about just kitting it out as a spare room for when Cassie or Robbie come to stay over. They'd love their own space here instead of those sofa bed, camp bed, fold up thingys? We could get bunk beds for them, and set up a game thing, you know a PlayStation or whatever they're playing on these days?"

"Erm...right," he replied slightly sounding a bit disheartened, "not quite what I was thinking actually," he paused to get another treat out of his pocket for the dogs, which was snapped up immediately, "my idea was more along the lines of something for us, for our future," he turned to face her after leaning down to get one of the dogs toys to throw, "I was sort of thinking, more like, well, erm…" he spluttered nervously.

"Spit it out man," she joked back watching Donut the cocker spaniel running back within seconds, toy in mouth, and drooling for more playtime and a treat.

Tom cleared his throat anxiously and looked back at her, "sorry. Well, what I was thinking about was, well," he stammered with an awkward tone to his voice, "how about a nursery?"

Sarah's eyes widened, her eyebrows raised, and she almost froze in shock. Her heart began to beat hard in her chest as the word nursery hit her ears. Her voice wouldn't work for a few seconds, and her hands seemed to freeze like statues. The remains of the freshly dunked biscuit started getting soggy between her fingers.

"You okay babe? You look like you've seen a ghost or something. It's not that bad an idea, is it?"

Her pounding heart began to thump wildly in her head, and she felt her pulse quickening, "Erm, yes, I'm fine. It's just, well, erm..." she replied, trying to keep her body calm, "well, a nursery? Aren't we a bit old for all that baby lark now?" she asked in a muddled slur, "I'm forty now Tom, hardly baby making material now," she stammered wiping the melted chocolate onto her paint-stained top without thinking of the mess it would make. The dogs were close at her feet waiting to help with any clearing up that was needed. She didn't seem to be able to function right and the adrenaline was rushing through her veins at a rate of knots.

"Oh, come on babe. People are having babies in their

fifties these days, you're in your prime darling," he answered, reaching across to wipe her chin of a dab of chocolate that had smudged on its way in, "imagine a little one of us running about the place. I thought we could paint the room as a zoo theme. I've always loved the zoo and the colours would look amazing with the sun that comes through the windows in the afternoons," he continued excitedly, waving his arms around as if he were painting all the animals in midair, "imagine it Sarah, I can see it all now…elephants, giraffes…a few little cheeky monkeys hanging from trees…"

"No," she interrupted loudly and abruptly, "I'm sorry but no, we're not having a nursery in that room," she suddenly stood up, spilling the coffee which was still very hot onto her shirt, "Shit," she cursed, trying to flap her clothing away from her skin.

"Sarah, be careful, what's the rush? I thought we were going to have a coffee break and a chat," he placed his mug onto the table, stood up and tried to help her.

"Tom, I'm too old to have a baby. I'd rather not talk about this anymore," she replied, pushing his hands away, "can we just go and get on with the rest of the painting?" she asked in a panic to try and get him to move off the baby subject, "I want to get the bedroom finished today so we can start building the bed. It'll be better than sleeping on that bloody air bed for another week or so," She was trying her utmost to change the subject, her heart ached feeling guilty as hell as she glanced up at his very confused face. He not only looked sad but also, quite shocked at the way she had just reacted. She felt emotional for him, for both of them. With her lungs feeling like they were being blocked from getting any air and her heart filling with searing pain, she hated herself once again.

At that very moment, all she wanted to do was to wrap her arms around him and tell him everything, confess to him her sordid secret and get it out in the open but the words just wouldn't come out. She had too much shame going on inside her already fragile body. He didn't need to know, what would be the point? He might hate her and think less of her or worse, leave her just like she had been treated all those years back as a teenager, abandoned to solve her own mess out. She felt sure this would be the case and the pounding drum of her heart beating right now could not take that hurt again.

He reached over to her again, holding her arms gently but with some reassurance that he was there for her. His hands met her chin as he lifted her head up to face him, seeing tears in her eyes, he said, "You're not too old darling. Just think about it hey. A son or daughter would be so cute and of course as beautiful as you..."

"No Tom," she cried back, "for Christ's sake, just drop the subject alright. I'm not having a bloody baby. Not at my age," she paused as she watched his expression change from a form of gentle excitement to shock at her sudden outburst, "I'm sorry," she said, with a lower tone in her voice. She reached towards him grasping hold of his hands which had fallen to his sides. His beautiful face now ashen white, this gorgeous face that knew nothing of her past and what she had done, "I'm sorry," she repeated, "I just don't want to have children. You and the dogs are all I need; please can we not talk about it anymore?" she asked as a few seconds of deathly silence fell on them. Even the dogs had stopped playing and sat on the grass in front of them, panting, "Look, I'm going to make another coffee seeing as I'm wearing this one, do you want a fresh one?" she asked in hope she hadn't ruined their day completely.

Tom couldn't speak for a few seconds from the shock of how Sarah had just lost it suddenly. He'd not seen her react that way before about anything, so he just shook his head and sat back down looking into the garden blankly.

Sarah gulped the massive lump down in her throat, she had really upset him, she could see that, but there was no way of making that alright now. She just had to hope that he would forgive her crazy freakish show and forget about the whole baby idea.

She made her way back into the kitchen and switched the kettle on to boil. Looking across the room towards the window where she could see her husband. He was just sitting and staring alone outside, apart from the dogs who were now laid at his feet like they knew he was upset. Why had she reacted that way and why couldn't she just explain the problem to him? Anger building up inside her body, she switched the kettle off and went back upstairs, passing the dreaded small room in question on her way. Glancing in, for just a bleating minute, she imagined it decorated in the pretty zoo scene Tom had just tried to start describing with all that joy in his voice. Her mind began stirring up the scene of a beautiful white swinging crib in the corner, fluffy teddies, and wooden toys on the windowsill. A rocking chair in the opposite corner where Tom would cradle their baby to sleep in the dead of the night, but no, she had to stop this. These thoughts were pointless, and they made her feel even more terrible than she did already.

Her heart ached thinking how much he would've made such a good father, she just knew it, and now she was taking that away from him. That chance to be a doting father, with his wonderful dad, becoming a grandfather finally as well after not seeing his other son's child, not even once being allowed. She hated herself so much right now but didn't have any choice, she just couldn't reveal her secret. It would just cause hurt and pain and moreover, it would change their seemingly perfect lives. No babies for the two of them, not in this life, it just wasn't going to be, and it was all her fault.

Later that evening as they sat down for dinner, Sarah felt there was more to be said regarding her outburst. They hadn't spoken properly for the rest of the day, and it had felt strained and horrible. After all the excitement of the wedding, the honeymoon, and then the decorating fun they'd had over the past few months, she had to try and make him understand why she had taken the idea of a nursery so badly, making him less angry with her for the whole argument somehow.

"Tom about earlier…can I explain?" she began.

"It's okay, it doesn't matter," he interrupted back, "I get it, you don't want kids, that's the end of it. I won't bring the subject up again," his tone was sharp, and it stabbed her heart a little bit more thinking of how he must be feeling knowing he wouldn't ever have his own children.

"No, I need to just say, well…" She needed to make something up that was believable, something that would be acceptable as an excuse as to why she had reacted so badly. Her brain ached from thinking but she didn't really have much to play with as she knew what the truth was deep down and she couldn't reveal any of it to him, "I just think our time has passed for that baby stuff. I've seen older mums come into the salon, telling me how they struggle, not only with the worry of pregnancy and the risks involved with it later in life. At my sort of age, it's not easy going and I am so happy right now with you. Meeting you was one of the best things that's ever happened to me, we have the dogs as our babies so, why spoil things?"

"Spoil things? Seriously? Having children doesn't spoil anything," he replied back angrily. Little did he know what he had just said had spiked so many memories of her younger life which had been spoiled. As she looked up into his stern eyes, he continued, "They can bring people together Sarah. We could be a little family, something James never got the chance to be, you know, how tragic was that situation?" he asked her, awaiting some sort of answer from her but without success, he continued again, "If it's an age thing, then how about adoption? You were okay living with your grandparents after your parents died, weren't you?"

Hearing the comparison to her childhood, she couldn't

help but become angry, "Tom. Do not bring my past into this. It wasn't my choice to have my parents die and have to live with nan and grandad. Yes, it was okay but that's not the same as adoption at all, don't you dare compare the two situations."

He suddenly threw his cutlery down which landed on his plate, the noise-making her ears ring, she'd never seen him so angry, so hurt and it was her fault. It was literally all her fault. She stood up and went around to his side of the table, slowly pulling the chair round and sitting beside him, trying to keep calm herself. She moved the plate away, touched his hand, and then he turned to face her with tears in his eyes, "I'm sorry Sarah, I didn't mean to say that about your folks. I love you so much and just thought having a baby with you would be the next dream for us, for our future together."

"I'm sorry too, I didn't mean to snap earlier today, you took me by surprise. It's just not something I've really thought about. I never even expected to get married, you know that. Jane's kids have been my stand-in babies."

"But they're not ours are they, they do belong to someone else," he paused, "Can we not even discuss adopting, think about all those babies who need loving homes? I see them come into the hospital and it's just heartbreaking seeing them have to go into care for years on end instead of being with people who can really care for them."

She took a deep breath, knowing that she didn't want it at all but couldn't bring herself to say it to him, "I'm not sure if…well if it's the right thing for us…" and before she could say anything else, her mobile rang making her jump.

She looked into his eyes lovingly and he moved his hand away from hers, speaking quietly, "Answer it, I think we're done here, don't you?"

Standing up from her seat, all she could do was try and smile back at him as she left to try and find her phone from the kitchen, only to find it was a withheld number, so she just declined the call.

A few minutes later, Tom appeared from in the lounge and wrapped his arms around her waist as she stared back at the phone screen. The background was a picture of her and Tom on their wedding day. It was one of her favourite photos of the day, one that Robbie had taken without them knowing. Such a natural, off-the-cuff moment and so much love in that one captured image, it warmed her heart every time she looked at it.

"I love you, Mrs. Cooper," Tom whispered as he kissed her neck.

She tilted her head to touch the side of his, and whispered back, "I love you too Mr. Cooper, I'm sor…" but before she could say sorry, he interrupted her whispering back lovingly into her ear, "shh, forget it." and they just held each other.

Chapter Seven

As the week came to an end, Sarah decided she needed a long overdue meet up with Karl at the park with the dogs. After the wedding and going on honeymoon, she had so much to catch up with work that she had completely messed up their weekly routine of seeing each other. She missed the kids too and had already texted both regarding a trip to London to check out some of the sights. They were both adamant they wanted to go on the London Eye although Sarah didn't much like heights or water but knew she wouldn't let them down and go for it, nerves or not. But this afternoon, she would chat with Karl and see how he was doing.

"How is everything?" Karl asked as they sat watching the dogs running and sniffing around.

"We're, okay. No, that's a lie. We are really good Karl,

honestly," she replied, taking a swig of the coffee he had bought for her on his way, "it's been such a manic time but no, we are just great and looking forward to the future now."

"Good. I've been so worried about you both," he replied, "after you texted me the other night saying you had that argument about having children. And well, I just feel it's my place to be there for you, you know, sort of take Jane's place as your male best friend," he sipped his coffee as he held her hand gently with the other, giving it a slight squeeze of reassurance.

He really had taken the place of her best friend. Always there whenever she needed him to be and when she needed time, he gave her just that too. They had both lost their beloved Jane and it had been so hard for them in so many ways but today, she felt just a little bit stronger for herself and him.

"Karl, you have been so amazing. I miss her so much but I'm glad we are staying as close as we are. It means a lot, and thanks for being so accepting of Tom, he really feels part of the family you know," she turned her head to look at him.

He just returned a knowing loving look to her, "He's a cool bloke, you've done well there and I'm glad you sorted it out with him. I'd hate to think you had just got started and then it fell apart just because of the children thing."

"Yeah, I think we will get over it, somehow. How are you doing anyway?" she asked. She felt like she hadn't asked this question to him for weeks, months and guilt suddenly flushed across her mind. Had she been so wrapped up in her own life, the wedding, the time away on honeymoon, work as always taking most of her days up. Her own memories that now kept popping up causing her to forget that he too was still grieving for the loss of his wife. He had two kids who had lost their beautiful mother so horribly and so quickly.

"Oh, don't worry about me missy, I'm doing fine too. The kids keep me busy with all their clubs and school, friends, parties...oh, and I think Robbie has a little admirer," he smiled back at her, winking in jest, "he's gone out this morning to the cinema with her and a few other mates I think, you know, safety in numbers," he chuckled.

"Aww, bless him. It's no wonder, he's bloody gorgeous Karl, although we will need to rigorously vet her before it turns into anything serious," she joked, making him laugh again.

Rufus suddenly bounded up with his tennis ball and dropped it straight into Karl's lap, mud, dribble, and all so it was quickly thrown back for him to fetch.

"Did you ever get round to reading Jane's letter? I kept forgetting to ask and what with all that's been going on, I didn't wanna bring it up," he wiped his hands down his trousers where the mud had splodged a nice muddy paw print or two.

"Sorry about that," Sarah said as she tried to help grabbing a tissue from her pocket, "I started to read it a few weeks after but then, well, I don't know. I just couldn't continue. It's five pages long Karl and I only got to the bottom of page one before my heart broke all over again for her and what she must have gone through before we all knew about it," she took a deep breath, "I think I may be ready to dig it out and get through it, or at least try. She's probably shouting at me now to tell me to get a move on and read it. You know how quickly she used to read books and that," they both laughed again remembering Jane's love of books.

"Yeah she probably is you know," he agreed, "anyway, I best get off now, I've got to pick Cass up from dance and then collect Robbie from the cinema, first date and all that, best make a good impression for him and not be late" he raised his eyebrows, checking the time on his watch, "let's sort a date out for you and Tom to come over for dinner, it's been too long," he leaned down and kissed her on her forehead just as Rufus appeared again with his ball.

"That would be nice, I'll speak to Tom and text you, thanks for today, Karl, it's been so lovely to catch up, finally," she reached down and grabbed the ball before he could get mud all over her this time, "give the kids a kiss for me and let me know how Rob's date turned out," she smiled up at him and they said their goodbyes.

Every time she had thought about reading the letter that Jane had left her before she died, it hurt like mad, but she knew deep down, her best friend had written it for a reason, and she had to man up now and take the time to read it. Tom was on some work mates stag-do for the weekend so she would use this time to get the letter out once more, maybe if she felt brave enough.

"Come on you lot," she called, giving them a sharp whistle to gather them all and securing the four of them with their leashes, "It's getting cold, let's get home hey?"

~

When she finally returned home and wiped all the dogs clean of mud, grass, and wetness, she again thought about her special letter. She had stored it in the safe under the bed so got the key and went upstairs. Maybe she could read a few pages before Tom got home.

'Dearest, dearest Sarah,' she began reading in her head, *'what can I say to you that you don't know already. I love you, no, you know that. I miss you, well I guess you should know that also. I wish I wasn't writing this - again, you obviously know that!'* Sarah paused for a moment. She could almost hear Jane's voice coming through the paper and it hit her just how much she wished that she wasn't reading this letter at all, wishing her friend was there with her instead.

'I hope you have behaved yourself and given out all the letters, I am in no doubt that you will have done so. Leaving you in charge of this job was, I think, the best option. I know Karl may be hurting too much to be able to deal with delivering my letters. I hope he's okay when I'm gone. :(

You really are...were, the most special friend to me. The bestest friend anyone could ever have imagined having next to them especially in the last months.

I'm writing this note because I know from my experience with pops that there will come a time when I just can't function exactly how I want to so it's so important to me to get these words down and express my utter and complete love for you.

I know the last few weeks will have been tough for you, but I honestly don't know what I and the rest of the family would've done without you.'

Extra-large tears were now forming in Sarah's eyes, and they were stinging as she tried so hard to keep them from falling but it was no use, she let them go and grabbed some tissues from the bedside cabinet to wipe them away again taking a deep breath before continuing.

'The times we had together when we were teenagers were awesome, I'll never forget them. You were such a funny teen and I know you went through some sad times with losing your parents and then your grandparents and I hope I did a good job at being there for you as you have been for me these past few months.

The utter craziness with boyfriends that we had, wow...what a time. That year that we had to spend apart was so hard for me, for both of us as I remember but you were so good and so brave to go and help your aunty in her time of need. You are an absolute diamond of a friend, an absolute diamond person. Therefore, I'm going to say what I'm about to say, and I know you might tell me to shut up, like you always have done but here goes anyway...You need a man! LOL. Honestly though Sarah. I really hope that you find someone to take care of you my beautiful lady, you deserve to have someone in your life to love and keep you safe. You know now that I can't do that job! Urghhh, I hate writing this stuff and please do not get upset or sad. I'd hate to think I'm upsetting you when you should be just keeping the happy memories that we built together over the million years. Lol.xxx'

Just as she smiled at Jane's silly humour, Elvis appeared at the bedroom door, "Hey boy, what are you doing up here?"

He gave a little bark, and she knew that meant he needed to go out to do his business, so she carefully folded the letter up and placed it back in the safe and locked it. The rest would have to wait, it was as though Elvis knew she needed a break from it. Reading too much at a time was so hard.

After getting all the dogs outside, she switched the kettle on to make a coffee and texted Karl. *'Started the letter again, got a few pages done this time, having a break again. Lol...see you soon. S. x'*

Then she gave Tom a call to see how long he was going to be.

"Hello gorgeous, I was just thinking about you," he answered.

"Oh? Hope it was good thoughts," she smiled as she stirred the spoon in the mug.

"Always darling, always. Yeah, I was thinking I could bring home a little Thai meal for us seeing as we won't see each other this weekend, what do you think?"

"Sounds perfect. Bottle of wine to go with it, I think we need a restock," she cheekily replied.

"Sure thing, got to go babe, my next appointment has just turned up, see you about six ish?"

"Okay, see you then, love you."

"Love you too sweetheart," and he hung up.

Charlie scraped on the back door to be let in, so she grabbed her coffee and watched them all bound in and get in their beds. Elvis curled himself into his blanket as usual.

She made her way back upstairs and changed into her favourite pyjamas. The ones from the hen weekend she'd spent away with Jane were still folded up in the drawer acting as a constant reminder of that special time. She'd not been able to wear them since but wasn't sure why. Maybe just the whole memory of the sadness she felt that evening. Jane had reluctantly told her about her terminal cancer after being quizzed about the tablets Sarah had seen. It had hurt like crazy to find out that her best friend would be dying much sooner than she should have but they'd had such a fun time afterwards messing about, dancing and singing and she would never forget that night with her.

Looking across under the bed, she contemplated getting the letter back out but decided not to, not for tonight anyway. It wasn't going anywhere, and she wanted to be able to take it all in instead of crying every two minutes and not being able to read it in full finally.

Tom arrived home just after six with a delicious takeaway meal and two bottles of sparkling wine for them to devour for the evening and Sarah had made it extra special with some candles on the table, special plates, crystal wine glasses and even the napkin rings that they had received as a wedding gift from one of his work colleagues.

"Have you been crying?" he asked after he'd managed to get in the door through the rabble of dogs greeting him.

"No, well not really," she answered, glancing across into the mirror above the fireplace to see her eyes. They did look a little puffy, "I had a read of Jane's letter earlier. That's all so nothing serious, it just got me a bit. I said to you it would be emotional, didn't I?"

"Bless you, did you get through it all this time?"

"Nope," she laughed, "it's going to take me a few years at this rate," they smiled at each other as they sat down to serve their meals, "this looks lush darling, thanks."

"No problem."

The evening was then spent watching a movie and finishing off the final bottle of wine before they went to bed. She was going to miss him so much this weekend, it would be the first time they'd been apart since they got married and although she had the dogs for company, not having him to come home to or get into bed with wasn't something she was looking forward to.

"It's only one night sweetheart and then you can have me back all to yourself," he said as he kissed her goodnight.

She just wriggled her body close to his and lay on his chest, listening to his heartbeat as they both fell asleep.

Chapter Eight

"So, girls, who's up for a little night out this Saturday?" Sarah asked as she began cashing up at work the following afternoon. It had been such a busy day at the beauty salon with clients back-to-back having their nails painted and toes polished ready for their weekends.

"I'm up for it," replied Tina, as she collected the towels from the workspaces.

"Brilliant," replied Sarah excitedly, "Shelley, Laila, what about you two joining us for a girly night out?"

"Sorry we can't, we're going to see our brother in London after work tonight and staying till Sunday night," Shelley replied.

Her and Laila were sisters and had started work at Sarah's salon at the same time. They'd both applied for the job and Sarah couldn't decide who she liked best so employed them both as nail technicians so she could focus more on the brows and lashes side of the business.

"Oh, that's nice, well, looks like it's just me and you then Tina."

"Great, looking forward to it, it's been a while since I've been out in town actually, shall we get a bite to eat before hitting the clubs?" Tina asked as she passed Sarah the keys to lock up.

"Erm, yes, why not. Tom is off for a stag night with one of his mates from work, so I'll be on my own eating anyway, yeah, let's do it, have a right girl's night," Sarah smiled. She hadn't had a good night out for ages too, "I'll have a look tonight at some places and text you later, have a nice evening."

"Ok, see you in the morning," Tina replied as she made her way to the bus stop.

Sarah's salon was becoming larger, and she had recently taken Tina on to help run the social media side of things as well as being a lash expert. Her Instagram and Facebook skills were incredible, and she had really helped to bring new customers in from all the posting and promotions that she frequently made. They'd become close as friends too but only been out a few times since Tina had started working there.

As Sarah walked home, she noticed a woman skipping along the path towards her with a little girl, hand in hand. The lady looked slightly embarrassed that she'd been seen but continued skipping along smiling coyly as they passed by. Sarah turned to watch them again and thought how cute it was. The little girl's hair was bouncing up and down, wonderful big curls with red ribbons trailing down from the bunches. How she wished she had got the chance to do that all those years ago. How would it be now if she had a little girl to walk along with and would she have cared about being seen skipping along like that? She would never know and something inside her panged. Maybe she should consider the adoption choice with Tom, maybe she could be a mother after all and get it right? Or maybe, just maybe, she wasn't meant to have that privilege. This is her life now; Tom and the dogs were her family that she had to look after.

As she approached the house, Tom appeared, "Hey darling, you ok," he asked, kissing her cheek as he moved the bin liner away from her that he was carrying, "I've started the dinner, just putting this smelly thing out and I'll make you a cuppa."

She smiled back at him, "thanks," and walked inside, kicking her heels off in the hallway and throwing her handbag over the banister. She sat on the stairs waiting for him to come back in.

"What are you doing sitting there," he asked as he shut the door behind him, "come here," he said, holding his arms out to her.

Slowly, she stood up, stretching her back and hearing a crack or two as she did so, "wash your hands first babe, then you can hug me," she laughed, turning away from him.

"Won't be a sec, dogs are in the garden, can you let

them back in," he called.

Sarah made her way to the back door where the four dogs were anxiously waiting to come back inside and when they saw Sarah, tails were wagging furiously. She loved how they made her feel every day when she got home from work.

"So, where's my hug then," Tom said, wiping his hands on the towel.

Sarah was crouching down with the dogs, so she stood up and hugged Tom tightly, burying her head into his chest and smelling his clothes, "Mmm, that feels good," she commented as he rubbed her back.

"Are you alright darling?"

"Yeah, just a bit tired, you?"

"All good, yep. Got home a bit earlier today so I took the dogs to the park for a run and started making us some dinner seeing as I won't see you for a few days."

"Lovely. Thanks. I was wondering if you wanted to have a bit of a chat again about the adoption thing," she said, looking into the oven to see what he had prepared. Turning back around to face him, she could see excitement in his face, he just stood there grinning from ear to ear, "Stop looking like that, I only said to chat about it," she sniggered, gently nudging him.

"Are you serious," he asked.

"Yes I am. I had a thought on the way home and just thought we could talk about it. I can't promise that it will happen or if we would even be considered but, well, look. Life is short isn't it, look at Jane. I saw this woman on the way home with a little girl and something just clicked," she paused. She didn't really understand what the feeling had been and if this was even the right thing to be saying to someone who desperately wanted children when she didn't even know if she wanted them herself, "we can talk about it okay Tom, just talk for now."

Tom leant forward and kissed her. He was overwhelmed that she had even considered talking about it after their argument a few days back and didn't want to push it, "Sure, let's have dinner and then talk about it." He smiled to himself as he turned to continue with the dinner plans. Deep down, he wanted to shout from the rooftops and was bursting inside.

After they finished their dinner and had fed the dogs, they sat down in the lounge with a glass of wine each. The atmosphere felt slightly tense, and Sarah was so nervous about it all, "So, do you know anything about adopting," she asked him as she sipped her drink.

"Well, I've learnt quite a bit about…" his words were interrupted by the sound of the front doorbell.

Sarah almost jumped up, "I'll get it," and made her way quickly to the door. It was like she had been saved by the bell and in some way she felt relieved. What was she thinking getting his hopes up like this? Did she really want to adopt a child when she did what she did?

"Hey, what's up?" It was Tina at the door, and she was sobbing.

"I'm sorry Sarah, I didn't know where else to go," she blubbed.

"Come in, come in. Tom, can you make a strong coffee, it's Tina from work," she called to him as she ushered Tina inside.

Tom had made his way to the lounge door and seeing how upset Tina was, decided to leave them to it, and make coffees in the kitchen.

"Sorry for being here late, you were the first person I thought of and the nearest too," Tina said as she wiped her tears away.

"Don't worry, it's fine. What the hell has happened Tina?" She passed her some tissues.

"Well, I've just found out that my husband had a baby with someone else when he was younger and I... well I can't have any you see. I just don't know what to do or what to say to him," she sniffed back as she blew her nose.

"Wow, really? How did you find out?"

"Tonight. I got home after work and he was like, ``I have some news…" she paused, "I mean, why didn't he think to tell me this years ago before we got married?"

Sarah didn't know what to say. She understood secrets and why people decided to keep them from loved ones more than anyone, "Maybe he didn't know?" she suggested as Tom brought in the coffees and promptly left to hide himself upstairs.

"Oh, he knew about it, he said he's known for years but he was too young to deal with it and thought the girl had got rid of the baby, you know, had an abortion. But she hadn't, she had it and gave it away. Now his daughter has found him and wants to find the mother too," tears rolled down her cheeks, she was really hurting badly, Sarah could see it and she felt so sorry for her, but something was hurting her too.

"Do you want something stronger than coffee; you can stay here tonight if you want, get a bit of head space between the two of you. We don't have the spare room set up, but the sofa isn't too uncomfortable."

"Oh Sarah, I couldn't impose."

"Honestly, it's fine. I think you need to have a bit of time to think and chat. I'm here for you okay," Sarah put her arm around her shoulders, she was quivering, "Let's have a glass of wine instead and you can tell me all about it, yeah?" With that, she went into the kitchen and grabbed another glass and the bottle of wine that her and Tom had started.

"Sarah, I can't stand the fact that he has a child when I can't give him one myself, I feel so...I don't know, worthless."

"Oh, don't say that. These things happen Tina. I'm sure it won't change anything between you," she was trying her best to make her feel better even if all the information was hitting a bit too close to home for her too.

"I really don't know at the moment, I just left, I told him I needed time to think about it all. We had accepted that we wouldn't have children and then we got this shock. She's a grown woman but just wanted some answers regarding her past," she gulped down the remaining wine in the glass and leant forward to pour some more, "she's so beautiful Sarah, a real stunner and she wants him to help her find her real mum. I think he's quite taken with the idea of being a father now and it hurts like crazy," tears fell heavily again, and she slurped another few sips of wine, "Apparently, his name was put on the birth certificate, that's how she found him, but the mother's name has changed. I guess she has got married maybe. Anyway, she's trying to locate her with Bens help. Oh, what a mess, what a bloody mess Sarah, can you believe it, how can someone just give their child away, it doesn't make sense to me."

Sarah's heart ached at hearing her talk like this. She understood the whole situation, but no-one knew what she had gone through. No-one would understand her if all was revealed, "I'm sure there were reasons, you never know what people are going through or why they have to do these things, it's a crazy world," she tried her hardest to shrug it off.

"I suppose so," Tina replied looking into her lap where her hands held the wine glass tightly, "It's just when Ben and I got married, we said we had no secrets, we promised each other there was nothing hidden."

"Ben?" Sarah replied.

"Yes, Ben's my husband, have I not told you his name before?"

Sarah's blood ran cold for a second, hearing that name, "No, I don't think you have." Her mind was frantically trying to remember Tina's surname, was it his name, no... her surname was Lords. That wasn't Ben's surname, she took a breath of air in relief. Then she felt stupid for even thinking it could've been him. There were plenty of Ben's in the world, why would it be the actual Ben from back in the day?

"Do you have any more of this?" Tina asked as she held up the now empty bottle of wine.

"Erm, yeah sure. I'll go get one," Sarah took the bottle and walked back into the kitchen. She felt sorry for Tina having to go through this but maybe drinking her sorrows away wasn't such a good idea. Maybe she should try and get her to sleep and then things may seem clearer in the morning, "sorry Tina, we are out actually," she said as she returned to the lounge.

"Oh ok, probably best I don't drink more anyway, thanks so much for listening to me going on Sarah, you're more than a boss to me."

"It's ok, look, why don't you try and get some rest for tonight, I'll go get some blankets and a pillow for you."

"Yes, good idea. I do feel pretty whacked out now, what about work tomorrow though and our night out?"

"You can take the day off, don't worry about that. You need to go home and see your husband; we can do it another weekend." Sarah placed her hand on Tina's shoulder, "don't worry, I'm sure everything will turn out fine," and smiled at her hoping that she would be right about it.

Chapter Nine

The next morning, Sarah got up early to take the dogs for their walk and crept into the lounge to check on Tina only to find that she had already left, leaving all the blankets neatly folded up on the sofa. Sarah noticed an envelope placed on the top of the pile where Tina had just written the word, thanks on. She felt better knowing that in some way she had helped her and would try and remember to give her a text after her walk.

Tom was just stirring when she returned home, so she filled him in on all the details from the previous evening with a coffee in bed. He'd been fast asleep by the time she had made it to her bed the previous evening, "will we be able to continue our little chat after the weekend?" he asked nervously, "I'm off on the stag-do in an hour or so," he asked, grabbing a last mouthful of his toast.

"Yeah sure," she replied. She hadn't really thought much more about the adoption subject, but she knew he would want to bring it up again at some point, "I best get ready for work," she continued, standing up, "the dogs have been on their walk, done their business outside and they've had a few biscuits each. I guess I'll see you Sunday night then," she watched him as he brushed back his wavy, black hair with his hands. They'd not had a weekend apart from one another since they met, and she knew she was going to miss him like crazy.

"Yep, I'll be back around lunchtime probably, maybe we can go out for something to eat in the evening?" he moved towards the edge of the bed to her and put his arms around her waist, pulling her back.

"That's a good idea, right, stop this," she chuckled, moving his hands away from her butt where they'd slowly worked their way to, "give us a kiss, I've got to get to work, we are one down today what with Tina's situation." With one more last long kiss, and a squeeze of her butt again, Sarah then set off to get ready for work.

As she passed the little spare room at the top of the stairs, she glanced in and tried to imagine what it would look like decorated as a nursery. Would it even get to that stage the way she felt about it all, she didn't know what to imagine? After her quick shower, she grabbed her things from the bedroom, and looked out of the window. Tom had made his way downstairs and was happily playing with the dogs in the garden. She smiled to herself and instantly felt enormous guilt deep down in her heart. So much guilt for not revealing to him the truth about her past and why she was so confused right now. Surely, he would forgive her if he did ever find out. They were the best of friends now as well as lovers. They were newlyweds, a husband-and-wife team and she loved him more than anyone she had ever loved before.

~

"Morning girls," Sarah called as she made her way into the salon finally. The roads had seemed extra busy this morning and even the parking had been a nightmare too, "Is my first client in yet?" she asked as she hung her jacket up in the office.

"No she's caught in traffic too, she called about five minutes ago to let us know so you're ok for about ten minutes or so i reckon," replied Laila as she began making some coffee in the new machine that they had just invested in, "there is a message on the desk for you though, some guy called for you, wouldn't leave his name, so just a number to call him back on."

Sarah walked round to the back of the desk to read the note on the message pad, "That's a bit weird isn't it, no clue as to what he wanted?"

"Nope, he just said you used to know him, and could you call when you get a minute, I did ask him his name, but he hung up quickly after giving me the number, sorry."

"Okay, no worries, I think I'll leave it till later. See if he rings back first," she closed the message book, "Right, best go get set up now. Oh, and Tina won't be in today, she's got some stuff going on at home so I said she should have the day off to get sorted, can you cover her appointments, she only had a few manicure appointments this afternoon."

"Sure, no problem, one of mine has cancelled anyway."

"Brill thanks, oh and if you can remember to take before and after pics so Tina can share them on the socials when she's back in."

"Yep, I'll bring your coffee through in a minute."

"Cheers Laila." Sarah said, as she went through to her room to set up her eyelash equipment.

The morning seemed to fly by with clients back-to-back for Sarah and by lunchtime, she felt exhausted. Maybe the late-night chatting with Tina had tired her out more than she had thought. Suddenly, she remembered that she was supposed to have texted her, so she quickly typed a message to ask if she was alright, which a return text pinged through moments after that confirmed everything was okay

Sarah felt relieved for her and slowly put her feet up on the desk in the office and rocked back on her chair wondering again who the phone call to the salon had been from this morning. Should she call the number and ask or was it just a sales guy trying to sell more lash products to her again. She would receive those types of calls daily, but usually Tina would deal with them. As she leaned forward to grab her water bottle, she noticed the note again on the desk with the number scribbled on it. Feeling a bit brave, and rather compelled to discover who it may be or what company it was from, she decided to give it a quick search on google. Nothing came up as scam numbers and no business numbers either, so she shrugged it off, screwed up the note and threw it into the bin across the room, getting it straight in. Giving herself a triumphant fist bump and smiling, she then returned to her work in the main area this time for her next eyebrow threading appointment.

An hour later, she was seeing her client out the front door when Tina appeared in the doorway, "Hey you," Sarah said, "you're supposed to have the day off."

"I know but I'm okay really and to be honest, I'd rather be here keeping busy and not thinking about stuff," Tina replied, "Plus, we were supposed to be going out together tonight weren't we, I didn't want to let you down, especially after you were so helpful last night."

"Oh Tina, honestly, it was no problem at all, glad to help. I'm just going to have a night in with the dogs now though. To be fair, I'm too exhausted to be bothered with all that getting ready and going out malarkey, it's been a manic day here," Sarah replied, clearing up her equipment, "you're welcome to come and join me if you like though, we could just have a girls' night in instead?"

"Erm...yeah okay, I'll check with Ben as to what he's doing but sure it'll be fine."

"Nice. Look, Laila is covering your clients this afternoon and I'm finished now with mine, so, do you wanna get off now? We could grab a takeaway on the way back to mine and a few bottles of wine?"

"But I'm in my work gear now?"

"I've got some stuff you can borrow for the night don't worry, unless you want to go home and get changed first or have things to do before, sorry, I'm babbling on a bit aren't I, ignore me, jeez, you'd think I didn't have any friends," Sarah chuckled to herself. She didn't know why, but she felt nervous about having Tina over somehow. It had been ages since she had spent any amount of time with another girlfriend after losing Jane. She kind of felt as though she was betraying her best friend by enjoying time with someone else again.

"Only if you're sure Sarah, I don't want to seem like I'm imposing, borrowing clothes and that? It wouldn't take long to go home again and change I guess."

"Don't be silly, I've not had a chance to do this sort of thing since losing Jane, so it would be really nice actually," Sarah put her hand on Tina's shoulder reassuring herself more than anything that it was okay to move on and have other friends now. Doing fun nights like this wouldn't hurt, "Tom is on a stag weekend now so it's just me and the dogs you have the company of, will your husband be okay to collect you later or you could stay over again?"

"I'll give him a quick ring in a minute, he doesn't drink so I'm sure it will be fine to pick me up, I can't impose on your sofa for another night," she paused to find her phone buried deep in her handbag, then glanced back up, "Sarah...thanks, I really need this support right now, I really appreciate your time and that."

Sarah just smiled back, then collected her things while Tina made her phone call.

~

"So, he's been trying to contact the birth mum but hasn't had any luck yet. I think maybe she's ignoring his calls and why would she want to speak to him after this long, probably wanting to keep her secret I'd imagine?" Tina said as she poured another glass of wine for them both. They'd got a Chinese takeaway delivered and were enjoying a girly chat and already one bottle of wine had been demolished. The dogs were waiting patiently beside the table in the hope something would fall into their mouths or that they might get a little treat soon.

"I guess so," Sarah replied knowing that sometimes, secrets needed to be kept hidden. She of all people knew that.

"We had such a good chat today though and I'm going to support him as much as I can," she continued, sipping on the wine, "I was just so shocked you know, but he's pretty taken with it all and if we can help the girl find her mother, then that's what we're going to do. I mean, imagine finding out you are adopted after all these years, I don't quite know how I'd cope with that, do you?"

"No," Sarah said, not even looking up from her plate. She felt awkward talking about this sort of thing so shoved a mouthful of chicken tikka in to avoid speaking.

"Anyway, thanks again for all this. It's been a really lovely evening. I told Ben to come and collect me at about ten, is that okay with you, not too late, is it?" asked Tina as she glanced at her watch. It was already nine o'clock and they had one more bottle of wine to get through.

Sarah pushed her plate away and rubbed her tummy, "Yeah sure, that's fine, do you want to sit in the lounge for a bit? I'll clean this up when you've gone, come through," she stood up, grabbing the wine bottle and her glass.

As Tina followed, her phone began to vibrate on the table where she'd placed it earlier, "Hello darling, you alright...oh, ok, yeah fine...ten minutes...yep...okay, see you then...ok...bye," and she hung up.

"Everything ok?" Sarah asked as she plonked herself on the sofa, bending her legs up behind her.

"Yes fine, that was the hubby, he's picking me up in about five minutes now, sorry. He sounded a bit upset actually. He didn't say anything really but just wanted me to come home," Tina placed her phone down on the coffee table. "I feel bad now, I should've stayed in with him really, he's had a shock as well as me, bless him."

Sarah glanced across at the phone as another text came through and lit the screen up. The background image was of a couple, quite obviously Tina and she presumed with her husband, but the new message was covering his face. "Is that the two of you?" she asked, nodding towards the phone.

"Haha, yes, it is," Tina replied, leaning forward, and picking it up, "blooming pizza place, they text me every day with their offers. Anyway, yes, this is us on our honeymoon," she continued as she swiped the text message away to reveal the screensaver image, "not the best pic but we had just come off a speed boat absolutely soaked through, such a fun day that was though," Tina beamed a massive smile down to the screen and Sarah's heart nearly stopped as she saw the side view of a face appear. It looked just like Ben, THE Ben that she knew from all those years back when she was a rebellious teenager.

Tina continued to tell her about the adventures on the boat, but Sarah wasn't really listening, the voice sounding more like a mumble now, she was in shock and had to try and hide it. What the hell was going on here? Did Tina know her secret, had she befriended Sarah on purpose and how was she going to get out of this one if that was the case? Her mind was racing ten to the dozen and she felt sick with worry. Surely it wasn't him, surely, he couldn't be back and surely not married to Tina, of all the people in Sarah's life right now. And why would he be back? Was his story true about a child coming back into his life and what did that mean for Sarah?

Her thoughts were suddenly interrupted by the sound of the doorbell and the dogs closely following with their barks towards it. She turned her head to look at the lounge door but couldn't move. She didn't want to answer it knowing who might be on the other side, she just couldn't imagine what the hell she would do if it was indeed him.

"Shall I answer it, Sarah?" Tina asked, looking blankly at her very still friend now frozen on the spot, "It'll be Ben," she paused, "are you okay Sarah?"

"Erm, sorry, no...err, I don't feel so good actually, do you mind seeing yourself out, I think the wine has gone to my head a little," and she got up and ran upstairs leaving

Tina gathering her coat and bag looking slightly confused.

A few minutes later, Sarah heard the front door close. She crept toward the front bedroom window to see Tina getting into the car. She watched intently as he held the door open for Tina as she got in and then made his way round to the drivers' side, closed the door and drove away. This guy that had just picked Tina up looked so much like him, the him from back in the day, but maybe the wine had gone to her head, and she had just imagined it being him, but why? Just because his name was Ben, didn't mean it could be him. *'There are millions of people called Ben for goodness' sake'*, she thought to herself.

Her mind seemed to be playing tricks on her and she felt dizzy with all the confusion. Too much wine and not enough sleep meant memories were starting to rear their ugly heads, taunting her of the past she had trained herself to forget about for so many years. She needed to get some rest, try to clear her head of this silliness, so she climbed into bed without bothering to get undressed. Within five minutes, she was fast asleep, with the four dogs joining her shortly afterwards at the foot of the bed.

Chapter Ten

Sunday afternoon couldn't come quick enough, Sarah had really missed Tom even though she had been kept busy with the eventful evening with Tina. The dogs all seemed to be extra playful this morning too and she hadn't even walked them yet.

All she could think about and all she wanted now was to be back in the arms of her beloved husband so, felt slightly upset when she got a text from him saying that he wouldn't arrive back until later than planned due to some train delays. The housework would hopefully take her mind off last nights' stupid thoughts and worries and then a quick walk to the park with her four buddies to work off their energy.

When Tom did eventually arrive home, just after half past nine, he was exhausted, "Urgh...I'm getting too old for this night club malarkey," he said as he sprawled himself across the bed after having a quick shower.

Sarah sat next to him, brushing her hair and at the same time, admiring his body which was only wrapped in a short towel, "Aww, old man hey," she chuckled.

"Haha," he joked back, "I think I'd forgotten what it was like, seems like forever since I've been to a club and that," he replied sitting up to get closer to her, "what did you get up to anyway? Anything I should know about?" he stroked her back lovingly and leaned forward to kiss her neck.

"Nothing really, a bit of work Saturday morning, some housework and dog walking today...oh and had Tina round last night for a bit, just a few drinks and a Chinese, it was nice actually."

"Oh, sounds fun. How are things with her and the whole secret child situation, any further news on that?" he asked.

Sarah didn't want to talk about it really as her mind had still been working overtime trying to work out if it had in fact been the person collecting Tina who she thought it was, "Oh it's all fine actually, they're working it out…" she paused changing the subject to food, "Do you want anything to eat, we could order a pizza for quickness?"

"Yeah, I wanted to take you out, but I'm knackered. Let me get some clothes on and I'll order it from the app, I think they have some Sunday deals."

He got up off the bed and grabbed a clean t-shirt and some joggers from his drawer. His pert butt looked incredible and under any normal circumstances, she would've taken the chance to grab it but tonight, she just wanted to take in the view and hope that their lives would continue to be as perfect as it had been so far.

"I'm not that hungry but order whatever you like, I'm gonna have a quick shower I think," Sarah walked over to the ensuite room, patting him on that gorgeous bottom she had been admiring, which made him smile.

As she began to undress, she got her mobile out of her pocket and something made her want to do a search on Facebook to see what Ben might look like now. She searched for Tina's name, but nothing came up. Maybe she just wasn't on Facebook, so she tried searching his name. A long list of people came up but only some of them had photos next to them. She scrolled frantically through them but couldn't see anyone who resembled what Ben used to look like anyway. Shaking her head, she sighed, locked the phone again and put it on the windowsill. What was she even thinking looking for him on there and why did she need to know? He had moved away, and it couldn't possibly be him who was married to Tina. It was all just too much of a coincidence surely, her mind was just working overtime. She needed to get this shower and enjoy the rest of this evening with her husband instead of thinking of the past. Tom was tonight's focus, no-one, and nothing else mattered.

The next morning, it was back to normality for the pair. Tom set off for work and Sarah made her way to the salon. She had eyelash and eyebrow clients back-to-back again today and had even booked an extra hour after closing to fit in a final eyebrow tint and wax customer who had emailed her for a quick spruce up before a big date that night. She didn't have to work late very often so didn't mind fitting people in especially if they were regulars.

"Morning ladies," she said as she arrived, "I picked up some doughnuts for you all today, my treat," her face beamed with a massive smile, she felt really good today. The fact that she had spent a romantic and, in the end, rather passionate night with her gorgeous husband had given her a real boost in happiness and she was ready for her day ahead.

Tina was already in the office doing her social media posting and replying to emails as Sarah went in and hung her coat up on the back of the door, "hey you, how's it going?" she asked her, "look at these yummy treats," placing the large box of delights onto the desk next to her computer.

"Hi Sarah, yes it's all good thanks, wow, they look amazing, we'll have to get some nice coffees to go with them at lunchtime, the machine doesn't seem to be working but I've emailed the company to come and have a look for us."

"Oh really, what a bummer. Okay, well, I can nip out on my break when everyone's ready to dig in, I know which one I've claimed. I have about half an hour spare today so can go then," she laughed, "right, better crack on, think my first lady is here for her lashes already, see you in a bit."

Tina nodded as she tapped away on the keyboard. She would spend an hour or so every few days taking photos around the salon, so she always had fresh content to post about on Instagram, Facebook, Twitter and sometimes even using their Snapchat account to get coverage. She busied herself continuing uploading images and hash tagging like crazy on all of them.

As lunchtime approached, quicker than Sarah had anticipated, Tina asked, "Do you want me to go to the coffee shop instead, I don't mind."

"No, it's ok Tina, I'll go. I need to pick up some pain killers from Boots while I'm out, my back is aching so much today, think it's all the lashes I've done this morning. If you could just text me through what everyone wants, I'll grab my coat and run around there." She felt super tired, her back was really aching today but she loved her job so much, it didn't bother her too regularly.

With her list of coffee choices text through, Sarah made her way to her favourite coffee shop which was just a few minutes' walk from the salon. She thought about how many times her, and Jane must have visited this place during their friendship and how much money they must have spent on coffees and cookies over the years. She wished she could spend more money here with Jane and as she remembered how beautiful her friend was, she sighed, and her heart ached for a moment. How long would she feel this sad for every time she thought about Jane? Why did she have to be taken away from them all and at such a young age? Not even getting to her big fortieth birthday that they had discussed so many times. She hated cancer with a vengeance for stealing her best friend, a mother, wife, and daughter who deserved so many more years to live.

Trying to get over her heartache, she made her way into the store, taking a deep breath to inhale the rich aromas into her nose. She loved coffee so much and couldn't wait to get her fix of her favourite beans in the form of a double shot americano today.

Patiently, she waited in line, checking her text messages, and scrolling through her Instagram feed, smiling to herself at various posts by Tina about the salon, giving them a like. She was so lucky to have found someone so creative who could make a simple set of eyelashes or new brows look so lovely in a social media post.

A text popped up on the screen from Tom saying he was on his lunch break and had gone to see her at the salon. Quickly, she replied, telling him to wait there and that she would bring him a coffee and a snack back as soon as she could. She finished the message off with three big X's.

She was then the next customer in line, so quickly opened the message from Tina on her phone to find the coffee list from the girls and added Tom's drink to the order along with a cookie. Once her order had been taken, she moved along the counter to wait for her drinks to be served.

Grabbing her phone once again to keep busy, she

opened her emails but as she stood there, she felt as though someone was watching her. Glancing toward one of the staff behind the counter, she noticed a young girl who seemed to be trying to make eye contact with her. Awkwardly, Sarah turned away to face the window but out of curiosity, she had to turn back to see if she had just imagined it. The girl had now turned herself away. What was wrong with her lately, thinking strange thoughts about people watching her, people turning up after years to mess her up. Maybe the menopause was hitting her early or something. She felt confused but shook it off and continued waiting, deleting the long list of junk email messages.

"Order for Sarah," called the voice from behind the counter, so she moved nearer to collect the haul of drinks. The young girl who had been looking at her a few seconds ago was putting the cookie into a brown bag for her and as she approached, she asked, "Sarah? Sarah Roberts?"

Looking straight back into her eyes, Sarah began shaking, not with fear but with shock at the impending situation that was now upon her. She just wanted to get her caffeine fix with her usual double shot Americano coffee and get back to her man in the salon where he was patiently awaiting his flat white and millionaire shortbread.

Married just six months ago, this wasn't how things were meant to start for them as newly-weds. They'd had their fantastic honeymoon in luscious Jamaica, bought their new home together and now, this normal daily trip to her favorite coffee shop, meant things were about to change, her life was about to get even more complex than she had ever imagined.

"You are Sarah, aren't you?" asked the timid voice from behind the counter, leaning forward as she passed the stack of takeaway containers and brown paper bag.

Spluttering back awkwardly, Sarah replied, "erm, well, I was Roberts…" she paused, "I mean, yes I am but, I'm married now so no, but erm…"

"I knew it was you. Oh, this is so exciting. Hi, I'm Kate," she held out her hand to shake Sarah's, "You may know me as Katie, Katie-Jane?" the girl replied, seeing the confusion in Sarah's eyes as she glanced around the room, "I've been looking for you for months, can we talk?"

Sarah's heart started thumping hard in her chest, '*Shit, it can't be? It couldn't be Katie standing right here in front of her. Surely not. But it was, it was Katie-Jane,*' she thought to herself as she swiftly plucked up the courage to finally answer, "erm, no sorry, I…well, I have to get going, I've got to get back to work, my husband, he's waiting for me, sorry, I can't talk right now," she flustered all her words, picking up the stack of cups and turning to walk away bumping into the next customer in line in a panic, "I'm so sorry, excuse me," she apologized.

"Sarah," the girl's voice remained strangely calm but slightly raising her tone, she called out, "Sarah, you forgot your cookie," and waved the brown bag in the air in the hope that Sarah would come back.

Turning around to see the strawberry blonde-haired girl holding up the paper bag, Sarah just stared at her for what seemed like minutes, but she couldn't make her feet do anything. They were frozen on the spot and people were starting to stare at her and began asking if she had finished her turn in the queue, but their words sounded strangely muffled. She had certainly finished here, and she didn't want to return in a hurry. She didn't have any interest in what she had forgotten to pick up.

"I'm sorry…," Sarah apologized again, bumping into another customer as she made her way out of the store, "excuse me, please, sorry, let me through, sorry, sorry," she continued as her feet finally led her to the doorway and out of the coffee shop in a sweat. She was walking as fast as her little kitten-heeled boots would allow, spilling the steaming hot liquids out of the top of the containers, and her mind began to race even more with question upon question, '*what had just happened, did it just happen? How had she found her and why had she found her, why now, what the hell was going on?*'

Nothing seemed to make sense and her head was full of everything but nothing at the same time. Dizzy and lightheaded, she felt sick and had a pounding ache in her chest from the panicked state she had got herself into. She needed to sit down before she made a complete fool of herself and fell in the street and what if Katie had followed her out, she couldn't faint in front of her, no, she couldn't do that. So, she quickly made her way to a side alley, slid down the wall, and crouched down breathing heavily, trying to calm down and make sense of what had just happened.

How was she going to explain this to everyone if Katie turned up at the salon or worse still, turned up at her home and told Tom everything before she had the chance to? Who would understand what she had done, and would they forgive her? Jane would have but she wasn't here anymore, and Sarah felt frantic as to who she could turn to about it all. Only one person popped into her head right now, it had to be Karl – her best friend's husband. She had always felt so close to him, even more so over the past few years helping each other deal with the heartache and grief that Jane's death had brought to them. He was like a big brother, and he was the only person she felt that she could turn to in this shock crisis. The nearest thing to Jane that she had, so he was the only option and she felt sure that he would not judge her or think anything bad of her. She hoped for that anyway. She had to see him, and it had to be today, like now, in her hour of need, it was Karl she had to get to.

Chapter Eleven

As she sat trying to gasp her breath, she glanced at the coffees she had nearly spilt all over the place now sitting beside her on the floor. There was no way she could deliver these to the salon now, not in this state so, standing up and dusting herself off, she threw them into a nearby bin and text Tom to tell him she had to go see Karl urgently and to let the girls know that she would be an hour and would have to get their own coffees.

Feeling terrible for lying to him, she began speed walking to her car in the hope Tom wouldn't ask any more questions in his reply text. He didn't, he just replied 'Ok darling', with an added kiss and that he would see her after work. She felt even worse after reading it, felt betrayal towards her husband but if she went to see him now, she would break down and reveal all to him and she wasn't ready for that. She didn't think he would be either.

The short drive over to Karl's house was simply a blur for her, with stinging eyes from the outburst of tears realising what was going on. Arriving in the driveway, she glanced into the rear-view mirror at herself and tidied her hair that she'd thrown up into a messy bun in haste, *'pull yourself together woman'* she thought to herself, *'everything is going to be ok, Karl will understand'* and she took a few deep breaths opening the car door. As she walked up to the front door, and rang the bell, she remembered the day she had returned from their girly weekend away for a hen do in Norfolk with Jane. Where her best friend had finally revealed to her that she had cancer and it wasn't going away. It had devastated her but now she had her own secret that she had to reveal to someone. Her stomach kept turning and churning over and she didn't know if she felt sick or relieved in some way. Karl would help her sort it out, she felt sure of it.

Jane's favourite garden gnome still sat by the front door, albeit a bit paint chipped with its bright red hat and boots. The cobwebs spanning from its larger-than-life button nose onto the brickwork of the house was a sign that it never got moved. Jane had bought it for herself one Spring from a local florist as she had been buying some flowers for her mum's birthday. Sarah recalled how excited Jane had been ringing her and sending her a picture through whatsapp on her phone. She smiled at the figurine for a moment as the door opened suddenly.

"Hey you. You gonna stand there all day or are you

coming in woman," Karl piped up standing with the door wide open.

"Oh Karl, yes sure, sorry, miles away. I was just looking at Jane's Gnomy thing, needs a bit of a dust and a paint job," she replied, trying to humour him.

"Yes, I've been meaning to do it but don't trust myself not to break the little man and Jane strike me down for it from above, you know," he smiled sweetly gesturing a striking hand across his neck, "come on in, you can make the brews," turning around, he began walking off up the hallway, so she followed him and shut the door. So welcoming all the time but in such a weird kind of way, he was so funny at times.

"So, what's this impromptu visit about then? You're not getting another dog are you and want my advice as to which breed you should get this time?"

She managed to chuckle nervously back at him, "No, no. I think four is enough for the time being although Tom would probably have another couple if he was honest. He's been showing me some pictures of some labradoodles lately. One of his work mates' dogs is pregnant with them but no, no more dogs just yet," she replied waffling on to avoid the subject in mind.

"Ha-ha, Tom is funny. You really lucked out on him mate. So, come on, the suspense is killing me, what is this visit about, aren't you working today?"

"Yes, well, no. I've taken the afternoon off because, well. Okay," she paused to compose herself, "so, do you remember Jane telling you anything about when my parents died, and I had to go and live with my aunt for a year?" she asked as she turned to flick the switch on the kettle as they got into the kitchen.

Shuffling some paperwork around the table to form a neater pile and to make some room, Karl replied, "erm, I think so yes. Weren't you quite young?" he then reached into the fridge to get the milk out and passed it to her.

"Yeah, that's right. I had to go and stay with Aunt Bridget to help her with some stuff after she got poorly, but it was only for a year and then I got a little bedsit with the money that mum, and dad had left me in their wills after my nana and grandpa died. It wasn't much but I just needed to be back here near Jane and that..."

"Okay?" Karl answered, puzzled by the conversation already.

"Well..." she paused for a minute wondering if this was really the right thing to do? The right person to turn to currently. Should she burden him with her problems? He'd had enough to contend with losing Jane and bringing the kids up on his own. But, yes, she had to tell someone. Feeling so bad for not confiding in her best friend at the time but now, somehow, maybe, just maybe someone would forgive her. She continued, "I went a bit crazy after mum and dad died, I sort of, well, went off the rails a bit, you know how teenagers can get even without their parents dying?" she poured out the steaming water into the mugs, trying not to spill anything due to her hands shaking.

Karl noticed her trembling. Concerned, he moved closer to her, "Sarah, are you ok? Why are you telling me this story? What's up?"

She felt the warmth in his voice, he had been Jane's rock – her soulmate. He was now turning into Sarah's best friend, and she loved him dearly for his compassion, "I don't know, I just…oh shit, I need to tell someone." Getting more frustrated by the second as the words just wouldn't come out, she was getting so angry at herself.

Karl took the mugs and ushered her to a chair to sit down, "Mate, come on, you know you can talk to me. I know I'm not Jane but, if I can help, I will. What's up, what's happened? Do you want a biscuit or something?"

Sarah suddenly snapped back, "I don't want a shitting biscuit Karl," immediately realising her awful tone towards him, she quickly apologised, "I'm sorry, oh god. I'm so sorry Karl, please, just give me a minute, I'll be back in a sec," she got up from the chair, sliding it back so hard it nearly toppled over. She practically ran to the under stairs toilet to compose herself. Her heart was thumping so hard it felt like a drum pounding inside her chest. She had tried to be so calm, but the realisation was just too much, and she hadn't told anyone before. This was the biggest secret that only her aunt and grandparents knew about. They'd managed to hide it from everyone else but now the truth was about to come out. She placed both her hands on the small sink, bowing her head down for a moment trying to take some deep breaths again. As she looked up into the ornate white mirror in front of her, thinking how awful her eyes looked, red and with blotchy skin reddening her cheeks, there was a gentle knock on the door.

"Hey, your coffee is getting cold, are you gonna come out?" his words, his quietness, his all-encompassing empathy. This man was pure first class. No wonder Jane had loved him like she had. Even in a crisis, he knew how to comfort people, even when he was still hurting himself. It hadn't been that long since Jane's death and he'd had the occasional break down on the phone to Sarah, but he really was coping better than everyone had expected him to. It's how Jane would've wanted him to be.

She slowly unlocked the door and pushed it gently open, to find Karl waiting on the other side, leaning against the wall with coffees in hand, just smiling so sweetly at her. "Come on you, let's get you sat down again hey? Tell old Karl what's going on in your crazy world," he passed her a mug of steaming coffee. It wasn't even near to getting cold, she thought to herself glancing down into it. He just wanted his friend out of that tiny cubicle of a toilet to check she was ok.

"I'm sorry Karl, I didn't mean to…"

"Hey, no worries. You know I understand you women and your woes, I have a teenage daughter remember," he joked back holding her hand to help stop the shaking which had subsided a little, "just talk to me when you are ready, okay?"

Looking into his eyes, she knew she had to confess to him now, more than ever, she just wanted forgiveness for what she had done all those years ago, some closure to her feeling like such a terrible person for so many years, "okay," she began, "so…I've not told anyone this, ever…and I just feel so ashamed Karl."

"Sarah, whatever it is, just tell me. I'm here for you. Seriously, if you hadn't been around for me after losing Jane, well, I'm not sure I'd be standing here at all. Take a deep breath and tell me what's going on," he pleaded with her and shuffled his chair nearer to hers. She felt at ease, slightly as he urged her to continue, "you went to live with your aunt, went off the rails, by that you mean?" he asked.

Taking an almighty inhale of air, she said, "I, well, here goes. Yes, I had to go and live with my aunt not long after losing mum and dad, but not for the reasons we told people. It was just an excuse to hide what was really happening, what really happened…she helped me sort out something, I… I had a baby Karl, I had a little girl," and then sudden silence fell hard in the room.

Staring at each other was all they could do. The aroma of coffee filling the air but sort of going unnoticed for the two of them. It seemed like minutes before anyone spoke and Sarah felt so nervous. What the hell must he think of her, after all these years knowing each other's lives inside out but not having a clue about that serious chapter, "Karl," she said, breaking the silence, "do you understand what I just said? Say something, please?"

He shook out of his shocked face and stammered, "Erm, OK. Give me a minute," he held up a finger, "So, when you say, you had a baby, you mean…?" he questioned looking down into his mug and then gulping at it as if it was really a big shot of vodka.

"Yes. I stupidly got myself pregnant and went away to

have it. Nana and grandpa sent me to live with my aunt so she could help me sort it all out. I had her adopted Karl, just a few days after she was born. It was all hush hush; we didn't want anyone finding out and thought it was the best option for the baby more than anything. But now, well, the thing is, she's just turned up. She has found me, and I don't know how to handle it, how to tell Tom, what to do with it, how to even begin to speak to her."

With a super confused look in his eyes, and looking quite pale from the revelation, Karl asked, "I thought you couldn't have children though Jane told me you had to have an operation or something and it caused some damage to your tubes?"

"No, urgh…I hate myself so much right now. I lied to her, Karl. I lied to the most special person ever to have been in my life. I should've told her, but I was so scared. My aunt said no-one would want to know me with a baby in tow, bloody bitch, that's why I never went back to see her," she clenched a fist and hit the table hard, "and that's what I've told everyone over the years, that I can't have children. The truth is, I've just been too scared to have them. Oh Jesus, this is bloody ridiculous. I told Jane off for not telling the truth about her cancer and now look at me lying to people, my whole bloody life near enough," she paused from her ramblings and looked again at Karl who still sat silent, his face empty of expression as to any idea what he was feeling or indeed what he may be thinking, "please say something Karl, I need help here, I don't know what to do, you were the only one I could think of to come to. I can't tell Tom yet."

"So, Jane didn't know anything then, about this baby?"

"No, my aunt said it would be better if no-one found out, so she swore me to secrecy. I wish I hadn't listened to her. But I was just seventeen Karl. What would I do with a baby at that age? I couldn't even cope now, let alone back then when I wasn't even an adult. Think about Cassie dealing with a baby when she was that age?"

"I'd rather not thank you," he abruptly answered, looking straight at her now with even more tearful eyes.

"You know what I mean though right? A kid having a kid, that's basically what it was, and I'd have never coped, I wasn't grown up enough. I really wish we could've kept her together, me, nana and grandpa, but they were old and didn't want to get into all the nappies and that again and their church friends would never have approved of the whole business so I had to, I had to give her up, I had to Karl," she explained, "When my grandparents died, the secret went with them and I kind of relaxed about it all, I never spoke to aunt Bridget again, I know she did what she thought was best but, well...I think we both just wanted to forget it all happened...I'm such an idiot Karl, I'm such a horrible person aren't I?" she sobbed.

"No, Sarah, look, try and calm down a bit. It's me you're talking to," he grasped her hands to try and stop them from trembling, "now, when you say, she's turned up, what do you mean?"

Sniffing back and grabbing a tissue from her pocket, she answered, "Well, I went to get everyone a coffee this morning at my usual place and there was a new girl serving. It was weird, I just felt like someone was watching me as I queued up and I kept looking over to this new girl pottering about trying to look busy and then, well, when it was my turn, she almost fell over herself to bring me the order and then, when I noticed her name tag, I just froze. I sort of knew what was going to happen next but, when she asked me if I was Sarah...I lost it," she paused to take a sip of her coffee. It had gone a bit cold now and she winced a little, placing it back down on the table and pushing it away, "I just knew Karl, I knew it was her. The strawberry blonde hair, just like mine, her striking blue eyes staring right at me, she looks just like me, she's my daughter Karl. And I have no idea what to do."

Chapter Twelve

Tomorrow will be my birthday and I'm turning seventeen years old already. That seems mad that the year has gone by so fast since my crazy sixteenth birthday.

This was supposed to be an occasion of excitement and happiness, when I should be getting all my hair done, makeup on, and choosing which new outfit I am going to wear to the big party or gathering and having some sneaky alcoholic drinks with Jane and our boyfriends. Well, that's what we planned anyway but it's not to be this year.

Instead of all that fun and instead of being with my very best friend celebrating, I'm stuck here, hidden away so no one finds out my sordid little secret. So that no one discovers our family shame that I have brought upon them.

I feel so bloody lonely and all I wish for is Jane to be

here with me. She would know what to say to cheer me up, to keep me strong right now, she always does. We've been best friends since primary school and we know each other inside out, going through all our schooling together, boyfriend troubles, the dreaded arrival of our painful monthly periods that we both suffer horribly with and now I can't have her with me when I need her the most. I need her more now than ever before, but I'm not allowed to see her and certainly not allowed to tell her what really is going on and why I'm away from her.

This bump, this mishap, this baby I have been hiding is the real reason I'm here with my aunt. It is now imminent and although I have grown to sort of love this little thing growing inside of me, changing my whole-body shape, and causing me to feel like some beached whale alone and deserted on an island somewhere obsolete, I am looking forward to getting my life back and giving it away is the very best option for everyone.

The father, well, he doesn't want to know about any of it. I don't think his family even knows about me and what has happened. It was just a one-time thing as far as he is concerned anyway, but in a few weeks, I'll be done with it all, back to my teenage life and can begin to forget about this sordid year of shock and disappointment that I have brought to my family. Well, what's left of them anyway.

This disaster all happened shortly after my mum and dad died. My world was thrown into complete turmoil in a few minutes. I literally fell apart at the seams and I couldn't grasp the fact that I had lost both my parents at the same time in such terrible circumstances. I just wasn't coping with it, hitting me so hard in the pit of my stomach and my heart bled losing them.

I mourned my beautiful parents in all the wrong ways a grieving child might do and some more. Becoming a rebellious teenager seemed to be the only way to deal with something so massively devastating. Instead of going quiet, locking myself away in my bedroom or turning to the one person who supported me throughout everything in my life, I resorted to secret binge drinking with older lads who could get hold of a bottle of vodka or two, skiving off school to go and meet them, and even smoking the odd joint so that I would fit in with their crowd of friends thinking that I looked cool and made them think I was older and more experienced than they thought. I didn't seem to pull that off though as every time I inhaled the horrid tasting weed, I'd then cough my guts up and splutter all over the place, nearly throwing up at the same time, embarrassingly.

But this was the only way I knew to try and mask the pain and sadness that I felt every day since they left, since my mum and dad died so suddenly.

It was April when we got the news. My parents had flown off for their fifteenth wedding anniversary celebrations. It was just a short few days in Venice together and I was more than happy staying with Nana and Grandpa in their quaint little cottage, getting spoiled by them with my favourite cakes and biscuits. My figure was nothing like my best friends. I was the short plump one and couldn't resist at least three or four biscuits at a time. Mum always said I shouldn't eat too many sweet things, for my figure as well as for the health of my teeth, but I was a teenager with raging hormones to boot. Being able to indulge while at my grandparents was more of an excuse to eat loads of what I loved, get a little bit plumper and not worry about it.

Mum and Dad had set off on the Friday morning after dropping me at Jane's house so we could walk to school together discussing all the girly teenage things there was to talk about. I was fifteen years old, and we had so much to chat about for our upcoming events. We were already planning for her birthday even though it was ages away. Just a few months before my big, sweet sixteenth birthday.

We loved to make plans in our special 'best friend' notebooks. We'd had these tatty things since we started secondary school and used to jot down ideas of our futures including wedding plans, our brood of kids' names that we would choose and what our new husbands would look like, what they would buy for us, what big houses we would live in and the amazingly expensive cars that the men in our lives would drive us around in like some sort of celebrity duo. It was all crazy stuff but so funny to imagine what we thought life would be like in years to come. We would wander off into our little dreamworlds of teenage girly stuff. I loved Jane so much, I don't know what I would've done without her during this awful chapter in my life and I vowed to her that my first daughter would have Jane as a middle name. She promised to use my name somewhere for her kids too. She wanted two children, I wanted four.

It was late on Sunday afternoon as me and Nana prepared a welcome tea party for mum and dads return that evening. They were due to pick me up around seven o'clock and we'd been busy all morning in the kitchen baking. We had prepared mums' favourite home-made sponge cake and baked heart-shaped, oat flapjacks for dad in the shape of fish as he loved going fishing on a weekend with grandad.

But they were never going to taste our creations because just as we were finishing up the icing on the cake, there was a loud knock on the front door. Me and Nana practically ran to the door but, on answering it, with pure excitement that they may have arrived early, we didn't get anything like we had expected. Instead of greeting my parent's happy faces and flinging my arms around them both, we were met by two police officers, standing there, taking their hats off and looking very serious. We opened the door fully in disappointment and confusion. With me still covered in cake mix and icing sugar around my face, Nana used her apron to wipe some away as the officers began to speak.

It wasn't those two loving faces of my parents, with smiles aplenty as they always had when I saw them, it was the police, looking serious and formal. These officers had arrived with the earth-shattering news that my parents had been killed in a road traffic accident on the way back to the airport in Venice. They'd died instantly with thirty other passengers when the bus had crashed and caught fire.

In a millisecond, the air around me went stale, time stood still, frozen as the awful news began to sink into my little brain. My heart crushed immediately, my stomach churned with sickness and agony, and the only sounds I could hear were that of my darling Nana's gasps and screams as her legs gave way beneath her. I watched her collapse right in front of me, weeping hysterically. Grandpa had run to the doorway hearing the wails of anguish and he was desperately clambering to catch her as she fell to her knees, sobbing and holding her head in disbelief. I stood motionless for what seemed like hours, unable to comprehend the huge tears that just kept falling down my face as I watched and listened in horror to my Nana's cries.

My world, their world, had been turned on its head completely and utterly beyond recognition right at that very moment and within seconds, I knew my life would be changed forever. It would never be the same from that day forward. My parents were dead, my precious grandparents only daughter was dead and their much-loved son-in-law, gone all in an instant and so tragically too. How the hell do you cope with losing your child that way? How the hell was I going to cope without my beautiful parents to guide me through the rest of my life now and, how would my grandparents cope with having to take care of me?

Within five weeks, we'd had the funerals and laid my beautiful parents to rest in our local cemetery. If I hadn't had Jane beside me throughout and especially on that horribly sad day, I think I may have fallen apart and run away or something worse there and then. She kept me upright, she kept me strong for my grandparents as well as myself and I will never forget that of her.

About two months later, Nana arranged for some counseling for me as she knew I wasn't coping too well with it all. She and grandpa had been amazing looking after me and looking back, I should've appreciated that they were in pain too. I mean, for goodness' sake, to lose a child like that must have killed them inside and there was me, being a complete brat and playing up, causing them even more anguish. What an idiot I feel now about myself, why couldn't I just have behaved and been good for them? Being the sweet granddaughter that they loved so much that they were now taking care of twenty-four-seven. At their age, they didn't need this nonsense.

Today I had really pushed it too far and I still hate myself for it. We'd gone back to my house to collect as many of my things as possible before the place had to be put up for sale and it had all just got too much for me to be there again. Mum and dads' room was as they had left it, exactly, down to the dodgy drawer on mum's sideboard, where they kept the birth certificates and important documents like passports and that. It would always be slightly open and hanging to the right as it never quite shut completely. The runners were worn out as it had been an antique from dad's father.

As I crept around the bedroom, I could still smell mum's perfume. I could hear dad's voice calling up the stairs to me as he did every morning to hurry me up for school or to ask me to turn my wretched pop music down a bit or call me for dinner. I glanced around the room wondering how this house could ever feel the same way again. It was heartbreaking to know I wouldn't live there anymore; all those years of memories would be erased when a new family moved in. We had lived there all my life and it was just too much, I had to leave. I just had to get out of there, it was time for me to be somewhere else, away from the painful memory of mum and dad not being there with me.

"Sarah, where are you going?" Nana had called as she saw me run to the front door and scramble to pull it open. My hands didn't seem to be working properly, it wasn't usually this hard to open the bloody door.

"I'm sorry nana, I don't want to be here anymore," I was turning the door handle but it just seemed to be jammed shut as I shouted back, "I just can't stand it, can we go back to yours now, I need to go Nana, please," my breathing was so heavy, I thought at one point that I would faint or burst a blood vessel with the quickening of my pulse racing through my veins.

She came to the door as quickly as she could, and as calm as ever, said, "darling I know this is difficult, but we need to get your things, so we don't have to keep bringing you back. You're the only one who knows what you'll need, you know school belongings and anything special that you want to have at our place."

I looked back at her kind face that was just trying to help me, to reassure me that everything was going to be okay but, in some way, I didn't understand it either. How was she being so brave and more importantly, why was I being such a bloody bratty child to her?

"But I just…" I whimpered as my head knocked heavy onto the wall beside me, with tears streaming down my face. I turned back again at her beautiful, calm face. She was crying too but the tears were silent, falling down her frail, wrinkled but lovely face, "I'm sorry nana, I just can't do this," yanking at the door handle once more, it opened and that's when I ran. I ran away from my home; I ran away from the person who was only trying their very best to cope with grieving herself. That gorgeous grandma who was trying to cope with the stroppy, moody, distraught and arse ache of a teenager that I was being, but I just couldn't help it.

I kept running not really knowing where I was going to end up until I got to the skate park, just near the swimming pool and playground where dad used to bring me on a Sunday afternoon while mum cooked our roast dinner. She loved an hour or so to get it all prepared for us on our return and dad used to climb the slide and pretend he was stuck halfway down, telling me I had to go to the top and push him through otherwise he'd be stuck there forever, or I'd have to call the fire brigade to come and hose him down. I looked at that exact slide as I passed the playground, almost seeing him again, stuck there, halfway down, wriggling his bottom, and waving his arms at me, laughing all the time. Man did that hurt right now. Knowing that he wasn't there and that he would never be there again now and once again, my heart shattered for the loss of such an amazing parent.

I slowed my pace and carried on walking around to the skate park, it was early afternoon, just after lunchtime. All my friends were at school, but I hadn't returned yet, unable to cope with teachers and lessons when my brain wouldn't function right as it was, so the school had agreed to let me have some extra time off. Time to grieve, time to heal but I felt like there would never be enough time to get over it all. I felt like there would never be enough years to get over something like this.

As I got to the back wall of the swimming pool building, there was a group of older lads with BMX's. They were smoking something which didn't smell quite like the cigarettes I had smelt before and a few of them were swigging on cans of beer, trying to not fall off their bikes as they did so. I just wanted to be alone so I slowed up and sat down against the wall, wrapping my arms around my knees, staring forward, away from the lads as best I could. I just wanted some me time really, but curiosity kept making me turn to glance at what they were doing. I wanted to know what they were smoking. The smell was really strong and fragrant, and it baffled me a little bit as to what it was.

One of the lads suddenly caught me looking, "you alright darling?" he called out.

I just nodded and quickly looked away again, turning my body a little so I wasn't as tempted to look but he came over to me, and stood right in front of me. He was blocking the sun, causing his shadow to be cast over my frail and still shaking body, "You want some sweetheart?" he asked.

His voice was deeper than the boys in my year at school so, I guessed he was around eighteen or nineteen. He had large gold rings on both hands, seemed on every finger, and a big thick gold chain around his neck. I remember seeing some rapper on the TV with similar jewellery adorning him but was sure this guy was not in that sort of league. This was real life for goodness' sake.

He held out the smoking thing toward me, "go on, it won't kill you, darling, it's just a joint, we don't mind sharing with ya'…go on, have a puff."

I looked at his face, he looked harmless enough, his hair was longer than the other lads just poking out from under his flat cap which had a skull graphic on it. I noticed that he had a large tattoo across the back of his hand of some sort of an eye, but he was just a lad, having a smoke and a beer with his friends, what harm could it do to join them. I thought it could maybe cheer me up, so I leaned forward to take it from him and took my first deep inhale, closely followed by a coughing and spluttering up of what seemed like my whole guts.

Once I had stopped the splutter and wiped my mouth of the spit, my head raised with pure embarrassment back up at him. My face was now even more red and blotchy from all the crying and now from this new smoking ordeal.

He knelt in front of me, holding my knee, "you're not supposed to do it that much darlin', look, this is how we do it," he inhaled gently and blew smoke circles into the air above him, then smiled back down to me. A smile which I melted into immediately for some reason and that was it, I was hooked. Not on the drugs, but on him. A complete stranger who I thought would be good for me during this sad time, someone to care for me and help me deal with my grief. He had arrived and made me smile for the first time in several weeks and I needed some sort of escape from someone that didn't know what was going on in my life. I was smitten and it didn't take long for me to realise that I had my first teenage love for the very first time and it felt nice.

Chapter Thirteen

Ben, that was his name. The boy, the man, who introduced me to all the good things in life that I thought would help me cope with losing my parents so suddenly.

The smoking drugs and vast amounts of shots of vodka were not a good mix and I knew it deep down really, but I couldn't stop myself. I'd fallen for this guy and without my mum and dad there anymore, I just didn't want to be a normal teenager, I mean, none of my other friends had lost their mum and dad. Everyone else seemed to have such a perfect family life except me, so this was my weekend life.

Jane warned me to stay away from him, she was the sensible one, but I would pretend, even to her, that I wasn't seeing him. I wanted to feel love outside of my home. I wanted to fit in with this crowd and pretend I was older than I was. But how was this going to end? I think Jane knew in her heart that I was still seeing him though. We had grown so close since primary school and I think she felt so bad for me and what I'd gone through, she didn't want to tell me what to do, all she could do was advise.

"Sarah, he's bad news, what do you see in him anyway?" asked Jane during lunchtime at school one afternoon.

"I don't know. I just like him, he makes me feel…special," I replied to her innocently, trying not to make eye contact with her so she couldn't tell if I was lying or not. Why did I feel the need to hide this guy from her? We'd always shared everything, always chatted about our boyfriends.

"Special? What do you mean?" she paused as she looked concerned, lowering her voice, "you're not actually, well, you know…doing it are you?" she whispered back glancing from side to side to make sure no-one could hear.

"That's a bit personal," I laughed back, making fun of the subject and the fact that she found 'it' meaning sex, such a secretive thing to ask about.

"Oh, personal? Come on, we share loads of stuff like that Sarah, so, come on, are you having sex with him?" her mouth muffled the S word in such a funny way, but I did feel annoyed slightly. Why shouldn't I? Just because she hadn't done it yet.

"No," I snapped back, shushing her a bit more, "not yet anyway," I paused as I moved a little closer to her, "but I think I might. I am legal now, so what does it matter if I do it with him?"

"Don't you want your first time to be with someone, well someone a bit more special?"

"He is special, Jane for Christ's sake, can't you just be happy that I have a boyfriend, it's alright for you with all your luscious looks and amazing tits. You can get anyone you like but look at me, I'm the fat one with goofy teeth and he's still taken an interest," I argued back at her as we left the canteen and made our way up the corridor to our next class.

She grabbed my arm as I slumped into my chair. We'd been sitting apart because we kept talking during lessons and passing silly notes to each other. We both didn't really enjoy science and Chemistry was the worst of the three, Physics being a very close second, "just be careful yeah, I'm sorry. I didn't mean to upset you. Still love me, bestie?"

I looked up at her beautiful face and couldn't help but smile back at her. She really was an amazing best friend, and I shouldn't have snapped at her that way. I just nodded back with a smile, and we blew an air kiss at each other before she made her way to the front of the class.

Waiting for the teacher to begin the lesson, I thought to myself that, yes, I did want to do it with him. I didn't want someone inexperienced for my first time and he seemed like he had probably done it loads of times before? Maybe he would be able to tell me what goes on, I mean, I had read about it all and we'd watched sex education stuff in class but, the first time is supposed to be different for everyone and I did feel nervous, but sort of ready to take the plunge. He was my first love after all, so what was so wrong?

It was nearing the Christmas holidays, and I was looking forward to being able to spend more time with him and maybe introduce Jane to Ben properly. Maybe then she would see how nice he was and finally accept that he was my boyfriend? Maybe he had a friend she could start seeing. Then we could have double dates, and all go out together to the cinema or bowling? All these thoughts ran through my mind as we made our way out of our last class of the day.

"Are you coming for a sleepover tomorrow night?" Jane asked me as I grabbed my stuff from my locker.

"Erm, no, actually. I can't. Nana has asked me to help her sort out some of her book collection to take to the charity shops. I promised I would help her decide which books to keep, sorry," I lied, "I could come around Sunday though?"

"Ok cool, do you want me to help, you know I love a good book, do you think she would have any I'd enjoy?"

"No, no it's fine. You know how Nana likes our special time together. I've not spent nearly enough hours with her lately and I don't think they are your sort of books anyway. They are very old, like classics, I think. I'm quite looking forward to just helping her out and spending some quality time with her."

"Aww, cute. Ok no worries, do you wanna come around for a bit tonight quickly. Mum and pops are at their dance group again till about seven. We could wrap some of the Christmas presents we got last weekend. I need to get organised with them all and you're so good at curling the ribbon."

"Can we just do it on Sunday instead? I'm going to get home. I've got that boring homework for English so rather get it done before the weekend." What I really wanted to do was get to see Ben. I wasn't even interested in homework but as per usual, she accepted my excuses and we walked home chatting about new clothes and trends that were coming out and what we hoped we would get for Christmas.

It was a strange time of year for me now without mum and dad there. Dad used to dress up as Santa and pretend to deliver my stocking late at night. He never knew, but I always pretended I was asleep when I heard him try to open my bedroom door without it creaking. I had to hold my breath so as not to laugh at his tiptoeing along the floor avoiding my clothes which I just used to throw across the floor as I undressed. What I would do to see that crazy outfit, the fluffy white pretend beard, and silly tiptoeing, just one more time.

When I got home, Nana was getting the dinner ready. It was my favourite meal tonight, bangers and mash with lashings of onion gravy and it smelt amazing, "Hey nan, it smells so good in here."

"Hello darling, yes it's your special dinner tonight, nearly ready now. Just waiting for Grandad to come in from his little man cave then I can dish up," she wiped her hands on her cute flowery apron and came over to me after

I had plonked myself at the table, "How was school my little cherub?"

"Oh, you know, the usual boring lessons, tons of homework, blah, blah," I moaned back at her taking an apple from the fruit bowl I'd made her at primary school, which sat pride of place on the table.

She laughed back, "Oh dear, well, don't eat anything else, dinner will be about five minutes, wash your hands darling, and why not go and give Grandpa a shout, I'm sure his clock has stopped in that shed of his, he loses track of time most days now and doesn't know when he's supposed to have come in."

I stood back up and made my way to the back door, just as Grandad came waltzing in whistling loudly, "Well, hello there little thing. How's my granddaughter this afternoon?" and he ruffled my already messy hair.

"Grandpa," I said, giggling back to him. He was so sweet and although I'd now turned sixteen, he still treated me like I was six. He was dressed in his tatty old blue dungarees that had what seemed like twenty years of paint stains, varnish splatters and God knows what else on them. They were his garden clothes and Nana had sewn up so many rips and holes, they looked more patchwork than the original denim.

We enjoyed our meal together and then, after doing five minutes of the homework and getting bored, I decided to go out for a bit. Nana and Grandpa were fast asleep in front of the TV as per usual, so I quietly grabbed my coat from the staircase and snuck out the back door, closing it as slowly as I could so they didn't wake up. I knew they'd be out for at least an hour; they always had a snooze after dinner and most times, wouldn't even know I had gone out. I was doing it all the time at the moment, and they hadn't found out yet.

I quickly made my way over to the skate park to find Ben who had lined the vodka shots ready for him and his mates to down, "HEY, look who's here," he called loudly when he noticed me walking over, "how's my special girl tonight?" he threw his arms around me so heavily, it nearly made me lose my footing. I realised that he must have been drinking already as his words were slurred and his breath stank of beer. I just smiled as his friends watched on and began taking it in turns to drink the shots. There were a few other girls tonight too. They were older than me too and were smoking normal cigarettes. I admired the skirts they were wearing and because they were so short, their legs seemed to go on forever. I loved how their make-up looked so flawless and wished I had made a bit more effort with my own face tonight. My hair was just pulled back from school, so I quickly tugged at the hairband and let it loose.

Ben wobbled as he began stroking my hair, "yes, that looks better darlin', don't it girls?" he called over to the gorgeous gang, who just smiled back and continued chatting among themselves, "so, you're sixteen now hey?" he asked me as he winked over to one of his mates, "you gonna have a bit of fun tonight for a change?" he laughed, and the girls sniggered a laugh. Were they laughing at me or laughing at the fact that Ben could hardly stand up properly? Probably at me, I thought. Look at the state of me? I didn't have the fancy clothes that they had, the gorgeous hair, the perfect figure, or the ultra-pretty makeup styles. I just tried to laugh it off, nervously.

After an hour, I'd had nearly half a bottle of vodka and my head felt dizzy. I couldn't walk straight and just kept giggling about anything and everything making a fool of myself, trying to chat with the other girls who casually moved away from me like I was some sort of vermin. I thought at that moment that I wished Jane was with me, she wouldn't have let me get like this and certainly would not have let anything happen to me.

Before I knew what was happening, Ben had taken me into the small alleyway round the side of the swimming pool building and that's where it suddenly happened. There and then, I lost my virginity in a dirty alley, both drunk and not at all how I had expected my first time to turn out. I didn't even really remember how it felt, how quick it was, or anything. I just felt numb and confused. Too drunk to take it all in and I swiftly realised, he was too drunk to care.

He left me standing there straightening my skirt and re-doing my hair into a tight ponytail again. I didn't quite know what to do with myself or how to act so I just left and ran home as fast as I could, only to find Nana making a fresh pot of tea in the kitchen as I tried to slyly make my way in the back door.

"Where have you been?" she asked, tipping her head,

and looking concerningly over her little half-moon glasses perched on the tip of her nose.

"Erm, I just had to nip to Jane's to pick up some notes from class today for my homework," I said quickly, feeling guilty about fibbing to her.

"It's getting late, you should have woken us. Grandpa would have run you there in the car instead, we don't like to think you are walking the streets when it's dark, you can't be too careful nowadays darling," she rummaged in the cupboard to find a tray to put the teapot and cups on.

"Nana, I'm sixteen now, I'm fine, you don't have to worry so much," I reached the tin of biscuits for her, "here, I'll carry that for you," and I took hold of the tray, arranging the items after passing her the biscuit tin. I felt guilty now and after having a quick shower, I sat with them for the remainder of the evening before going up to bed.

I lay there with just my side lamp on low, thinking of what had happened and wondered if, hopefully next time, it would feel better and maybe be somewhere a bit more romantic or warm even, but it didn't and it wasn't. Over the next few evenings, when I went to see him, he would either ignore me completely, flirt with other girls right in front of me, or just not be there when he said. I felt heartbroken and used and I still hadn't told Jane about that first night because I wanted to tell her about it when it was a bit more special. But that wasn't going to happen. The next time I saw Ben, I got a big wakeup call about him.

I had missed my regular period and when I told him

that I thought I might be pregnant, he had freaked out completely and told me not to go there again, adding that he didn't want to see me ever again.

"I ain't being no sodding daddy, I've got shit to do in my life so bugger off and have the sprog by yourself," he pushed me away like I was a bit of trash, or worse, like something he had just stepped in, and it was heart-wrenching. Stupidly I had thought he may be able to help, have some idea of what I was supposed to do but how completely and utterly wrong I was.

His spiteful words hit me deep down into my stomach, like a knife stabbing inside of me, I felt completely torn apart, but more than that, I felt cheap and nasty with it. Why hadn't I listened to Jane? She knew he was bad news; she'd said it that very day to me but, stupidly, I hadn't listened, I didn't want to listen to what I now know was the truth, and I felt like a complete idiot. What an absolute mug I had been, thinking he cared for me and worst of all, for thinking I was in love with this boy.

Chapter Fourteen

When it finally dawned on me that I was pregnant, I bravely told Nana and after having a good old cry together, and telling grandpa, we all decided it would be best for me to go and live with my aunt who could sort it all out for me. I couldn't keep the baby, not at my age, I wasn't ready for it so, once I was over the three-month stage, I was picked up and taken to live with my Aunt Bridget in Oxford.

Every day, I wanted to phone Jane and tell her the real reason I'd had to go off for a year, but the words just wouldn't come out. I felt too ashamed every time I went to call her thinking that she would hate me or tell all our friends who in turn would hate me too. But tonight, I thought I may try again and tell her all about Ben and what happened that fateful night. Why I was here and what I was going to do with it all.

"Hey, you, how's it going?" Jane asked as she answered the phone that evening.

I was trying to get a phone call every few days to her. Just to hear a friendly voice on the other end of the phone was what I needed to keep me sane. I really intended on telling her the truth tonight, but for some reason, again, my guilt and shame took over and I just couldn't bring myself to reveal what I'd done and what was about to happen to me. The fluttering in my tummy reminded me of what was in there and how terrible I was for hiding it.

"Hi, yeah I'm good. I really miss you though," I replied to her quietly trying to rub the feelings away, realising it was the baby moving around.

"Aww I miss you too, when do you think you'll be back? Mum said you can come and stay with us if you wanted to get back a bit earlier."

What I would have done there and then, in that one moment to just tell her and go and live with them. But no. Why was it so hard? What was stopping me from revealing all my sins to her? I couldn't.

"Really? That's so lovely of her but I can't. I've got to stay here and help out a bit more but hopefully, it'll only be another few weeks now."

"Are you doing anything for your birthday? We had so much planned, didn't we?"

"I know we did, I'm sorry Jane. I wish I could be with you instead, but I promise, it won't be long, and we can make up for it, yeah?" I was bursting at the seams.

Literally. I felt as though my insides were going to explode any moment. My sadness at not being able to spend my birthday with my best friend was killing me and in that second, I thought I may tell her, "I've got some news actually, something to tell you about Ben."

"Oh. The guy from the skatepark? I thought you weren't seeing him anymore?"

"I'm not, it's just, well. Oh, it's nothing really," I paused and bit my lip in anger, "I just wanted to let you know that I told him where to go before I came here. I know he's probably with someone else already, so I wanted to end it before he had the chance when I'm back." I lied putting my head in my hand with shame yet again raising its ugly head.

"Ok good, I've not seen anything of him actually, someone said he moved to another town, so that's good," she paused as I heard her mum calling her name, "ok mum, coming, look I've gotta go for dinner now. Can I phone you again tomorrow?"

"Yeah sure, speak then," and with our normal air blow kiss down the phone, the call ended, and I felt even sadder than I had before the phone call. Why was it so hard to just open up and tell her? Again and again, I've had the chance but every time, something stops me, and I feel terrible each time.

"Was that your friend Jane again?" asked my aunt Bridget as she walked through the hallway. I just nodded back as she gave me a short glance, "It's probably best you don't call her that often for the next few weeks, you have to concentrate on the matter at hand child," she pointed to my belly which had expanded rapidly over the past week or so and I felt ready to burst.

I clambered myself up from the bottom stair and made my way back up to my room. As I laid on the bed, I lifted my top up exposing the bump. My belly button didn't seem to exist now, it was flush with the rest of my skin and tight. Stretch marks were red and angry looking. I placed my hands over the bump as much as I could and felt heavy tears fall down the sides of my face onto my neck. I wanted to love it, this big bump, I really did but I wasn't allowed. Aunt Bridget had been making enquiries to the church about couples who wanted to adopt a baby, all on the quiet obviously but no-one had come up so far. I sort of hoped that they wouldn't some days, so we could keep her, him, it. Maybe Nana and grandpa would change their minds and help me bring the baby up between us? They'd make lovely great grandparents; I just knew it. I missed them so much and although I imagined us all being a big happy family, deep down, I knew that they were far too old now to cope with me let alone me, a silly teenager with a baby in tow now.

Keeping it. What was I thinking? How stupid. This was the best thing for this child right now and I just had to go along with it and hope someone would take care of it and love it as their own. I straightened my top back up and wiped my eyes clear, switching the tv on to watch the latest dreadful soap operas that played in the evenings before dinner. No stories of teenage pregnancy on them this month, I was being my own soap opera for now, living the real-life nightmare so this would be my escape from reality for now and before long, I was fast asleep with the tv still playing.

In the morning, Aunt Bridget came into my room early with a tray consisting of a hearty bowl of porridge with a dab of jam in the middle and a cup of tea. She knew I preferred coffee or juice even but said that this green tea was good for me in my condition. I wasn't convinced.

"Good morning Sarah, did you sleep well," she seemed to be almost gliding across the room with a joy to her step and before I could answer, she continued, "I got some good news late last night but I looked in on you and you were fast asleep, so, I thought I would wait until this morning to tell you all about it...you know you left your television on again dear," she perched herself on the side of my bed as I sat up, wiping my eyes clear and yawning. I didn't even remember what I fell asleep watching last night, I must've been so tired, I even had my slippers on still.

"What news?" I asked her, pushing the porridge away and reaching for the tea. My appetite was not great now. In the first few months, I couldn't stop eating but as my belly grew and everything got more and more contained and squished, it became more uncomfortable, and I had to force myself to eat just one meal a day sometimes. I'd even hide snacks and chuck bread from the sandwiches she brought me up out the window to the birds. A cute family of sparrows had become my daily visitors on the windowsill over the last few weeks.

"Well, this little bundle we have here, it seems we have found a lady who will be its new mother," she replied, reaching across to me, and for the first time, she stroked my bulging belly. Like she was saying goodbye to it or reassuring it that it would shortly be in a better place than here in my teenage tummy. I didn't like her attitude towards me or the bump but again, I knew that all she was doing was trying to help me out and she had promised nana and grandpa that she would do her best by me.

She lived in the heart of Oxford and was an avid member of the church community actively helping girls like me in these predicaments. She had told me about the babies that she had found homes for and the fact that they were in a much better situation now than they would've been. A few girls had changed their minds and kept their babies but what with losing mum and dad and having to live with my elderly grandparents, we all just assumed that this was the best thing to do, for all of us but especially the little baby inside me.

As she continued to tell me about the lady who they had found, I began to imagine what life would be like for me in a few months' time. Would anyone notice that I had been pregnant, would anyone find out that I'd given the baby away? All these questions would have to wait and must stay locked in my mind for now. I had to concentrate on getting through the next few weeks as my due date rapidly approached, and I was getting even more tired day by day.

~

"So, when do you think you'll be back then, it seems like so long since I've seen you, I've got a new boyfriend, remember Donnie from gymnastics?" Jane said excitedly as I sat at the bottom of the stairs once again on the phone to her.

"I should be back by the end of this month. Aunt Bridget is getting on so much better now, so she doesn't need as much help with things," I lied once more. I hated it so much, all the lies to my best friend who had a heart of gold. I thought to myself over again, that she would never lie to me. That's not what best friends do. Surely not but I had promised what was left of my family that I would obey their rules and keep this secret forever and that's what I was going to do.

"Great," she replied, "I can't wait, we need to re-do our birthday plans and find you a boyfriend, maybe Donnie has a mate he could set you up with," she said thoughtfully.

"I'm ok Jane, really. I don't need a boy in my life right now, I'm quite happy being single," I said back to her, feeling a little sad but honestly feeling that's exactly what I wanted. Another boyfriend right now would not be a good option for me to get into.

"Oh come on Sarah, it will be fun, we can double date and that, get over that horrible Ben character once and for all," she was trying so hard to cheer me up, I was sure she could sense how sad I felt right now, "what's up Sarah, you're not sounding like your usual self?" she asked as I went silent for a minute.

Maybe this was the moment when I could tell her the truth, just spill it all out right now, there, and then, once and for all get rid of this secret? "I'm just a bit fed up with things at the moment Jane. It's boring here and…"

"And what, what's going on, has something happened?" she asked, concerned.

"No, I mean, well…" Aunt Bridget appeared at the lounge doorway and just looked at me as if she knew I could crack at any minute and tell Jane everything, "No, it's nothing really, sorry," I turned away from her stare, "I'm just missing you I guess and nana and grandpa, I miss them so much. They want me home."

"Yeah, they do, I went to see them after school today, they said how much they missed you too."

"Oh really, did you? Are they okay?" I was surprised that she had been round, she had only ever come round to the house with me there. She was so thoughtful, so I just put it down to her wonderful, caring personality.

"Yeah, they are alright. I just wanted to give them your birthday card to see if they could send it to you. They said they would so hopefully you'll get it in a few days, I wanted you to have it on your birthday, I've put a little gift in it too so let me know when it arrives," she said lovingly. She was so caring like that; I'd not even thought much about my birthday. I was so lucky to have her in my life.

"Thanks Jane," I replied as a stabbing pain hit my tummy hard, "look, I better go, I need the toilet," I said as I tried to laugh off the pain.

"Oh ok, I'll phone you tomorrow then, maybe we can arrange to pick you up from the station when you do get back?"

The pain seemed to be getting stronger and it hurt like crazy, "Ok, love you," I said quickly gritting my teeth but trying not to let her hear the pain in my voice as she said goodbye back.

I put the receiver down carefully and grasped hold of the breadth of my vast tummy. It felt like bad period pains but ten times worse so I just sat for a few minutes curled up as much as I could with this big lump in front of me. Taking some deep breaths, I wondered if this could be the start of it all, the birth of this little being inside me. I knew it was going to be painful, but I was trying to be the tough little thing that I made myself out to be. Inside though, inside my very fragile heart, I was weak and broken and just a young girl. I'd lost my parents, I'd let my grandparents down, and now I was about to lose this other person who I had grown for the past nine months. Was I such a horrible person to deserve this sadness and heartbreak? How much more could I take in life? How much more would it throw at me?

I vouched from then on, that the minute I got back to normal life, I would live life to the fullest, be a free spirit and enjoy what years I had left. I wouldn't be tied down; I wouldn't answer to anyone but myself. And I would tell Jane, at some point I would tell her my secret because she would understand, she would still love me the same as she always has because she's my best friend and she deserves to know the truth. I just had to have enough courage and be brave enough to face my demons, one day. One day surely, I would be able to.

Chapter Fifteen

The next few hours grew even more intense and stressful. The griping pain across my now very hard lump of a belly got worse and worse and the contractions became even more regular, causing me to rile in agony while they did their thing each time. My Aunt sat with me the whole time, thank goodness, trying to keep me calm, trying to get me to use the breathing techniques that she had taught me herself, until we both knew that it was finally time to go to the hospital and let the professionals take over.

The bump that was my belly was on its way, my baby was about to arrive in the world. This little bump was going to make its appearance very soon and I was petrified. I was more scared than I had ever been about anything ever in my life before. I was scared to think about the fact that it was happening, it was real. I was scared about how

I was going to cope going through it and ultimately, scared beyond belief to finally see my very own baby whom I would have to then say goodbye to very soon afterwards. That was what scared me the most, that I would be forever living with the guilt of not being the mother my mum always hoped I would be. I was letting her down and my grandparents, but the time was coming, and I had no way back.

The dreaded moment came much quicker than I or Aunt Bridget had imagined it would and, in just under two hours, all the pushing, pain and screaming was over, for me anyway. A little girl had been born, arriving quickly but safely with an almighty screeching cry that almost pierced our eardrums. She was absolutely beautiful. So, so beautiful beyond words, and once again, my heart crashed to the floor of my body and shattered into a million pieces. The hurt that I had inside me was like nothing I had ever felt before, it almost hurt more than the labour itself. It seemed like a pain that would never leave my body, a pain I would never be able to forget.

"It's a little girl Sarah," exclaimed my aunt holding my sweaty head as she kissed my cheek. She seemed more excited than I thought she would be, but I sort of guessed it would be momentarily a happy time.

I couldn't speak back, I just lay there in that hospital bed stunned, exhausted and in pain, not physical pain, but mentally hurting while they cleaned me up, and took the little screaming bundle off to the side to check all her vitals.

The birth itself had been straightforward with no

complications for the baby and luckily no stitches or cuts for me. I had the usual gas and air for the pain but that was it, which Aunt Bridget told me was very brave.

The baby was tiny though, weighing in at just six pounds exactly. Her little fingers on delicate hands, her little toes on long skinny feet and her pink scrawny skin didn't fail to melt my heart too. I watched her as she lay there peacefully sucking away on the dummy that the nurses had given her for comfort. She was oblivious to me being her mother and in some way, I thought that was best. For all of us.

The hours passed and I hadn't held her since she had been born. I couldn't bring myself to, in fear that I would never want to let her go again. The reality that was running through my mind of the fact that I had to say goodbye very soon to this gorgeous little package that I had created over the past nine months. A truly remarkable package that deserved so much more than me as a mother. She deserved all the love in the world, and we knew that the lady Aunt Bridget had chosen would give this all to her unconditionally and much better than I ever could. I didn't even deserve such a beautiful thing in my life, with no father to help, it just wasn't right. She had been made from my stupidity and I messed up big time.

My thoughts and fears were interrupted as the duty nurse came to check on us and take my blood pressure around nine o'clock, "How are you feeling now Sarah?" she asked, wrapping the cuff tightly around my upper arm.

I didn't answer, just smiled, and turned back to face my

bundle of pinkness again. I wanted to take in every inch of her skin and savour every moment of her beauty.

"She's very pretty," the nurse said as she tried to make conversation again, pumping the monitor which was now squeezing my arm, "You are a very lucky mummy."

'I am not lucky and certainly not a mummy', I thought to myself, I may be her mother, but I will never be a mummy to this lovely little thing, and I shook my head in reply to her statement as tears began to well up in my already swollen eyes.

"I'm sorry if I upset you. Do you want to have a quick cuddle with her?" she asked as she put the monitor away on the trolley and went over to the cot straightening the yellow blanket that covered the little sleeping body. Aunty had taught me how to knit not long after going to stay with her and I'd snuck it into my bag as we left for the hospital in the hope that maybe I could see her wrapped in it. She looked so warm and cozy with it. I watched her as she stirred from the movement of the nurse's careful touch. Only her lips were moving as she sucked on her dummy. I remember chuckling to myself at one point, thinking she looked like some cartoon character but so much cuter.

"Oh, I... I don't know," I finally managed to answer, "I might drop her or hurt her, I've never held a baby before," my heart began to race as I thought about the conversation that me and aunty had just had only a few weeks previously. She had advised me not to hold her after giving birth, no matter how much I might have wanted to. Just in case I got too attached or changed my mind about keeping her somehow. She said it was so easy to fall in love with a newborn baby and I shouldn't hold her for this very reason.

But my Aunty wasn't here, and she wasn't going to be coming to see me anymore tonight now, so what harm would it do? No one would find out, just one little moment of holding her would be alright surely. I had made my decision and plans were in place so I couldn't change my mind.

"You'll be fine Sarah, and I can stay with you. Would you like me to lift her out and bring her over to you?"

As I glanced back into the cot, her little eyes began to blink open and shut so gently and then she gave a wide yawn, stretching one arm up out of the blanket. My god, she was so cute, maybe I should have a little hug with her, just one? I nodded back to the nurse and quietly replied, "Yes, yes please," smiling through my eyes at the little pink thing who was about to be with me.

I pushed myself up into a sitting position, breathing deeply through the stinging pain I still had and more than that, to try and contain my nerves at what I was about to do. I was disobeying my aunt doing exactly what she said not to do, but she didn't know and although I felt slightly guilty, this was my choice and I just had to do it while I had the chance.

I watched intently as the nurse gently lifted the baby up into her own arms, cradling her softly. Then, as if in slow motion, she walked those few steps over to my bed with my baby in her embrace, wrapped snugly in her blanket with the pink knitted bonnet slipping off making my heart melt again at the sight of her lovely head of thick hair.

The nurse leaned towards me and placed the little bundle in my trembling arms, "Now just support her head with your arm there Sarah, that's it, and try to relax a little bit," she said reassuringly, "There you go little one, there's your mummy," and then she sat at the end of the bed watching us.

I looked down at this precious package in my embrace and in that moment, I felt everything inside of me change. She was utterly the most beautiful thing I'd ever seen, and she peered up into my eyes which were now awash with tears that wanted to drop like a waterfall. I tried to hold them back but as a massive teardrop fell onto her cheek, causing her to jump a little, the nurse moved forward again and just held my hand softly. I think deep down, she knew the situation, it must have been on my files but the warmth and care that she was giving me right now was something else from today that I would never forget. Thank God she was there tonight. I may not have got the chance to do this otherwise. Hugging this baby cradled in the special blanket that I had made for her, I treasured this moment, a special moment of my whole life that I would never bear to forget.

For over half an hour, I held her with the nurse staying with me the whole time chatting to me about what programme was on the television, but I didn't really listen, I was too intensely concentrated on this little warm bundle of loveliness. As time went on, I knew I had to let go and it made me silently weep with her still in my arms. I cried for this baby that I would not see grow up, who I would not see walk or talk for the first time, who I wouldn't see go to nursery, start school, fall in love. The thoughts spun in my head, and I wondered if I was really making the right choice. It was though, I knew way down in my heart that it would be best for her and me really. What could a teenage mum living with her grandparents provide for this beautiful child, not as much as I would like to. I had to do this for her sake, for her to have a better life and grow up in a more secure family. Someone at the right age to take care of a baby, not a teenager with problems and struggles of her own. A teenager who was still very much in the grieving process. I probably wouldn't be in this situation at all if I hadn't lost mum and dad so suddenly and I hated myself for getting into this mess and having to even contemplate doing what I had to do the next day.

Suddenly, she spat her dummy out and began to get a bit grizzly, making some cute little noises, so I asked the nurse to take her from me so she could tend to her. From that moment on, I didn't hold her again. I felt in my heart, I had said my goodbyes to her. I had my wonderful cuddle in secret, just me and the nurse knew and that's how it remained, our secret.

"Please don't tell my aunty I held her will you, please" I begged the nurse as she took her from me, "she would be so angry with me if she found out," I continued as she sat down in the rocking chair in the corner preparing to bottle feed her.

"Of course not, I promise. It's our little secret Sarah," she winked, "I just hope it helped you a little bit, I know how hard it can be, for you young mums," she smiled at me knowingly. She must have been in this situation before and her kind face was one I felt very thankful for and especially for what she had done for me that evening, I wouldn't forget it or her, not ever.

"Thank you," I replied sleepily, laying myself back down against the pile of pillows behind me.

"Have you picked a name for her?" she asked, lifting my baby onto her shoulder to wind her. She had gulped down her bottle so fast which I was told was a good sign.

"Well, I have but it might be changed when, well, you know," I paused, frowning back at her, "I've named her Katie-Jane. It's after my best friend, Jane," I told her.

"Oh, what a beautiful name for such a beautiful baby," she replied, "now you get some rest, I'll put her to bed once she's done, you look exhausted."

I was exhausted and although I didn't want to miss a second of seeing my baby, I had to close my eyes and get some sleep, ready for tomorrow, the day I had to say my very final goodbyes to her. Within minutes I was fast asleep until the morning when Aunt Bridget arrived bright and early.

The following afternoon came round quickly, and they would be the last hours that I would lay eyes on my baby girl. It was time to say goodbye for good and let her go and live with her new family. Time for my past to be left in the past, time to move on and try and live the remainder of my teenage years with this secret hidden away for good and well behind me.

Her new mother had shocked me by agreeing to keep her name, saying it suited her, but she would obviously have a new surname. My details would be on the birth certificate of course as was Ben's information too. It was the right thing to do for all parties involved apparently. I didn't particularly want to share his details but, according to my aunty, it was for the best.

The hours flew past, and I watched out of the window as Katie's new mother placed her into her car and drove away. Swallowing a big lump in my throat, I took one last deep breath and promised myself to be strong. I had to be, I had to be that normal teen now, so no one suspected anything else other than I was helping my aunt out.

Aunt Bridget busied herself and collected all my belongings from the bedside cupboard and then began straightening the pillows on the bed, "Right sweetheart, let's get you home for some rest, shall we? Nana and grandpa are ringing this afternoon to sort out when you will be returning to live with them, so we best get a move on," she said all regimented. I knew she cared about me really, she was a very tough lady but had my best interests at heart. I had to be thankful to her for all that she had done for me these past months and the whole process had been easier than I thought it would be with her dealing with it all. At the end of the day, she had lost her brother, my dad and I knew how sad she felt over it still too. In some way, she felt even more responsible to help me out as he wasn't here to do it. "Are you okay to walk to the car?" she asked, finally fluffing the last pillow on the bed, and grabbing my overnight bag.

The whole situation hurt like mad, and I knew deep down, it would never be something I could just 'get over' but I reassured myself each minute it seemed that I had done the right thing for everyone involved but especially for my little bundle of pinkness.

"Yes, I'm fine to walk," I replied, grabbing my cardigan from over the back of the chair as she still wasn't happy with the bed and kept straightening out the sheets with her hands.

We made our way out of the hospital and as I looked back down the very long corridor, the lovely nurse that had helped me have those last few magical moments with my baby, stood there smiling sweetly. I mouthed, '*Thank you*' and she gave me a thumbs up. What a beautiful lady, I thought to myself as I turned to catch up with Aunt Bridget who was lugging my bag of clothes to the car park. If only we were carrying Katie home, if only she was coming back to have more cuddles and mesmerising eye moments. But she wasn't and I had to snap out of it. I had to let go. I let go of that notion and clung to the only thing I had left of her, the yellow blanket that she had been wrapped in. The nurse had kept it back for me when the new mummy had brought in her own blanket. I'd managed to squeeze it into my backpack before my aunt had arrived. I knew this item would be the only thing I had left, and I would not let anyone take it from me, not ever. It's all I had, and it was mine.

From that day forward, from the very last moments I laid eyes on my beautiful baby girl, my daughter, I vowed to myself that I would never go through that type of heartache again. I would never have any more children as I didn't deserve another chance at motherhood. I promised myself in my own head that I would live life to its fullest whatever the cost to my mental health. I had to try my hardest to forget this episode in my already complicated and emotional drama of a life. I had to move on and leave this behind me, somehow. Put it to the back of my mind for good. Ignore my broken heart.

The thoughts were so difficult, but it had happened, and I had now said goodbye forever and would try my utmost to not look back at this year of my life. My brain would get rid of the chapter that was letting go of my secret baby. The cutest, most adorable baby I had ever laid eyes on. That beautiful pink bundle that I had made, my gorgeous, wonderful, unforgettable, Katie-Jane.

Chapter Sixteen

Nana and Grandpa were so happy to see me when Aunt Bridget dropped me off a few weeks later. I had been checked over by the doctor before leaving my aunt's home and I finally felt well enough to start getting on with what was left of my teenage years.

My dreams had been getting weirder and weirder as the days went on after the birth and I would wake up in a sweat, panicking that the baby, my baby was screaming at the top of her lungs beside me in that cute little crib from the hospital bedside that I had stared at her in for hours on end. But she wasn't there, her little voice wasn't being heard by me anymore, and every time I woke up with that realisation, it kicked me hard in the pit of my stomach a bit more but, at the same time, I was getting there, and each day hurt less in a strange kind of way. The kicks got less painful. I knew it had been the right decision even though my heart ached and would forever be missing a part but, I knew now it was time to move on and start to try and enjoy what was left of my teenage years.

The first thing I wanted to do once I had seen my grandparents was to see Jane. I had missed her terribly and I knew she would be waiting anxiously to see me and tell me all about her new boyfriend and any antics or plans that she had been making in my absence. I just hoped she wouldn't notice a change in me and the few stretch marks that I'd been left with.

~

"How are you darling, are you feeling alright, do you need anything, do you need to have a rest, something to eat...?" Nana asked nervously as she watched me unpack my small suitcase.

I smiled at her sweet little face to try and reassure her, "no Nana, I'm fine, honestly. I'm going to unpack this and then go and see Jane," closing the case back up, I plonked most of my clothing into the washing basket in the corner of the room. I'd not really worn my normal clothes as nothing had fitted much during the last six months at least. The maternity trousers and tops that had been brought for me were going in the bin, so I chucked those bits towards the bedroom door to go downstairs on my way out.

"Oh, do you think that's such a good idea, so soon, are you sure you are ready to face your friends?"

"Nana please don't worry so much, I just need to get back to some sort of normality now and I've missed her so much. I just want to be a normal teenager again," I replied looking over to her worried face. I knew she meant well but Aunt Bridget and I had a good chat on the car journey home about keeping strong and getting on with things, so I had to do it. I couldn't keep thinking what may have been, what had happened or who would know. I just needed my life back, "I've missed you so much Nana, but you know what us teenage girls are like, and you know how much I love Jane. I need to catch up with her, but I promise, I won't be late back, okay?" I made my way over to her and gave her the biggest hug since mum and dad had died. She felt warm but also very frail. I had to grow up and look after her while I could. This whole experience had made me realise how lucky I was to have them in my life and how important they were in my future. I would not let them down ever again.

"Okay my little darling, I know you need to do this, just, well...we've missed you so much, especially Grandpa. I tell you what, why don't you ask Jane to come over here instead? I can make us all a nice supper and then she could sleep over maybe?" her face was suddenly beaming with her usual smile and excitement, and I loved seeing her like this.

"Yes okay, that's a great idea. Can I phone her and ask before she makes other plans for dinner?"

"Of course, let me know what you'd like to eat, or shall I just do your favourite, bangers and mash yes?"

"Nana, that would be perfect, thank you." I hugged her again before she left me to finish unpacking.

The last item to come out of the case was the blanket. That very special piece that I had made and got to have my dream come true and see my baby girl wrapped in. I lifted it to my nose and took a big inhale of breath. I could almost smell her and once again, my heart had another little chip carved out of it. I placed it at the bottom of my wardrobe under a big pile of other bed blankets so no-one would see it. It would live there until such times as I could let go, if ever that would be.

Shutting the wardrobe door, I made my way down the stairs to the phone excited to talk to my best friend once again and after so long, finally, I would get to see her and hug her in person. It would be the best hug we would ever have; I was determined to make it special.

The phone seemed to ring for ages but then I heard the wonderful friendly voice of Janice, Jane's mum answered, "Hello?" and repeated her phone number twice. Jane and I always found this so funny that people would say their number to you when you had just rung it, like you didn't know who you were ringing.

"Hi Janice, it's Sarah, I'm back. Is Jane about?"

"Oh Sarah, hello my dear, yes she is, I'll just give her a shout, she has some rather loud music playing in her room so I may need to go up there, one moment, oh...and how are you my dear and how's your aunt doing?"

"I'm good thanks, yes we are both good, I'm just dying to see Jane now, it seems like ages."

"Oh, that's fabulous, good news, good news. Oh, Jane will be so pleased to see you, she's been lost without you here sweety. I won't be a minute my dear, bear with me," I heard her place the phone receiver onto the table, and I then waited patiently. Within minutes, I heard Jane's thundering footsteps coming at a million miles a minute. The stairs were solid wood so you could always hear anyone coming down, especially when they were excited to get to the phone.

"Sarah, Sarah, yay, are you back?" she cried slightly breathless from the running.

"Yes, I am, I got back about an hour ago. Can you come round, nana is going to make us some dinner and maybe you can stay over if it's okay with your parents?"

"Yes, I'll ask pops to drop me round as soon as, yes, I have missed you sooo much," she cried again, "I'm so excited to see you."

"Me too, I can't wait to hear all about your news. See you soon." And no sooner had we said our goodbyes and I'd had a quick shower, the doorbell rang and there she was, standing with her arms out wide to welcome me back loaded up with a big bag of my favorite chocolate bar and sweets.

My best friend, my absolute beauty and the nicest person in the world smiling her massive grin back at me. We just squealed with delight as we made our way to my room, almost flying up the stairs, hand in hand with nana laughing at us at the bottom of the staircase.

I had considered telling Jane that evening about everything that had happened over the past six months or so, but it just didn't seem the right time. She was too excited and had so much to tell me. We had other things to start planning for our lives ahead, so I dismissed the idea to the back of my head once again and just enjoyed our time together munching on our sweets and devouring the chocolate bar.

We talked about how she had been accepted into her chosen university and the new boyfriend that had lasted only a few weeks. I just seemed to take it all in, I mean, there wasn't much I could tell her, and she was chattering on so much, I was just enjoying listening to her and seeing her gorgeous face again. She didn't need to be told of something so horrible, it would have taken the smile away from her gorgeous face, I couldn't do it. Not that smile of hers, so I just watched and listened to her for now.

~

"Sarah, it's so good to have you back, is everything sorted with your aunt now, do you have to go back there anymore?" Jane asked as she took a breather between mouthfuls of sausage and mash.

Nana looked at me as I felt my cheeks flush with panic as to what to reply, "No, she's doing fine now," I replied, looking down into my dinner to avoid further eye contact. The fear of thinking Jane might see I was making stuff up hurt like hell, but she was so busy pouring another portion of onion gravy onto her mountain of mash, she didn't notice anything out of the ordinary. She loved her food and sometimes I wondered how she managed to keep her hourglass figure. I had struggled for so many years now with weight issues and always felt like the fat friend if we went out with others. As always, Jane continuously managed to make me feel better about myself, even down to helping me find flattering clothes to hide my lumps and bumps. Of course, now I had even more lumps to cover but not from eating too much this time although that's what I would have to tell her if and when she did notice.

When we had finished our dinner, we went back upstairs to my room again where we chatted all night and ended up falling asleep fully clothed. It was so nice to be what was classed as a normal teenager once more, having a girly night in with my bestie. My sadness and hurtful thoughts were kept at bay with her near so from that night, we spent every living moment we could together. It helped me cope so much quicker with my ordeal of the past year, and I couldn't even tell her why it meant so much, why she meant so much to me right now.

The months flew past and before we knew it, we had left secondary school sixth form, Jane went off to University and I studied hard at the local college to get my beauty qualifications and even managed a few diplomas. I wanted to have my own beauty salon one day so I threw myself into learning as many procedures and treatments as possible so I could choose a few to specialise in.

Grandpa passed away from a heart attack when I was nineteen and then nana left us a few months afterwards. I think she died of a broken heart because after Grandpa died, she just couldn't seem to function the same. She missed him so much and night after night I would hear her sobbing so gently in her room. She would still lay the dinner table space for him, even down to putting his favourite bottle of sauce on the table too. It broke my heart and I tried to spend more time with her to help her cope. She had been so good to me through everything, but she wanted to be with grandpa, and I think she knew deep down I was now old enough to go out on my own, so she died peacefully in her sleep on one Sunday evening. I held her hand as she went off for her afternoon nap in Grandpa's chair knowing that she was ready to go be with him finally.

Mum and dad had left me a large lump sum in a trust fund, and this enabled me to easily buy my first little flat. My grandparents had put the money from the sale of my parent's house into an account for me too. So, with that and the surprise bit of money that they left to me in their wills, I started up my beauty salon soon after.

The year I turned twenty-one, with the last of the money from my grandparents' house sale, I paid to go abroad and have a tummy tuck as a birthday present to myself. The final few stretch marks from the pregnancy were now gone and I just told those close to me, who knew about the surgery, that it was because of my weight issue as a teenager. Always being slightly plump, it turned out to be a no brainer when it came down to fibbing to people why I was getting it done. No questions were asked, and I felt so much better about my size from then on. I was still no catwalk model, but it worked for me.

When Jane returned from university with qualifications galore, she also had a new man in tow, an engagement ring and so many plans for their future. I was so happy for her, she really deserved it after all her hard work and studying and I loved Karl from the get-go. She still didn't leave me out at all and helped me out so much getting the salon up and running, taking control of the decor, and offering to do my accounts. She loved numbers and got a great job with a new accountancy firm in town.

Before we knew it, Jane had got married and became a mother to twins. The pregnancy and the birth brought back some memories for me but again, I kept them hidden and spent many nights where I cried alone for what my life could've been like if I had kept my baby.

I used to watch Jane with her babies and only imagined in secret what my little girl looked like. I wondered if she still had my hair colour, the hue of strawberry blonde. Or maybe it had turned darker over the years and more like his dark locks. Did she have my dodgy nose, my plump structure or those piercing deep eyes that he'd drawn me in with?

Jane's love for her twins was incredible and I told myself time and time again that she just wouldn't have understood if I'd told her the truth. She was the bestest friend in the world and I know she would have done anything for me but for some reason, I never was able to bring myself to tell her my secret. There's been so many times I have wanted to, mostly when we'd had too much to drink and I could've just blurted it out but no, stupidly, the one person I knew I could trust with this secret, I never plucked up enough courage to reveal all. I would lay in bed thinking about it, thinking that maybe one day when we're old and grey and there's not enough days left to hate me for what I did or for what I hadn't told her, I could finally confess. Finally tell her that I could've also had a family for all these years. But no, they were all the family I needed.

Chapter Seventeen

"I'm sorry Karl, I shouldn't have put this on you, I'm going to go, I shouldn't have come round here," Sarah grabbed her bag from the chair and made her way to the kitchen door.

"Sarah, stop, please," Karl said, turning around on his feet as fast as he could and holding his arm out to try and stop her.

She stopped in her tracks and faced him again. Looking into his caring eyes, she knew she was in the right place and with the right person. As she made her way back across the room and felt his embrace, her heart melted knowing that she had made the right choice in coming to him. He wasn't her husband, but he was the perfect person to help her and be with her in her hour of need. They'd been through so much over the past year and now it was her turn for some friendly support.

"God Karl, I'm sorry."

"Hey, stop it. We will sort this out, I promise, I'll help as much as I can. Come on, let's make a fresh drink, or do you want anything stronger before you fill me in on the details?" gently moving her chin up to face him, he smiled that all-encompassing grin at her worried, sad face.

Sighing with relief, she replied, "coffee is probably the best thing at this moment in time, thanks Karl and I'm sorry again for…"

"Stop it will you. Do not apologise one more time okay," he interrupted her, "come on, sit down and tell me everything."

Before she knew it and to her surprise, she had told him everything, the whole truth about her past. Leaving no stone unturned, she had opened up for the first time in over twenty years and in some way, it felt good, but she was also still so worried about how he would react, how he would see her now as a person and more importantly, how the future would be from here on in for her and as part of his family.

Her worries didn't last long though as he was even more understanding that she could ever have imagined. He listened intently, wiping away the tears which kept flowing out of her sad eyes, holding her trembling hands and supplying the all-important extra strong coffee fixes, mug after mug of it.

Just as he stood up to make a fresh round, Sarah's phone rang, it was Tom.

"Hi darling…" Sarah answered, trying her best to compose her voice to sound 'normal', "yes, I'm fine, I just popped to see Karl for a bit, you know, teenage issues that only I could sort…ok…yes that's fine, love you, see you later then…bye darling." and hung up breathing a huge, relieved sigh.

"Everything ok?" asked Karl, stirring the mugs of fresh coffee.

"Yes, he was just letting me know he might be a bit late home tonight, some guy's birthday at work so they're going for a quick drink afterwards," she replied, staring down at her phone, admiring the screensaver image of her and Tom, "Oh Karl, what is he going to think of me? We had a bit of a row the other week about not wanting to have children and now this happens. He's going to leave me I'm sure…after finally finding someone I truly love and want to spend my life with…he's bound to leave me when he finds out what a bitch I've been, what I did back then," her eyes filled again like an overflowing tap that just kept gushing out.

Karl sat down and again, held her hands tightly, "Sarah, listen. Tom is a good bloke; he will understand, and I will be there with you if you want me to. I know we've not known him for that long but I'm pretty sure he's not like that, he'll be there for you, he will, he's different," he continued, "he's been through shit himself hasn't he, he knows people have history."

Sarah had her doubts but thinking about it and listening to what Karl was saying, what Tom had been through with his own family, the truth was, he was an amazing person and she loved him so dearly as much as he loved her. She had to face the fact that she couldn't keep this secret from her newlywed husband, he deserved to know why she was so adamant about not having children. The real reason she felt she couldn't and didn't deserve to have anymore even if it was with the most beautiful person she had ever been with. She had to confess to him and help him understand why it hurt so much to even think about babies let alone having another one herself.

~

The drive home gave her a little bit of time to get her story together, to get her explanation in place and try to know exactly how she was going to be strong enough to speak about her past. She had to be strong, and she felt she had to do this by herself, it wasn't fair to drag Karl over there so they'd decided she would text him or ring him after if she needed him. This was her time to be brave and reveal her secret.

As she pulled up in the driveway of their house, she noticed Tina's car was parked out the front. Her heart began to race wondering why she was here and if she had come along with her husband, the guy who looked so much like Ben. What would she do if it was him, what would she do if he was in her house now talking to her husband, revealing everything to him before she could? She had to be the one to tell him, not them. Her brain hurt from all the thinking and worrying, she had to get in there.

Grabbing her bag from the passenger seat, she got out

of the car and looked toward the front window where she noticed Tom standing looking towards the sofas. He was chatting and laughing away happily oblivious to her arrival. She hoped it wasn't them but why else would Tina's car be outside. Maybe it was work stuff.

Hurrying, she made her way to the front door, unlocked it and stepped in. She could hear voices, more than one, more than two and suddenly, she felt scared to go any further. Hanging her keys onto the key rack, she took her coat off and hung it on the end of the staircase as Tom appeared in the hall doorway.

"Hey there darling, I thought you'd be home before me. Everything alright with Karl and the kids?"

"Yeah, sorry, yes, all sorted. We got a bite to eat as I thought you were going out." she replied busying herself with her bag trying to not make eye contact with him for now or listen out for the other two voices that she'd heard before.

"Well, we did have a quick drink with all the other and then thought it would be cool to introduce you to the birthday boy himself. We grabbed a few bottles of wine to have here with you and your mate."

"What do you mean?" Sarah asked, finally looking up at him as one of the dogs appeared at her feet, rubbing its wet nose onto her leg.

"The guy whose birthday it was at work, turns out you know his wife, come on in, I'll grab you a glass. Come on," with excitement, he turned and went back into the lounge, and she heard the glasses chinking and wine bottles clinking together.

Her heart was beating as hard as a bass drum inside her chest, surely this was not happening. Surely her thoughts of what could be meeting her eyes any moment would not really happen. She fussed Charlie as he settled down on a pillow in the hall and took a deep breath.

Almost creeping into the lounge with anticipation and dread, she was met with the image she had hoped wouldn't be. The stark picture she had thought about but hoped would be just a nightmare and she would wake up quickly, very quickly.

There he was, there they were, Tina, Tom, and him. Him being Ben - the Ben from that awful teenage chapter she had tried so hard to forget about for so long. What the hell was she going to do now? What the hell was he doing in her house, with her husband? And why? Why had he come here at all, what was he playing at?

As she stood motionless in the doorway, Ben got up and began walking towards her. It all seemed to be happening in slow motion and she was hating every millisecond of it. As he met her gaze and was a matter of inches away from her, he smiled, and her blood ran cold. It was that same smile she had fallen for all those years ago, the same one that had drawn her stupid teenage self into and given her the biggest mistake of her life. She just looked at him in shock and said nothing.

"Hey Sarah, Ben," he reached out his hand to shake hers, making out they didn't know each other, but she didn't respond, and he lowered it again as well as toning down that beaming smile on his face.

Tom was busy pouring himself and Tina another glass of wine so was oblivious to the cutting knife in the air atmosphere that Sarah and Ben had between them. Tina was chatting away to him about something, she couldn't make it out as everything noise in the room seemed muffled, but they were out of earshot, so she needed to ask him what he was doing, "Why are you here?" she whispered through gritted teeth.

"I wanted to see you again darling," he answered, whispering back, and leaning toward her, "we have something to sort out and I think you know what? We will have to have a chat," he said as he turned away from her and joined the others grabbing his glass.

Sarah watched him as he put his arm across Tom's shoulders like suddenly, they were the best of mates. Her skin crawled and the anger inside felt like a volcano about to erupt.

"Come on babe, grab your glass and let's toast to Ben's birthday, it's not every day you turn forty-three, is it?" Tom said joyfully unaware of what was unfolding for his wife.

"I'm alright actually Tom, I just need to go upstairs for a lay down, I think I have a migraine coming, you lot carry on, sorry."

As she turned to walk away, Ben called to her, "Oh come on Sarah, Tom's been looking forward to us meeting, he's told me so much about you," he smiled that smug grin again, "tell her Tina babe, you have some migraine pills in your handbag she could take don't ya?" his sarcastic voice drained Sarah's mind. Why was he being so matter of fact and acting this way?

In her head she wanted to turn around and shout at the top of her voice for him to get the hell away from her husband and get the hell out of her house, but she couldn't. She just couldn't bring herself to do that, not in front of everyone and not before they knew the truth. With all the strength she had inside of her at that moment, she reluctantly went back and stood close beside her husband, as far away from Ben as physically possible in that small lounge knowing that tonight would not be the night that she would be able to tell Tom what was going on and what had happened during the day. He looked so happy to have some friends over, but little did he know, this new friend of his would not be someone he would want around.

The evening went on longer than she had hoped and as it got close to midnight, Tina, who had now become very tipsy from the four bottles of wine that they had devoured between the three of them, started to fall asleep on the sofa.

"I'll ring a taxi for you, none of you are fit to walk really," said Tom wobbling himself and patting Ben on the shoulder as he went to the kitchen to find his phone, "it's been a great night mate, good to have you and the wife over," he called disappearing into the kitchen.

Sarah sat rigid and completely sober in the armchair as Ben came and sat on the coffee table in front of her, "It's been lovely to see you again," he said quietly, tilting his head towards her and then glancing to the kitchen to make sure Tom couldn't see them.

"Get lost Ben," she sternly replied.

"No need to be like that," he touched her knee as he leant forward.

"I mean it Ben, I don't want you anywhere near me or Tom," she said, immediately changing her sitting position so he couldn't touch her again. She felt repelled by him and couldn't believe his tone toward her. His wife was lying just feet away from them with no clue as to their former relationship. She was the sweetest person Sarah had met since opening the beauty salon and employing her and it wasn't fair on her for him to behave this way.

"Sarah, look, we have some unfinished business to sort out, I think you know what I'm talking about don't you?"

Before she could answer, Tom appeared, "Taxi will be about five minutes mate, want another one for the road?" he said as he dangled another bottle in his hand.

"No mate, I think we are all wined out for tonight but bring it to ours next time, we could grab food too, soak it up a bit so the missus doesn't fall asleep," he laughed moving over to Tina, gently rubbing her shoulder to wake her, "she's always sleepy with wine, bless her cotton socks."

"Yeah ok, sure, that would be great wouldn't it babe?" Tom answered looking at Sarah who just smiled back at him. She knew she would not be entertaining that idea anytime soon. There was no way he would be getting close to her husband again.

"Right then, come on darling, let's get you outside for

some fresh air before the cab gets here," Ben said as he lifted Tina from her seat trying to make out what a gentleman he was but Sarah knew he was a bad egg, she knew how he had made her feel way back then and even right now. She hated every bone in his body for it. She just wanted him out of her house and away from her and her husband.

She listened to them saying their goodbyes and as the front door closed, she heard Tom coming back, whistling to the dogs for their nighttime toilet duty. She started clearing away the glasses and the bottles from the table.

"Hey gorgeous, come here," he said as he reached his arms around her waist as she bent to collect the last glass, "it was nice to have some friends round at last, wasn't it?" he swayed slightly but lovingly cradled her totally unaware how she was really feeling about the evening and especially the company. She had nothing against Tina, apart from her bad taste in men but she just couldn't even think about being friends with Ben again, not with their history together.

"Yeah, lovely," she nonchalantly answered, "come on silly, let me get all this cleared up," she tried to release his hold.

"Why don't you leave that. I can clear it all up tomorrow, let's get upstairs, you never know, it may be your lucky night," he whispered in her ear, running his hands down her sides now, rather tipsy.

Sarah was in no mood for all that nonsense tonight, not the way she felt after this evening. She had way too much on her mind to even contemplate sex. As much as she adored her husband and could see how happy he was to have spent the evening drinking wine and entertaining his new so-called friends, she just couldn't, "oh Tom, go on, you go up. I'll be up soon. I really don't want to leave these glasses here. Just in case the dogs bound in and knock the table or something," she said waving her hands at the low table, "I'll be up soon alright?" she repeated.

"Oh, come on babe…" he slurred trying to pull her in towards him again.

"No Tom, Christ," she said raising her voice, "You know I hate leaving a bloody mess…" she paused realising immediately she had snapped at him, "look, sorry, I'll be up shortly okay, you go and get the bed warm. I'm just going to give them a little rinse." she turned to face him, "sorry for snapping, I'm just really tired." With that she gave him a kiss on the cheek and made her way to the kitchen.

He didn't argue, he was too drunk to even notice she had snapped, maybe he just didn't want to start a row or maybe he just knew she needed space. Whatever the reason, she listened as he hummed a tune making his way upstairs.

Placing her hands on the side in the kitchen, she felt angry and upset. She was supposed to have told him everything tonight, revealed her horrid past and how ashamed she had been her whole life about it but again, Ben had ruined it and now she was back to square one with having the secret to herself. All she wanted to do was hit a wall, or smash something up and scream with anger and frustration. When would she have the courage to tell him everything about her sordid past now? When would ever be the right time to tell him the truth? And what would he say when he found out?

Chapter Eighteen

Morning came and Sarah hadn't slept much at all spending as much time downstairs clearing up as she could. All to avoid getting into another argument or confrontation with Tom about the previous evening.

Thankfully, Tom had fallen asleep quickly when she did eventually go up and she felt relieved in some way. She felt bad for snapping at him again and had laid watching him sleeping for what seemed like hours. Watching the funny way his lips moved as though he was trying to talk to someone. She loved his gorgeous face so much and every part of her ached right now for being such a bitch to him and hiding her secret for another day. He didn't deserve to be on the end of her temper, a temper that had been built up by her own stupid past and some guy that looked suspiciously like he was about to cause her more trouble and bring sadness into her life yet again.

She knew that she was going to have to face Ben at some point, tell him to stay away, tell him to keep away from Tom but for some strange reason, she had a feeling he wasn't going to disappear anytime soon, and this certainly wasn't going to be something that could be sorted out easily or indeed quickly.

Her brain was working overtime yet again with thoughts running around her head until finally falling asleep in the early hours of the morning. It had been so late she had remembered listening to the morning birds beginning to chirp outside their bedroom window. A few hours' sleep done and dusted, she crept out of bed and made her way downstairs into the kitchen, grabbing her phone from the bedside cabinet and shoving it into her dressing gown pocket.

With her extra strong morning coffee brewed, she sat down for five minutes to check all her socials and emails but nothing exciting was happening there and thankfully, there were no messages from Ben or Tina. Maybe he was going to stay away. Maybe she had dreamt it all or just overreacted to something that was never going to happen anyway. Whatever was going on, she had to deal with it later. All that mattered now was getting back on track with her husband, so she decided to make him his favourite breakfast in the hope that he wouldn't mention her outburst the previous evening. There had been too many shock rows just lately and she didn't like it one bit.

As she scrambled some eggs, fried some bacon, and

popped a slice of bread into the toaster, she heard him coming down the stairs, chatting away to someone on his mobile phone.

As he walked into the kitchen, he smiled at her in a puzzled sort of way and continued to speak on the phone, "Felicity that would be great, I don't know what to say...thank you, thank you so much," he looked at Sarah pale faced as he then sat down at the table listening intently to the person on the other end and then replied, "okay, great, yes, fine, I'll see you then, bye." before hanging up and sitting blankly, staring at the screen in silence.

Sarah looked at his confused face and then looked down at the phone, but it had gone off the screensaver now, "Tom? Are you okay?" she placed her hand gently on his shoulder, "who was that on the phone?" she asked him now worried at his still blank expression.

"It, it was Felicity," he stammered, still staring down at the blacked-out screen.

"Felicity?" questioned Sarah, "Tom, who is Felicity?"

"Oh sorry," he apologised, shaking his head, "I thought I had mentioned her before..." he reached up and rubbed her hand on his shoulder still, "It's James' wife, well, his ex-wife, remember me telling you about her that day? She left him to move to Paris with her girlfriend and his baby," he pushed the phone towards the center of the table.

"Oh my god, really? One sec," she said as she went over to the kitchen counter to give the bacon a flip and stir the eggs, "How long has it been since you spoke to her?

What did she want?" she asked, grabbing the slice of toast that had just popped up and quickly buttering it.

"Well, since the funeral really, she came to it, but stayed way off in the background. She didn't want dad to see her there. I only noticed her when everyone else had left. She was in quite a state to be fair; I mean...I guess she did love him at one point, she did marry him after all." He moved the phone again a bit more as Sarah dished up his breakfast and placed it in front of him.

"Wow, what did she say, and what does she want after all this time?" she said, passing him his cutlery, the bottle of tomato sauce and then went back over to the worktop re-boiling the kettle.

"Well, you won't believe it but...she wants me to meet my nephew, you know, James' son," he squeezed a blob of sauce next to his eggs, "she was still pregnant at the funeral, so we've never actually seen him...the baby. I'm going to finally be an uncle to him Sarah, I'm finally going to meet my brother's son," he paused as he looked up towards his wife with a massive grin on his face, "I'm going to meet my nephew." he was beaming with utter joy in his face and began tucking into his breakfast excitedly.

As she watched him continuing to try and talk at the same time as feasting on his food, she knew how much this meant to him. His dad and him had missed out on being there for that baby but now they would have the chance to be family to it; to him, to his nephew and Henry's first grandchild. She knew how excited he got regarding children, he loved them, she knew that more than anything so to actually have a child in the family now was amazing for him, for them.

As he munched away, he continued to tell Sarah more from the conversation he had had with Felicity as she brewed another mug of coffee for them in the new cafetiere they had received as one of their wedding gifts, "He's nearly five already, she said he looks just like J. His name is Albert, they called him Albert James, AJ for short, it's cool, isn't it?" talking ten to the dozen with so much elation he went on, "they've decided to come back and live here in England. Well, Felicity and Albert have anyway. I'm not asking the ins and outs of why but they will be closer now and I can see him whenever I like, that's what she said," he slurped a sip of his coffee as soon as she placed it in front of him, swiped up the final bit of egg onto his toast into his mouth and sat back in his chair, rubbing his now full belly, "this is awesome Sarah - hey, ha-ha, I guess that'll make you Aunty Sarah, for real this time," he chuckled to himself, "oh I've gotta call dad and tell him, he will want to come with us for sure. Thanks for that babe, it was delicious...I'm gonna go give dad a call now," and with that he started tapping away at his phone dialing his dad's number, quickly kissing her cheek on his way out the room.

Sarah sat alone at the table as she listened to him relaying to his dad all the news. She was so happy for him but selfishly thought about her own situation again, how could she tell him her secret now? Now that he was so excited about having a new family member after all they'd been through. She would have to try and meet with Ben and ask him to not say anything. She would have to meet with Kate and ask her to not say anything - not for now anyway. It was the wrong time to reveal such a thing to her husband. He needed to have this happy moment with his new nephew, for James' sake, he needed it. Last night's outburst seemed to have been forgotten thank goodness so at least she didn't have to go through that with him. All his focus was on this morning was this news of his nephew and she felt a sigh of relief come over her.

Putting the breakfast washing up into the sink to do later and scribbling a quick note to Tom, she decided she needed a walk to get her head straight as to what she was going to do next with her ongoing saga.

She grabbed the dog's leads from the hooks next to the fridge and went out the back door to fetch the four of them who were now chilling on the decking in the morning sun.

There was a fenced in area at the park towards the end of the street where dogs could be off their leads, so she went into it and sat on a bench watching them immediately smelling the butts of the other dogs that were in there. She smiled as she noticed two other dog owners laughing and pointing at the very same thing. She could never grasp why dogs did that and it made her chuckle, especially for Elvis the sausage dog who could hardly reach other dogs butts at the best of times.

Thoughts of Kate and Ben soon entered her mind again and she needed to get things straight in her head, so she started making some notes on her phone. Excuses of why she hadn't told anyone, reasons why she had to and what hell she had gone through over the years. For some reason writing them down made it seem clearer in her head and maybe it would be easier to relay back to everyone eventually and maybe it would be easier for them to understand even.

After writing for a few minutes, she then googled the coffee shop where Kate had appeared to see if she could find out any more information. No success there, that led to nothing, their Facebook page hadn't even been updated for over a year and the staff album only had the two owners' photos in it.

She then decided to look at Tina's Instagram profile - she knew she didn't use Facebook as much so she set off scrolling through her photos and after a few seconds, she found some images that she really had hoped wouldn't be there. Tina, standing with Ben. It was as though he was staring right back at her, smiling from ear to ear with such a slick look on his face. Her skin crawled at the thought of him and how horrible he had been to her all those years ago and even the other night in her own house, he had been creepy. She had never hated anyone so much in her whole life and it made her sad, her eyes began to fill with tears. She took a deep breath to hold them back, looking up to see her dogs jumping around with another dog owner who had brought a bubble gun contraption that they were shooting out for all the dogs to play with.

As she had a glint of no stress for a few seconds, watching them all with delight, her phone began to ring.

She looked back down at it and, not recognising the number, just answered softly, "Hello?"

"Sarah, it's me, Ben, can we talk?"

Shocked and with the pit of her stomach wrenching with nausea, she just replied sternly, "Ben. How did you get my number?"

"I got it out of Tina's phone last night when she was out of it," he replied almost whispering, "look, I really need to talk to you, I'm sorry if I was a bit of a twat last night. It was just, well, seeing you after so long, I guess I just lost it in the moment. You look amazing by the way."

She didn't know what to answer so just kept quiet, shaking her head, and pouting her lips to herself. How dare he try and compliment her now, she thought. How dare he even have the balls to seek her out and phone her without permission.

"Sarah?" he asked as the line fell silent.

"What?" she replied again abruptly.

"Look, can I come over to yours or meet you somewhere, we just need to talk about, well I think you know what it's about don't you?"

Still, she remained silent, she didn't want to meet him, she didn't want to talk to him, see him, listen to him trying to compliment her, why should she? Why did he deserve to even be near her? But something deep down ached, she knew he wouldn't leave her alone unless she at least met with him. Maybe then, she could make it clear that Tom doesn't know her past, and she wanted to keep it that way. Maybe he would respect her now that she was an adult and understand her reasons. Surely, he knew that Tom wouldn't have known. From her reaction last night, he must know.

"Sarah...are you still there?"

"Yes, yes, I am, but…"

"Can we meet then," he interrupted, "I promise to not be a twat, I just want to see you and explain some stuff,"

"Explain what Ben? That you left me to deal with being pregnant at just sixteen and wouldn't even help me, didn't even wanna know about it? That I had to go through that all by myself and give our baby away, what is there to explain any further than you are a twat and always have been," she exclaimed, losing it for a second with his audacity.

The other end of the line went quiet for a few seconds and then he spoke with a lowered tone of voice, "where are you, you sound like you're outside somewhere, can I come and meet you now?"

She had obviously hit a nerve with her comments, and it kind of felt good in a sadistic way, "I'm just out with my dogs, I told Tom I wouldn't be long. I'll drop them back home and meet you at the skatepark, you remember that place, don't you? I'm sure you do," she said with an angry and sarcastic tone to her voice.

"Yeah, that's fine. Thanks, about half an hour work for you?"

"Fine," she replied and ended the call. Now it seemed it was her turn to stare at the blank screen. What was she doing agreeing to meet up with him and why on earth did she suggest the skatepark, of all places? Tom would never think to go there so it seemed like the only place she wouldn't be seen meeting up with some bloke, some idiot bloke at that. The vivid images of that night in the alley were parading across her mind and her brain was flooding with questions for him when they got there.

Just then, Charlie came bounding up to her and disturbed her racing brain with his muddy paws going all over her trousers, snapping her out of her mind trap. The dogs always seemed to sense her sadness or when she was worried, and she loved them so much for it. She ruffled his fluffy face in her hands and smiled, "you scruff bag you," she said to him, kissing his nose and then whistled to the others to come and get their leads back on to get home. The puppy training had been useful for them all except Elvis who was slightly deaf so always took a bit longer to learn the command of come. His little legs took longer to catch up with the other three too.

"You have some beautiful dogs," said a voice from behind her as she finally managed to get the last lead on Elvis.

"Oh, thank you, yes they are my babies," she replied standing up wrapping the leads around both her hands, two each side.

The woman speaking was the one who'd been playing with the dogs and the bubbles, "they certainly liked the bubbles, I've never seen dogs jump so high to try and catch them, bless them" she said smiling at Sarah's brood, "my name's Linda and these big scruffs are George and

Ringo," she paused looking at Sarah, "my mum was a big Beatles fan, anyway, lovely to meet you, hopefully the dogs can meet again soon."

"Yes, that would be great, thanks, they do love their bubbles, oh and I'm Sarah," she replied smiling.

"Cool, see you again soon then, come on dogs, let's get home," and she walked out of the fenced area towards the high street.

Sarah stood and thought for a moment, why couldn't she just have a simple life, why did it always have to get complicated and why couldn't Jane be here to help her with this. Why did her best friend have to die? She needed her advice right now more than ever.

She decided to give Karl a quick update by texting him. She had completely forgotten to let him know the outcome of last night, what with all the Ben business now impending doom on her life once again. Tapping a quick, *I'm ok, long story short, not told Tom yet, I'll ring you soon and explain, sorry. XX'* text to him, she then took a deep breath and made her way back home.

Now she had to face meeting up with Ben and reliving the memories again. Those memories she had tried to keep hidden away for so long. She just hoped and prayed to herself that she could keep it together and be the responsible adult that she had tried to grow up to be. He would not hurt her again, not this time round.

Chapter Nineteen

When she returned home, Tom had gone out already, leaving a note back to her saying he was going to a toy shop to buy some bits for Albert. Her heart wrenched open at the thought of her beloved husband in a toyshop buying toys for a child he had never even met yet. She also imagined him if it had been a shopping trip for their baby and how excited he would be if it was that. Why was she having all these selfish thoughts, why couldn't she just be happy for him and focus on this new nephew they were both gaining at the end of the day.

In some way, Tom not being there made it easier to get back out for her meeting with Ben. She didn't have to make anything up or indeed, lie to him about where she was going. She just had to get through this, as always so she chucked down some biscuits for the dogs, freshened up their water bowls and left for the skatepark feeling even more anxious and almost sick to the stomach at the whole thought of it.

Passing by a mobile coffee van, she decided maybe it would calm her nerves a bit so ordered herself a large double shot latte and a small cookie to go.

Within a few minutes though, she felt terribly sick and had to run into the toilet block just next to the skatepark. Throwing up in a public toilet made her feel even worse and to make things even more frustrating, she dropped the latte on the way in too. In the panic of getting through the door, she had bumped into it, knocking the drink out of her hands with warm coffee splashing up her legs and over her shoe.

Wiping her mouth with some tissue, she washed her hands thoroughly and made her way outside to get some fresh air. She picked up the coffee cup which lay waiting for her a few feet away from the doorway now and put it in the bin nearby.

She always hated being sick, she hadn't even had any breakfast this morning, worrying too much about making Tom his and then the big news about James' child coming on the scene, she'd totally forgotten about herself eating.

Her ribs ached from the heaving of trying to bring up nothing and she had an instant headache coming on. She rustled through her bag and grabbed a couple of painkillers, swigging it down with the last of the water bottle she had in there. Now she had to focus on pulling herself together and finish what she set out to do today -

meet the person she never wanted to meet again.

When she arrived at the skatepark, Ben was already there, sitting on a bench, tapping, and scrolling on his phone. His ripped jeans and smart polo shirt were a contrast to each other. His hair was still thick black as she remembered, but now showing signs of grey flecks in it. She hadn't taken much notice the other evening, trying her hardest to not even make much eye contact until now, then he glanced up like he had sensed she was standing there staring.

He stood up, tucking the phone away in his jean pocket and smiled at her awkwardly. She made her way over to the bench and sat down staring straight ahead as he then slowly sat down again beside her.

"Thanks for coming, Sarah," he said after a short pause of awkward silence.

"You're welcome," she sharply replied, unable to turn her head towards him, "now what do you want?" She wanted him to get to the point. This all needed to be quick, and she didn't want to be here any longer than ten minutes.

"Okay, look, I know this isn't ideal but well, we had...," he paused correcting himself, "we *have* a child together," again he paused and Sarah looked at him confused at the sentence she had just heard him say to her, "Sarah, she has got in touch with me, a few weeks back now and she wants to get to know us, she wants to meet you too, you're her mum."

Sarah gulped down the lump in her throat as memories

came flooding back to the saddest day when she had said goodbye for that final time. It never felt any easier, no matter how many years had now passed, it still hurt so much to remember that day. And now she had turned up and contacted him. She was in shock and didn't speak for a few seconds, "I'm not her mum Ben, I gave up the right to call myself her mother when she was a few days old, not that you knew about any of that shit, hey?"

"Look, I know. I'm sorry Sarah. I was young and stupid and just couldn't handle the fact that I would be tied down with a baby. I had ambitions, you know?" he turned to face her, "at the end of the day, you are her birth mother and the least you can do is meet her, you have to, for her sake."

"Do not tell me what I should do," she replied, raising her voice now turning her face, glaring at him, "you do not have a clue how hard it was for me to give her up, no idea in the slightest, so do not ever talk to me like that, do not ever tell me what I should and shouldn't do where this is concerned, you have no right."

"Okay, calm down," he said, holding his hands up in front of him which annoyed Sarah even more.

"Don't tell me to calm down," At this point, she just wanted to tell him where to go and walk away but seemed frozen in the seat for some reason.

"Look, again, I'm sorry, it's just, well, she's found me, mum's fallen in love with her and it's like we've been given a second chance to be parents. My mum never thought she'd have a grandchild after all my antics, so this is a huge deal for her," he paused, "you know Tina can't have children, so this is a chance for us to become a family in some way. We are going to be in each other's lives now. I must make things right for once in my life. Please Sarah, Kate's asked me to ask you. Just one meeting, that's all she wants, just one time to meet her real mother," he was pleading almost, and it was coming across as genuine. Like he really did want to make things right. But she wasn't yet convinced of his purity.

"She obviously didn't tell you about our meeting then?" Sarah replied, turning her face away from his again feeling as though she might explode with anger any minute. All she wanted to do was punch him and tell him where to go, then all this mess would be gone too.

"What meeting, when did this happen?" he asked.

"She found me already. She's working in the coffee shop near my salon and tried to talk to me."

"Oh right," he replied back, "Did you not stop and speak to her then?"

Immediately feeling silly about the fact that she practically had run off to avoid speaking to her, she replied, "not really, I," she paused and then glanced back at him feeling embarrassed, "well I just freaked out and left when I realised who she was."

"Oh right," he replied, sounding shocked.

"Stupid really but she just took me by surprise, you know, all of a sudden, there she was looking back at me as if nothing ever happened, it was a shock to say the least."

"Wow, I bet it was, she hasn't mentioned that,

although I've not spoken to her for a few days, she's been busy working two jobs."

"Ben, I never expected to see her again so for her to turn up like that…you know, just out of the blue…and in public, it was all just a bit too much for me at that moment."

They sat in silence for a few minutes both thinking about what the other was going through and thinking about. There were a few older children in the park practicing their skateboarding tricks so they both just watched while they thought.

"She's so much like you Sarah," he said, suddenly breaking the silence.

Sarah closed her eyes, that hurt so much to hear, "Don't say that" she replied, her heart pounding as she stood up again and began pacing in front of him, "I can't handle that, Ben. I can't handle all of this, you, her, Tina even, it's just too much for me, I'm not strong enough at the moment," her pacing was getting quicker and her hands were shaking at her sides, "I've just lost my best friend, I've started my new married life with Tom and now you, Kate, this…this whole situation, I just can't cope, with it all right now," tears began to escape as she got more and more flustered and anxious. She really did feel as though this just wasn't the time to try and cope with something so huge and something that would impact their lives at such a high level. Something so painful to think back on as well as trying to think about a future for the three of them.

Ben stood up and grasped hold of her arm, "Sit down,

try and breath, come on," he rubbed her arm gently, but she pulled away from him, "Sarah, I know I was a dick the other night but honestly, I just want to help you and her to meet and then I'll get out of your life, I promise. I'm taking a new job in Germany, so Tina has got to give her notice to you soon anyway. I'm telling her later tonight."

Not even realising what he had said about Tina leaving work, she sat down with him again and took a few deep breaths. She felt like this was the worst thing for her right now. How could she even contemplate being here with him, where it all started, where it all went wrong all those years back? What was she doing?

As he reached into his jacket pocket and proceeded to light a cigarette, she bravely asked, "can I ask you a question?"

He nodded as he sucked in the potent fumes, "sure, anything."

"Did I mean anything to you? You know back then when we...did you care about me at all?"

Blowing out a huge puff of smoke away from her, he replied, "look, if I'm honest, I was a teenage prick, most boys are at that age. You were a pretty little thing, you still are,"

She shook her head. He was still trying to be charming, and it was ridiculous. She let out a huff to let him know he wasn't impressing her with his charm.

"You are Sarah, but I wasn't after anything other than fun, like most teenage boys. I was too young, and I could never have handled being a father back then. I was high on drugs most nights, I couldn't stop drinking and getting into trouble, what good would I have been to you and a child? I liked you yes, but it was just a bit of fun, you know, sex?"

"Oh my god. So, I was just another notch on your belt then? Cheers for that."

He choked back the smoke, "I guess so, yes, if that's how you wanna put it. I didn't intend on hurting you like I did. I just, well I was shocked I'd got you pregnant and hoped you would get rid of it to be honest."

"That's lovely," she said sarcastically.

"I know, I know...I feel like an even bigger prick for saying it out loud and now I've met her, our kid, well, that makes me even more of a prick for not sticking by you and standing up to what I did, to both of you," he paused inhaling his poisonous stick again, "I can't say sorry enough times I know and I don't expect you to just sit back and accept it. I just want to make it happen for her and, Sarah, I think you would really love her too. As I said, you are very alike."

Tilting her head up towards the sky, she knew deep down that he was probably right, she would probably love her. If she was honest with herself, she had never stopped loving her from even before she had been born. It would be good for them all but how could she face her. How could she be that mother to her when she just gave her away to someone else so many years ago? Her mind was smashed in right now, her heart broken once again, and she couldn't stop the tears that now fell down her flushed cheeks. She felt sick again and became lightheaded, her face turned pale.

"I, err, I don't feel so good…" she leaned forward holding her knees, gasping for air, then that feeling was there again, she held her hand to her mouth and suddenly turned to throw up behind the bench. Totally embarrassed to see Ben crouching over her, she managed to utter, "Oh god, do you have any tissue."

"Here, use this," he passed her his jacket, "it's all I've got, don't worry," he said as he saw her face grimace at the thought of wiping her sick laden lips on his jacket. "It's fine honestly, I don't much like it anyway."

As she sat back round on the bench, red faced and eyes full of tears, she smiled at him and he smiled back, taking the jacket carefully in the tips of his fingers which made her chuckle, "Thanks," she said, "I don't know what's wrong with me today, that's the second time today."

"Maybe it's the stress I've put you under now. Look, I know this is a shock, it was for me but once we'd had a good chat, me, and Kate, that is, she was fine. She's been brought up proper-like, you know. Her mum who adopted her died of cancer, so she has been through a rough time, but her aunt and uncle took over. She's so…respectful, polite, she's really lovely Sarah, she really is a great person."

"Okay, okay," Sarah snapped again and then instantly felt bad for doing so. The word cancer struck a chord pulling at her heartstrings, "I just need some time, a few days or something to get my head round it all. I don't want to throw up in front of her now do I?"

They sat for another fifteen minutes mostly talking about their lives and what they had done during their years apart. Memories of the skatepark and the things they ended up smoking and drinking all those evenings. Sarah eventually relaxed and enjoyed chatting with him which shocked her. He really wasn't so bad after all; well, he'd grown up at least and he wasn't being a prick like he had been the other night.

As they made their way out of the skatepark, her phone began to ring. It was Tom. "Hey babe, you alright?" Sarah said as she put her fingers to her lips and shushed Ben then mouthed that it was Tom on the phone. "Yeah, I'm just walking back now, I just nipped to the leisure centre to see about booking a badminton session," she lied, "Yep, okay, see you at home, won't be long darling, bye, bye" and she hung up relieved that she'd been able to think quickly.

Ben had just watched her the whole time, "everything okay?" he asked.

"Yes. It was Tom. Look, I can't meet you again like this, I'll text you when I'm ready okay, please don't come to my house again and please do not tell Tina or Tom. I just need time to think, time to get my head round it all, yeah? I will be in touch, but I need to get my head around everything first, you know."

Ben gently reached for her arm, "Sure, no problem. I'll speak to you soon, yeah?"

"Yep, and thank you," she replied, honestly, "oh and sorry about your jacket," they both chuckled as he looked down at the sick laden jacket he was holding, "best get that in the wash asap," she laughed, squinting her nose as he wafted it away from their bodies.

"Haha, yeah, probably just chuck it in that bin, save on any explanation to Tina maybe. Speak soon, yeah?" and with that, he left her standing there feeling alone, sad, embarrassed and more than that, totally confused. She didn't know whether to hate him still, to forgive him, to respect him for being so honest or anything. Her life was now even more complex than she had imagined it would be.

When she finally arrived home, Tom was back too. He had arranged all the shopping of new toys onto the kitchen table, and he was busily trying to decide which wrapping paper he should use. He looked so happy, so excited and she loved seeing him beaming that gorgeous smile back at her as she made her way into the chaos of present wrapping.

"Hey darling," he said as he noticed her walk in, "I can't choose, what do you think, you're the best at wrapping presents aren't you, do you think they need wrapping, I mean, don't children enjoy that ripping open of presents more than just a gift bag, I don't know, I did get some of them too but, well, the children at the hospital seem to love the paper option when they get gifts, what do you think?" he flustered rapidly talking ten to the dozen.

"I think he'll love both darling, I'm sure it'll be fine whatever you choose...but I do like the superheroes wrapping the best," she smiled and rubbed his back making her way over to boil the kettle, "he's a very lucky little boy to have you as his uncle."

"Aww, thanks babe, what a lovely thing to say...and he's very lucky to have an aunty like you too. Aunty Sarah and Uncle Tom, love it, I just love it," he exclaimed excitedly, grabbing the sellotape from the kitchen drawer, "did you book a session?"

"Session?" she asked, confused.

"Badminton, you went to see about booking in?" he replied innocently.

"Oh," she felt her heart beating faster, "no, nothing available," she lied, remembering the stupid excuse she had told him on the phone earlier.

As she watched him wrestling with finding the end of the tape, she thought again about the meeting with Ben, the future meeting with Katie-Jane and how all that would affect her relationship with Tom. How would he feel being a stepdad to a grown woman almost? How would he feel knowing it was Ben that Sarah had had the baby with in the first place? Her mind raced, her heart hurt, and she felt terrible for all the sordid details that were now in the fore front of her life once again. After all these years, to feel this worthless and this confused again, just worried her more than anything ever before and she just wished Jane was here to help. She would've known exactly what to do in this sort of situation and would've put Sarah's mind at ease somehow.

Just then her phone pinged, and she saw that it was Karl answering her text. *'Sorry it's taken so long, been in a meeting all day and then had to pick Robbie up from his mates. Talk soon, yeah. I'm here whenever you need me, lots of love, K.x'.*

She smiled down at the message, it was as if he knew that Jane was on her mind at that very moment. She was so lucky to still have him in her life and she must remember to go round and fill him in on what was going on. But for now, her husband and his exciting news was all that she needed to concentrate on. Her news would have to wait a few days more.

Chapter Twenty

The next morning, it was time for them to meet their nephew and Tom was beside himself with excitement yet again. He'd not slept much, got up early with the dogs for a run in the park but was still fiddling around with the presents that Sarah had finally helped him wrap perfectly last night, adding some blue bows to the bigger gifts.

"Do I look alright?" he asked as he straightened his shirt, tucking it into his jeans, then swiftly untucking it again, nervously.

"Babe, you look fine, come here," she walked over to him and cupped his face in her hands, "he's not going to be looking at your clothes sweetie, especially when he sees all of those," she nodded over to the table where the pile of gifts stood proudly awaiting their new owner.

"I guess so. Thank you darling, you're always there

keeping me sane, aren't you?" he replied, "I just want him to like me, that's all. Be a great uncle for him. I want to tell him all about his dad too. He should know everything about James, you know," he sighed, "oh god I wish he was here to see this, to meet his boy...his son."

"I know babe but I'm sure he's looking down on you both today and he would be so proud of you too," she kissed him gently as they stood motionless together, no words needing to be spoken on the subject, "let's have a quick coffee before we set off, yeah, to calm your nerves a little bit. What time do we need to be there?"

"Well, Felicity said midday and then we can all have some lunch together. Dad and Janice are coming over in about half an hour. I said they could ride with us, save on taking two cars into town."

"Aw yeah, that's a good idea, I'll make the coffees and just check in with the girls at work to make sure they're all okay, do you want a few biscuits with yours?"

"No thanks, I'm good. I think I'm too nervous to eat now to be fair," he chuckled back, checking himself again in the mirror, flattening down his hair with his fingers, "I'm gonna sit outside with the dogs before it rains, get some air, see you out there?"

She nodded back as he lovingly rubbed her shoulder on his way past. The dogs shot up from their beds and closely followed him, one grabbing their favourite toy along the way. Elvis waddled his little legs as fast as he could to keep up and it made Sarah smile. He was her favourite out of the four of them. Her little sausage dog always managed to make her beam with happiness because he was the cutest of them all.

As she switched the kettle on, she grabbed her phone and sent a quick text message to the salon girls. She had taken the day off to make sure that she was able to meet her nephew with Tom. A few seconds passed and a text pinged back saying all was fine and she didn't need to worry. She did though, it was her business, and she loved every part of it including her wonderful staff who held the realm when needed. As the kettle started to boil, she wondered if Tina had gone in and if Ben had told her about Germany yet. Would she just up stick and leave her job to go with him? He was her husband after all so Sarah guessed she may be down a staff member soon. She just hoped that Tina wouldn't know about her connection with Ben. She didn't want any bad feelings between them or any of the other girls finding out about it all.

Preparing the coffee into the cafetiere and fetching their favourite mugs from the cupboard, she stopped her mind racing about it all, began to relax until her phone pinged again. She smiled as she picked up the phone once more thinking one of the girls had forgotten to tell her something, but this time, it was Ben. She immediately felt on edge.

'*Hey, I know you said you needed time, but I just wanted to make sure you were okay after the sickness?*'

She texted back quickly, almost thumping the letters with her fingers, '*yes fine thanks*' and turned her phone over facing down on the counter. Strangely, in one way, she felt angry that he had messaged her but on the other hand, at least it showed he cared, even if it was a bit late to bring his caring side out for her now. She hoped he wouldn't keep messaging her though. What the hell would Tom say if he saw it, she kept thinking to herself. Thoughts about that very scenario in a split second, she quickly picked her phone back up and deleted the message, then continued to make the drinks, glancing out to see where Tom was with the dogs. It was safe, he was crouched on the lawn wrestling the pull-toy with Charlie. Their perfect life had just begun and now this little hiccup appearing could jeopardize it all and she hated that fact and couldn't let it happen, not until she was ready to face it head on at least.

As they sat together on the outside furniture, finishing off their coffees, dogs laying at their feet, the doorbell rang. Tom got up to answer it closely followed by Donut who was bounding around the garden with his ball just moments earlier. They never failed to ensure that they saw who was coming into their home.

It was Henry and Janice, both looking their very best. Henry was donning a beautiful grey suit and Janice in a stunning red floral dress. This was such a special occasion for them all but, especially for Tom and Henry - they all looked lovely, and Sarah felt proud to be part of this family and this exciting event today.

As half eleven approached, they all decided it was time to leave. Tom locked the back door, settled the dogs in their beds, and then proceeded to transfer all the gifts into the boot of the car as Sarah rinsed the mugs quickly. Janice was explaining something about a new dance class that she and Henry had just started attending but Sarah's tummy began to feel weird again and she went pale and dizzy for a second. She held the side to steady herself.

"Are you alright my dear?" Janice asked as she noticed Sarah slightly wobbling, holding onto the kitchen worktop tightly.

Sarah wiped her forehead that now felt clammy and hot, "Erm…I don't feel so great, I…" and before she could say anymore, she realised what was coming. With her feet moving as fast as she could get them to, she rushed to the upstairs toilet and there it was, more sickness, head down the loo time.

Janice appeared a few minutes later peeping through the unlocked door. Seeing Sarah on the floor next to the toilet, she went in and closed the door behind her. "Oh sweetheart, have you eaten something a bit peculiar my dear," she asked, concerned, rubbing Sarah's back, "here, wipe your mouth you poor darling," and she passed her some tissue.

Sarah slowly stood back up, cheeks both looking flushed now and feeling more embarrassed than anything, "sorry Janice. Something definitely hasn't agreed with me," she said as she wiped her mouth clean, "I was sick yesterday too, maybe it's a twenty-four-hour bug or something," she threw the tissue into the toilet flushing it away and then moving to the sink to wash her hands.

"Oh, bless you, yes maybe, there have been some unsightly bugs going around just lately," replied Janice.

"Do you think it's okay for me to still go today, I wouldn't want to pass anything on to Albert or any of you?"

"I'm not sure darling. Do you want me to fetch Tom my dear, maybe ask him his thoughts on it? He's a lot more medical than I am, isn't he?"

"No, no," she answered quickly, "I'm sure it's just something I've eaten, I can't spoil his big day. I'm sure I'll be fine now. I'll just keep my distance in case, thanks Janice. Oh, and please don't say anything to Tom or Henry, I don't want them worrying and fussing over me, not today anyway."

"Of course, I won't say anything my dear. You know I'm good with secrets hey? It's just between you and I, my promise."

They just smiled at each other knowingly and made their way back downstairs. Tom and Henry were waiting patiently outside by the car, so Sarah closed the front door behind them, took a deep breath of the fresh air and hurried up the path.

"Where have you been, we've got to go?" said Tom, concerned and anxious to not be late.

Janice replied to him quickly, "sorry my dears, we had some lady business to attend to in the ladies' room, you know us old girls. When we need to go, we need to go," she chuckled, giving Sarah's arm a reassuring squeeze so she didn't have to answer. She really was the best mother replacement for Sarah and again, she thought how lucky she was. Since Jane had died, they had become even closer than ever and supported each other through their grief. Janice had always been there for Sarah and not having a mother from such a young age meant they had grown closer even more.

~

The afternoon flew by, and Albert was as gorgeous as they had all imagined him to be. His beautiful olive skin, his amazingly curly black hair and super cute button nose with a smile that pulled on everyone's heartstrings. The smile in particular reminded Tom of James so he was constantly making him laugh just to see that grin again and again.

Sarah was thrilled to see them together but kept in the background just in case the sickness she'd been experiencing was actually a tummy bug. It was so lovely to see them playing with the toys which had been ravishingly opened.

She imagined how Tom may have been if he had gotten the chance to be a father. She knew that he would have spoiled their kids to the max and would have loved every part of it. Suddenly, she thought about the sickness again, could it be something other than a bug? When was her last period? Now, an even weirder feeling was fluttering in her tummy at the thought that this sickness could be...no, surely not that, she thought to herself feeling fraught with worry. She wouldn't even be able to contemplate that she could be pregnant with his baby. Shaking her mind free of those mad thoughts, she watched Tom chatting quietly with Albert's mother.

"When can we meet up again?" Tom asked as the afternoon drew to a close. Albert was exhausted and had fallen asleep on the bench in the restaurant after his massive ice cream sundae.

Felicity collected her jacket as Henry and Janice helped load the presents into her car, "whenever you like Tom. He loved it so much and I'm so glad we got to do this finally," she moved forward to hug him and whispered in his ear, "I'm so sorry about James, I really am."

Tom didn't know what to answer but as he stood back, he just gave her a smile to let her know he was alright with it. Too many years had passed and now was all that mattered. The joy of finally meeting his nephew was plenty of an apology.

He gently picked Albert up in his arms and they all made their way out to the car park settling him into his car seat, still snoring away sweetly.

Sarah linked into Tom's arm as they watched Felicity drive away, "Happy?" she asked, laying her head on his shoulder.

"Over the blooming moon babe, how bloody cute is he? I mean, come on, he's the cutest kid in the world, isn't he?" he excitedly answered.

He was so cute, but Sarah couldn't help but think about another cute baby that she had once laid eyes on, and the all too real reality hit home for her again. That baby girl, her baby girl, that precious little bundle of baby cuteness that had been unloaded on her all those years ago. And now, it was her turn, she had the task of meeting her blood relative, but it wasn't as simple as this meeting had been. It wasn't going to be anywhere near that simple and she felt even more bewildered by the minute about it all.

~

Another morning of throwing up for no apparent reason was the start for today and she felt even worse than the last few days.

She had concluded that it could, and probably was down to the recent amount of stress she had been trying to deal with? But how could stress make her so sick, was it some sort of food poisoning? Did she eat something dodgy; she racked her brains trying to think of something she may have eaten to make her feel so rough for the past week, but nothing came to mind, she'd not been out anywhere recently, home cooked meals were the only food they had been having so it could only mean one thing? She went through her period app on her phone and noticed one small detail that she had been hoping wouldn't be in there - her period was late. She hadn't had her monthly cycle which was usually dead-on time.

"Oh Christ," she whispered to herself as she sat down on the toilet in the staff room.

"Shit, shit, shit," she whispered again to herself, her heart pounding. Maybe this was a sign. Maybe it was a sign of good things to come after all the recent worry and fretting she had been doing. But how could she have another baby, how could she whilst knowing her past and what she gave up already. The baby she gave up whom she was supposed to be meeting with at the weekend.

She had messaged Ben after they'd got home from seeing Albert and agreed to meet with them Saturday afternoon. He'd agreed in turn to not contact her again until Saturday morning. She couldn't risk Tom seeing the messages between them. Ben had also agreed to not contacting Tom regarding the four of them going out for dinner as previously discussed. For what it was worth, Sarah felt relieved that he was playing ball with her demands.

She decided she needed to find out what was going on inside her once and for all so gathered herself together, met her final client of the day, finished off a beautiful set of Russian lashes and then left the salon early to get to the chemist.

"Are you okay Sarah?" Tina asked as she got to the office door.

"Oh, you made me jump," she replied, slightly startled. She seemed to be in a daze and hadn't noticed Tina there, "Yes, I'm fine, I just need to go early. Gotta pick up some bits from the dry cleaners before they shut, are you okay to lock up tonight?" she was feeling awkward about even making eye contact with Tina right now, knowing what she did, knowing even more than Tina knew herself about going away soon with Ben.

"Yes, of course, no problem, see you tomorrow?" and she went off to sit back at her computer, tapping away happily.

Walking briskly down the street towards the chemist, she sent a quick text to Karl, *'Hey, are you about, just need a chat, may have news? X'*

On arriving at the door to the store, a reply pinged back, *'sorry, got meetings until six tonight, then dance with Cassie, wanna come over around eight? K x'*

'It's okay, don't worry, I'll text you when I get home tonight x' she pinged back.

Throwing the phone into her bag, and taking a deep breath, she began braving the walk towards the pregnancy test shelving aisle, head down in the hope no-one would see her.

Chapter Twenty-One

As she looked down towards the white stick in her hand, her heart pounded in anticipation. She had all kinds of emotions running through her body right now. Would there be that word 'pregnant' on it in a few minutes? Was she overthinking the sickness, or could she have messed up somewhere along the lines with her period app and forgotten to note down her last cycle properly? If not, if this test was positive, what would it all mean for her and Tom, for her and Ben, and more urgently, for her and Katie-Jane? Would this change everything for their future? How would she even feel about being pregnant again or how would Katie feel knowing that Sarah was pregnant and was going to keep this one. Sarah felt confused with everything running through her brain, she really didn't have a clue what to think at the moment.

Her emotions about this little stick in front of her were mixed and it seemed to be taking forever to just pluck up the courage and pee on it. She'd never been late since that chapter in her life which she had tried to put behind her for so long. This time it felt different though, different in a right sort of way. Although she had set herself up for never having children since Katie was born, vowing that she was not deserving enough to have them for giving her baby away maybe, just maybe, this was her chance to put her life right again? Right the wrongs that she had done as a teen.

Finally, she stuck it down in between her legs and peed on it, not knowing how she would feel but at the same time knowing for sure that Tom would be over the moon.

Seconds seemed like minutes as she lay the stick on the basin beside her while she pulled her knickers back up and fastened her jeans. Drying her hands, she glanced over towards it, and then, saw that all important word had appeared stating her fears, 'pregnant' and she let out a loud gasp in shock, arching her eyebrows in disbelief.

She *was* pregnant, she was actually pregnant. She was having a baby again but this time, things were going to be a lot different. This one would be staying; she would not let anyone take this from her. Nobody would talk her out of keeping it. She was in charge now, she was old enough to make this choice and this time, it would be the right one for her, not anyone else.

They were going to have their own baby and she began to feel elated at the idea but also had a huge sense of self-doubt in the same instance. Questioning her ability to finally have a child, something she never thought would happen to her again. How could she have this baby and not meet or have anything to do with Katie now? Would Tom even want her and the baby once he knew the full truth of her past? Questions, questions, all running around her brain like little lemmings.

She now had an even more important choice to make and even though she felt like bursting out the news, she decided it would be best to wait to tell Tom, at least until after she had the meeting with Katie and Ben. This would be the closure of secrets and finally, she would make all the future choices right for everyone involved.

She hid the test in her knicker drawer and threw the wrapping paper and box in the wheelie bin out the back, as deep as she could get it to go down.

Just as she reached the back door, she heard Tom arrive home. He looked exhausted after another hectic day in the hospital, so she set to making dinner, trying not to heave in the process from the smell making her feel sick again.

Once everything was cooking, she took him a glass of wine as he sat on the couch tapping away on his phone, "Oh thanks babe, here, look...Felicity has sent me through some baby pics of Albert. His smile kills me, isn't he lovely?" She looked on as he began scrolling through the images on the screen, smiling like a Cheshire cat right back at them. She imagined what he'd be like when it was his own child he'd be admiring. Fluttering butterflies niggled her tummy at the thought. In one way, she couldn't wait to tell him but in another, she was reluctant and just wanted to sort out everything else first before the news of a new beginning in their lives started.

"He's really gorgeous darling, I'm so happy for you," she replied, "he really took to you, didn't he? You're a natural. Maybe he could come over for a sleepover one weekend?" She laid her head on his shoulder looking down at his phone admiring the pictures he was still scrolling through.

"That's a fab idea, I'll text and ask her now," swiping the screen, he began tapping away a message to Felicity.

"Hey, leave it for now. How about we grab an early night?" she squeezed his thigh and he immediately stopped what he was doing. Smiling cheekily back at her, he gently placed the phone onto the coffee table, grabbed her hand and led her upstairs to their bedroom.

As she lay beside his warm body, watching him now fast asleep, she glanced down at her tummy. Running her fingers gently over it, she remembered all those years ago when she felt her first baby moving inside her huge teenage belly and how fond she had become of it. She recalled the feelings of anxious hope that she would change the minds of her aunt, nan and grandpa and keep it, knowing deep down that wasn't an option all along.

She wondered how much different it would be now, knowing that she had someone to support her this time, having a family together with someone so special and so loving. She smiled to herself and decided that she would tell him tomorrow evening, after meeting with Katie and Ben. Draw a line under that madness and maybe they could all be a big happy family in time, just not with Ben of course. She hoped he would leave as promised.

~

The next morning, Tom was up early for work. He'd already been on his run and made Sarah some toast and coffee before she had even got up. She hated him working on a Sunday, but it was only a shift that he had to do every other weekend and he loved his job so much.

"I'll be home at about five tonight, I hope. I said I'd cover Gary's shift for a few hours. Shall I bring a Chinese back, save you cooking?" he said as he grabbed his hoody from the wardrobe.

Sarah stretched and yawned a reply, "Mmm, yes that would be nice babe, thanks," and sat up to eat her toast. He'd put lashings of butter on it just as she liked it with a touch of marmite which he hated.

He came back over to the bed and kissed her on the head, "You keep your marmite breath to yourself," he joked, "see you later babe...oh, and the dogs may need to go out to do their business, they were all asleep this morning," and with that he was gone before she could answer.

As another drop of butter fell into her lap, she looked down again at her plump tummy. She could barely see the scars from the surgery anymore, they had faded to thin silvery lines now. She would have to be careful not to put on too much weight with this pregnancy, she didn't want to undo her tummy tuck. She loved her new belly button and smoother middle.

The dogs began to bark as the post flew through the letterbox, so she got out of bed and made her way downstairs. Without fail, she was promptly greeted by her crew of wagging tails and smiling long tongued fluffs. "Hey, you lot, come on, let's get you outside, come on," she picked up the post from the doormat and made her way to the back door. They all ran outside and began their morning business.

She watched them laughing at Charlie as he played with his soft toy, throwing it up in the air and then leaping on top of it. He was one of the older dogs, but he didn't act like it. Elvis was waddling about on his little legs, sniffing the grass. Rufus and Donut were in the bushes almost doing synchronized peeing up them. They were brothers and always did everything together.

The inside silence was broken as Sarah heard her phone ping where she had left it on the kitchen table last night. It was a message from Karl. *'Hey, hope all okay, I'm free later this afternoon if you need anything. Working from home. Speak soon. K.x'*

She'd completely forgotten to message him last night as she had promised so, immediately feeling bad she swiftly text him back. *'Sorry I forgot to text yesterday, got some news but will meet up soon, promise. Meeting with K today, so nervous...eek. Will let you know how it all goes. S. x'*

'Wow, good luck, here for you whenever you need me. K x' Came back a reply.

'Thanks. X' she smiled as she rapidly texted the message.

With the dogs safely back in, she locked the door, gave them some biscuits, and went to have a shower.

Just as she went to get in, her phone pinged again but this time it was Ben.

'Still on for today?'

'Yes, see you at 12' She typed back quickly feeling slightly frustrated that he'd text her again. If Tom was here and saw these messages, what the hell would he think? She deleted it and continued with her shower feeling even more nervous about the meeting. Thoughts ran through her mind about how to react, how to greet her, just basically how to be about the whole situation.

Another quick round of nausea hit her as she began trying to decide what she should wear. She wondered how long this sickness would last. Apparently around three months she read as she googled it after wiping her mouth once again. She hoped she would have the chance to tell Tom before he saw her throwing up. Morning sickness they call it, but it seemed to be hitting her whenever. Or could it be nerves today? She hadn't suffered with being sick the last time and again her brain ached from thinking things over and over. Maybe this meant she was having a boy this time. A son for Tom would be amazing.

She looked down at her watch, it was nearly half eleven and she needed to start making her way to the meeting. They had decided to meet just out of town at a small farm shop and cafe. It seemed like the ideal place and Sarah just hoped she wouldn't see anyone she knew.

As she drove into the car park, the sickness returned but she managed to stop it this time, inhaling air and taking more deep breaths once she was parked up. This round of sick feelings must be nerves she thought to herself. She hadn't been able to stop the pregnancy vomit so far. Her tummy had been doing somersaults ever since she got in the car back home. She wasn't even sure if she was doing the right thing by meeting them, making her even more confused than ever. But she was here now, and she had to finally close this chapter of her book. Apologise, talk it over and say goodbye to Ben for good this time, forever she hoped. Even if he had said sorry and seemed a lot nicer than that horrid last hour, she had seen him as a teenager, she didn't want to be friends with him, she didn't want him in her life ruining everything. More importantly, she didn't want him in Tom's life.

Locking the car and taking a final, and much deeper breath, she walked into the farm shop through to the outside patio area.

There they were, the two of them waiting patiently to meet her. Katie looked a bit nervous; Ben just looked his usual brazen self and Sarah felt sick to her stomach.

For a few moments, she just watched them laughing, chatting, and sipping on their drinks like they'd been friends forever, father and daughter out for a bite to eat together like everything was normal. Like there was no history between them, no past to think about. It felt weird, strange, not real to Sarah and she sneaked back behind a tree feeling so worried about what to say to them when she could pluck up the courage to finally go over to the table.

Suddenly a voice came from behind her, "Can I help you madam?"

Sarah turned around, feeling embarrassed, "Oh erm, sorry, yes I am meeting some friends, I think they are over there," she replied to the young waitress pointing to the table in the corner where her past and future problems now sat waiting for her arrival.

"No problem, I'll come and take your drink order as soon as you're settled, this way please," and she led the way to the table in the direction of Ben and Katie.

Sarah followed slowly with a slightly red flushed face as the waitress reached the table and pulled the chair back for her. Ben stood up and Katie just stared at Sarah.

"Thank you, could we get the same again here and Sarah, what would you like to drink?" asked Ben as he sat back down.

"Oh, just water for now please," Sarah replied, taking her seat trying not to make direct eye contact with either of them.

There was a hew of silence for what seemed like minutes as they all composed themselves and then Kate spoke, "I'm sorry if I startled you in the coffee shop the other day. It's lovely to finally meet you," she smiled sweetly as Sarah looked into her gorgeous blue eyes. It was like looking in a mirror, but she couldn't speak, and this made her feel so childish and stupid, she just smiled back.

"I'm just nipping to the loo ladies, won't be long," Ben said as the atmosphere grew a little bit more tense.

Sarah watched as Ben disappeared behind the bar area and then turned back to face her daughter, "Katie...I... I need to say something," She could feel her hands trembling so much she had to grasp them tight in her lap to try and keep them still.

"Please don't say it Sarah," Kate replied, "You don't have to say sorry," she paused, "Ben told me everything. I know the story and I understand the reasons you did what you did, honestly, it's okay," she reached out her hand across the table but Sarah just looked at it not knowing how to react, "and please call me Kate, no-one has called me Katie for many years now," as she moved her hand back, she continued, "I don't want to cause you any stress Sarah, I just wanted to meet you, to see you properly, meet my birth mother finally, even if you can only do it just the once."

Sarah glanced down into her lap and then up at her again. She could feel a lump growing in her throat, her eyes felt sore from trying to hold back a waterfall of tears that wanted to cascade down her face. Why was she being so nice? Why didn't she hate her for giving her up? It seemed almost dream-like, movie like but it wasn't, and Kate meant every word she was saying.

"It's just been a shock you know, I never expected to see you again, not ever," Sarah whimpered as she finally managed to string a sentence together.

"Yes, I would imagine it has been a shock and it was for me when I found out that I'd been adopted but honestly, I get it. Along with my coffee shop job, I work with young mums in the local youth club, so I know how tough it must've been for you to make that decision. Things were very different to how they are now. I don't envy the choices teens have to make in that predicament."

Sarah looked over to the toilets to see if Ben was returning anytime soon. He was now chatting to someone at the food counter. Obviously avoiding coming back over to them. Or was he being nice again and giving them time, the time they so needed together?

"It really was tough and I'm so sorry I had to do it, but..."

"Sarah, I told you, you don't have to apologise. Not ever. Look, let's just chat, you know, like two normal people who have just met for the first time. Tell me about yourself, I want to know everything. And you can ask me anything about me too, anything. We can decide where to go after today, yeah?"

As she stared into her daughter's beautiful eyes, she felt relaxed, happy. Ben was right, Kate had turned out to be such a beautiful person inside too and she had made Sarah's broken heart a little bit fixed at last.

Chapter Twenty-Two

The afternoon seemed to fly by and before they knew it, it was time to leave.

"I have to be at work tonight, extra shifts to pay for my new car I've been saving for," chuckled Kate as she gathered her bag and jacket.

Ben had joined them after leaving them be for an hour together. It had been so strange for Sarah, but she had enjoyed every moment of it once the nerves took a back seat. Even with Ben there, she had felt happy and was glad that they had all met up.

"I'll run you there Kate," said Ben as he tucked her chair under as she stood up.

"Oh, that would be great thank you Ben," she replied sweetly, "Sarah, it's been really lovely today. Thank you for meeting me." She moved towards Sarah and hugged her, taking Sarah by surprise but she slowly reached her arms round her daughter, and they embraced each other.

"It's been amazing Katie, I mean Kate," Sarah whispered.

"Eh, can I get some of this love?" asked Ben, holding his arms out wide but Sarah just gave a stern glance back at him and he knew she was having none of it, "Joking…" he said back with a big grin, pulling back his arms.

The three of them walked out to the car park, Ben got into his car as Sarah and Kate said their goodbyes.

"I feel like I'm saying goodbye to you all over again Kate, I don't want to lose you again now," a lonely tear escaped, rolling down her cheek.

Kate wiped it clear, "Sarah, don't be sad," she said calmly, "like I said to you earlier, I don't hold any grudges and I forgive you, it wasn't your fault," their eyes met as she continued, "Ben was too young as well. I see it all the time in my job, but girls get so much more support these days. It's very different for them, but these things happen, and you did what was best for you at the time. And the main thing is you did what was best for me. I appreciate that, I really do. I had a great childhood because of the difficult choices that you had to make, so you don't have to feel guilty about any of it, not at all, okay?" she held Sarah's hands like she was the adult, "look, if you want to meet up again, that's absolutely fine but if you don't, that's fine too. I know your life now and I don't want to cause any trouble or interfere with that. I just wanted to meet you, just once to see if we looked alike which now sounds weird, so I'm more than happy you were brave enough and came."

"Wow," Sarah replied, astounded by the words coming out of Kate's mouth. Her very grown-up attitude at this very poignant moment was truly astounding to hear and be a part of, "Kate, you are such a beautiful person, I feel proud to call you my..." then she paused, "sorry," she stopped herself from uttering the word that she so wanted to say.

"Your daughter?" Kate said, "Yes I am and always will be so text me yeah, whenever. I'm living locally now for a while so I can meet up when I'm not working," she smiled at Sarah wiping another random tear from her face, "Look I really have to go otherwise I'm going to be late, speak soon yeah?" she squeezed Sarah's hands.

They had one final hug goodbye and then Sarah stood watching them drive out up the long gravel exit and onto the main road. She couldn't quite believe how amazing this afternoon had been and suddenly felt a little bit more excited about the prospect of revealing all to Tom. Two lots of news were now in line for him. This would make three new members of the family in a matter of days. She decided she had to tell him tonight, not wanting to hold back anymore but which news should she share first - her baby or their baby? Maybe Karl could help her make the decision? She rifled through her bag to reach her phone and text him quickly.

Within a minute, a reply pinged back that he was at home for an hour, so she jumped in the car and made her way to his house smiling and thinking of the future, the future for her and Kate and all the new additions to their family.

~

"So yeah, it was all very...civilized, she is so lovely but," said Sarah as she sipped on her extra strong coffee that Karl had made her, "I just can't help thinking it's all too good to be true you know? I mean, Ben turns up acting all ignorant and arsey, then arranges the meeting, is kind enough to leave us alone to chat, and Katie, Kate, forgives me...but why? I can't even forgive myself for abandoning her like that, just giving her up, you know. Or am I being paranoid or overreacting about stuff?"

"People are so different Sarah, I cannot imagine how I would feel or what I'd do in this situation, but it all sounds positive, just go with it and embrace it I say," he smiled knowingly at her now flustered face, "Look, life's too short mate, we know that with what happened with Jane don't we. Grab it by the horns and enjoy your daughter," he touched her hand gently.

She knew he was right, she now had the chance to put some past things right, to right the wrongs she made and forgive herself for the mistakes. This was her time to rein it all in and reveal memories she never thought she would utter. Just then, feeling slightly sick, she remembered the new bit of info that only she knew about. The new baby, she hadn't told anyone about that yet. Taking a gulp of coffee to try and aid the sickness, which this time, she knew was just nerves, she took a deep breath, "I err, I have some other news too actually, I need to tell someone..."

"Oh, blimey Sarah, you are full of surprises today aren't you, go on, shock me again," he laughed getting up to get some biscuits out of the cupboard, "Do we need the chocolate ones for this news?" he juggled two packets of digestives towards her.

She just giggled back, "I think so maybe…" she replied.

As he sat back down and began opening the packet, he asked, "right let's have it, what dog are we getting next, what salon extension do you have for us, men's treatments going a bit further?"

"Haha, no, sorry, none of those. I, well I've been a bit sicky lately, so I took a test,"

He suddenly stopped mid rip, "test?"

"Yes…a pregnancy test. It says I'm pregnant Karl. I don't know how, well," she laughed, looking into his blanked expression, "I know how of course but, well, I've been under so much stress with all the Ben and Kate stuff, I think I just forgot to take my pill for a few days or something and then bang, morning sickness arrived, and the test was positive," she paused again, "Karl?"

"Sorry…" he replied, shaking his head free of the shock, "that's great news, right?" he said in hope that she was happy about the predicament.

"Yes, I think so. I didn't really know how to feel at first but maybe this is my chance to make everything better, turn things around with how bad I have felt all these years. Maybe finally, life is good and going my way," she dunked a biscuit into her coffee after finishing off the unwrapping for him. "I've not told anyone yet, not even Tom. I want to make it special and of course, I have the Kate news to tell him first I think, do you think he should know about that in the first instance?"

"Mmm, that's a tough one as I don't know how he'll take it but, you know what, he's a good guy and he loves you so much, I think whatever you throw at him, he'll still love you the same, if not, even more than he does already. Oh Sarah, I am pleased for you, for all of you" he held up his coffee mug, "here's to new lives being built."

Sarah chinked her mug against his, looking at his face, beaming and smiling widely back at her. She knew how much Tom loved her and knew one hundred percent that he would be ecstatic when he found out they were going to have a baby, she just wasn't sure how he would react to the other news. The fact that his wife actually had a child already and who was now going to be part of their lives as well as his new nephew and their new baby.

"Man, my life gets ever more complicated, doesn't it?" she laughed.

"It certainly does my friend, but you have dealt with so much already in your life, this is just another hurdle for you to jump the hell over."

She chuckled again, "Thanks Karl, I knew I could turn to you with all this craziness."

"My pleasure darl, now, go on, get over to your man and tell him your news...and text me after to let me know how it all went, yeah?"

"I will do."

As they said their goodbyes, she felt excited to get home but still didn't know which news to reveal first. The good news about their baby or the awkward news about Kate and of course, then there was the fact of Ben being her ex-boyfriend from years ago. Her thoughts returned to that night he was in their house, and she pretended to not even know who he was, how would Tom feel about that deception. She had already lied to his face right there and then. Now she felt sure she couldn't bring that subject up just yet, maybe when Ben had moved away like he said, maybe that would make things easier to reveal the details then, yes, that's what she had to do for now. Her mind wandered frantically. Tell him about their baby and bring him in closer, prove to him how much she loved him. She had only just told him she wasn't having children, that she didn't want them and now she was pregnant with his baby. It had to be this news immediately, just in case.

Pulling up the driveway, she pinged Karl a quick text, *'thanks again for today, K, I'm home now and going in! LOL...Going to tell him about our baby first, speak soon, lots of hugs. S. x'* and threw the phone into her bag as she locked the car and made her way up the path excitedly and with butterflies in her tummy.

The dogs came bounding up to her as soon as she opened the door, nearly knocking her back. She loved seeing their faces, tongues hanging and usually drooling, tails wagging like mad, from side to side. Nothing quite like a dog's greeting. After finally getting through the hallway and letting them out the back door to run off steam, she went to the fridge to grab a bit of cheese. She'd not eaten all day apart from the chocolate digestive at Karl's and immediately felt guilty for the little peanut growing inside of her now. She wanted to look after this new life, protect it and help it grow perfectly - just like Kate had grown.

She took a big bite out of the block of cheddar but then almost immediately felt sick once again and ran to the toilet trying her best to not actually be sick this time.

As she took some deep breaths, Charlie's wet nose rubbed against her arm as if to kiss her better. She ruffled his curly fur on his head and smiled back at him. Sitting on the floor for a moment, she hoped this sickness wouldn't continue for too long.

Half five came and went but there was no sign of Tom yet. She had been busy tidying and cleaning since getting home and setting the scene with candles ready to light and the dining table set out awaiting their Chinese meal. She'd written him a little note and placed it in her pocket ready to give it to him during dinner. She'd put just two words on it; 'Hello Daddy' with a smiley face and love heart drawn underneath and she couldn't wait to see his face when he opened it. They loved writing notes to each other and this one would mean so much.

Getting a little anxious, she decided to try and call him, he was rarely late without texting or calling so she was a little bit concerned. After three attempts, he answered, "Hey babe, sorry, had an emergency come in so I've had to stay on and my phone has been in the locker, are you okay?" he said, sounding tired.

"Oh yes, I'm fine, I was just a bit worried you weren't back."

"Sorry darling, I should've called but you know what it's like sometimes here when they come in. Quite a bad car accident but should be able to get off in about an hour. Do you still want food brought back?"

"No worries, babe, yes can do. I've not really eaten much all day. I'll have a quick bath while I wait, I love you."

"Cool, see you soon babe, love you too, bye," and he was gone again.

As she stared down at the blank screen, she turned to the dogs who were all surrounding her, "Well guys, it's just us five for a bit, daddy's gonna be late," she said as the dogs watched and waited for their dinner. "Let's get you all some munchies, shall we?" She filled their bowls with biscuits and made her way upstairs to run her bath. Filling the tub with her favourite bubbles, she checked on her social media pages and emails while the bath was filling. She felt so happy tonight and couldn't wait to see Tom as soon as he got home.

When the bath was half full, she slid into it with the tap still running when her phone pinged. Wiping her hands dry on the towel next to her, she looked and saw that it was Ben. What did he want now? Didn't he say he wouldn't message her? She swiped to open it angrily. *'Need to talk urgently, please call me Sarah. URGENT!'*

She deleted the message and put the phone back on the

side, why should she answer his beck and call whenever he felt the need to contact her. She would do it when she had finished her bath at her convenience. She swirled the bubbles over her tummy, smiling at it.

Two minutes later, it pinged again but she just ignored it. She knew it would be him again and was getting annoyed. So much so, that after the fourth ping sound, she got up out of the bath, splashing the water with frustration.

The messages were all similar.

'Please call me Sarah, really need to speak to you'

'Sarah, it's urgent, please call me asap'

She dried herself off, got her dressing gown on and sat on the bed. He wasn't going to give up, so she dialled the number. She would tell him finally to stop messaging her no matter what he wanted. She didn't want him in her life right now and certainly couldn't have Tom see him messaging her. He may have been playing Mr. nice guy and she knew he probably meant well getting her and Kate together, but it didn't mean she needed him interfering in their life.

He answered before even the first ring it seemed and she was ready to have a go at him but the sounds from the other end of the line stopped her in her tracks. The sounds she could hear was of him crying and so much so, he had to compose himself before speaking.

Chapter Twenty-Three

As the line went deathly silent, with just the small sounds of sniffing and breathing, she asked, "What the hell is the matter, Ben?"

"I'm sorry," he replied, "I'm so sorry for bugging you but…" he took another deep breath, "It's Kate, oh god, Sarah, it's Kate."

Sarah's blood ran cold, and her skin immediately produced goosebumps, "What do you mean, what's happened? Is she okay?" she asked in a panic.

"There's been a crash. She's been in an accident, a car accident, someone hit her and it's bad, it's really bad Sarah," he gasped as he began crying once more.

"What?" she cried standing up in shock, "when? Is she okay, where is she, are you with her?" she asked him, fraught with worry, her hands beginning to shake.

"I'm at the hospital now, can you get here, I think you ought to. It's not looking good Sarah, she's in surgery now but they've told me to expect the worst," he replied sounding terrified, his voice croaking in between sniffing back his tears.

"Oh my god, shit, what hospital is it, I'll get there as soon as I can."

When the answer came back, her world shook again, and she felt as though her heart was stopping. It was where Tom worked, and he was still there. How could she go with the chance of bumping into him? He didn't even know about Kate; he didn't know she knew Ben and what their history was. Now she was torn between her past and the future and she didn't have a clue what to do.

"Sarah, are you still there?" Ben asked.

"Erm, yes I am, it's just, well that's where Tom works and he's there dealing with a car accident, what if it's the same one, I've not told him about all this yet?"

"I'll text you when she comes out of the operating theatre yeah, I don't want to cause any trouble for you."

"No, no Ben, I need to be there, it doesn't matter, I have to come, what if...what if she doesn't pull through?" She started grabbing some clothes from her wardrobe, chucking the dressing gown onto the bed, "I'll be there as soon as I can. I'll ring when I get to the entrance." She hung up the phone, quickly pulled on her hoody and joggers and bunched her wet hair in a hairband.

Just as she got to the door, grappling with her trainers, it opened and Tom was standing there, Chinese takeaway bag in one hand, flowers in the other, juggling with trying to find his keys, "That was good timing babe," he said grinning and holding up the food bag and flowers, "I come bearing gifts," he smiled but then saw her expression and now very pale, distressed face.

"Tom, I'm sorry, I have to go out, someone...a friend has been taken to hospital, I need to go and be with them, sorry," she felt terrible lying to him, but she had to just go, she had to get to the hospital, and she didn't have time to explain everything to him right now.

"Oh jeez. Do you want me to run you there, who is it?" he placed the food bag and flowers on the step, "Sarah, you look terrible, let me take you," he asked, trying to stop her as she made her way past him.

"No," she snapped back, "I'm going in my car, I'm fine. I'll call you later," and she ran to the car driving off at speed, leaving Tom standing there none the wiser and confused.

~

The hospital car park was super busy as usual, and it took her ten minutes before she finally found a space then she ran all the way to the front entrance. She had been grabbing her phone to ring him as she approached but Ben was outside pacing up and down, biting his nails looking frantic with worry. Her heart felt for him for a split second, he really did look upset.

"Ben," she called to him, and he glanced up to see her walking towards him.

With a despairing expression on his face, he held out

his arms and she could see he was still crying. He looked terrible and she couldn't help but envelope herself in those arms. It felt weird but strangely right at the same time.

He sobbed for what seemed like minutes and then she led him to a nearby bench to try and get some more information about what was going on, "Ben, how is she, is there any news yet, is she out of surgery?" she rubbed his shoulders as he composed himself.

Placing his hands on his knees, he gently spoke, "I can't believe we were all together earlier laughing and chatting and now this."

"Ben, what do you mean, can we go and see her now, is she out of surgery?"

"Oh god Sarah. It's too late. She's...she's gone," he looked across into her eyes with his glazed over and a large tear fell down his cheek. He held her hand so tightly, it almost hurt, "she didn't make it, I've just spoken to the doctors. She's dead Sarah, our daughter is dead."

Sarah just looked at him, stunned and unable to speak or move. It all seemed like a nightmare, and she wanted to wake up so badly from it. Her heart was broken again, and she had now lost another person in her life who she had only just met. How the hell could this happen? It was only hours before they had been in each other's arms and thinking of the future together. Her little girl who had grown up to be such a wonderful person was now suddenly gone and she would never have the chance to love her anymore.

She couldn't speak as she sat back on the bench and

just stared forward as the constant streams of traffic fell silent. She couldn't hear anything or anyone, everything was numb, and nothing made any sense. Her life was getting even more complicated by the hour.

Without even realising what was happening, Ben led her inside towards the room where the doctors had given him the tragic news. He sat her down on the chair and went to find the doctor. She just sat silent thinking of the whole horrid situation and this predicament. This was her punishment; she was sure of it. She was being punished for not being a proper mother when she should have been. She didn't deserve to have Kate in her life for giving her away. She hated herself so much right now and all she wanted to do was turn back time, turn the clocks back and make Kate stay with her. She should've taken her straight to Tom then she wouldn't have been in the accident at all. She would still be alive and in her arms. Her brain was racing with all the thoughts about why, when and what she had done to deserve this.

The doctor sat with them both and explained the injuries that she had sustained but nothing was registering in Sarah's head, nothing was sinking in as she was in too much shock. His words became muffled to her ears, and she didn't even want to hear what Kate had gone through in the past few hours. The pain she must have felt and being alone.

"I'm very sorry for your loss, would you like to see her? Her guardian relative has agreed that you can both see her," the doctor said as he collected his paperwork from the table.

Sarah just nodded in stunned silence.

"I have to inform you that there were significant facial injuries."

"It's okay Sarah, I'll be there with you," Ben said assumingly, now holding her hand which was bitterly cold and shaking.

"No. I'd rather do it on my own," she replied as she moved her hand away from his grasp and carefully got to her feet, "I have to do this alone Ben."

The doctor ushered her to the door and as she followed, she briefly glanced back to see Ben lower back onto the seat and put his head in his hands. This was all too surreal and weird, like a dream...like a nightmare. It was just like the crappy soap operas she used to watch, drama after drama, and she felt sick to the pit of her stomach about everything.

As she made her way along the corridor, her sickness reared up, "I just need a minute," she said, holding her hand over her mouth.

She ran to the nearest toilet and locked the door. She tried to take some deep breaths to stop it, leaning back against the door but it was no good and there was the bowl of a toilet once again. This time though, she sobbed as she threw up, thinking of how horrid this whole situation was and thinking that she now had to say goodbye to her daughter once again. In a hospital just like the day she was born, just like that awful day where the first goodbye had taken place. This time it really was for good though and it killed her to the very core.

For once in her life, she wanted to feel good about herself but, right now, she felt like the worst person ever. All this just seemed like punishment and the most beautiful people were being taken from her one by one.

"Are you okay Mrs. Cooper, do you need a glass of water?" the doctor asked as Sarah reappeared in the corridor, wiping her face with some tissue.

"Erm, no it's fine, thank you," she replied, rummaging into her handbag, and swigging on the bottled water she had.

"This way please," he said as Sarah composed herself once again. As they approached the room where Kate was, he said, "I'll get a nurse to come in with you or she can wait outside, whichever you prefer."

Again, all Sarah could do was nod, her mind felt numb as she prepared her heart for complete shattering as the door was slowly opened. There she was, laid on the bed, like she was fast asleep peacefully resting but she wasn't asleep, and it hurt like mad. Sarah gasped at the sight of her beautiful daughter, the daughter she would never have the chance to know more about, never have the chance to truly say how sorry she was to her. Kate was taken from her once again and right now, life felt as crap as it could get for Sarah.

She slowly walked toward the bed and looked up and down the silent, still body. The cuts on her face had been cleaned up as best they could, bruises to her forehead purple. Her beautiful face, hurt and scarred but still so pretty to Sarah.

She made her way beside the bed and touched her hand, "Katie," she whispered, tears freely flowing down her face, "I'm so sorry."

She just couldn't believe it, she wasn't going to get an answer back and Sarah's heart bled, shattering into a billion pieces for her baby, again.

~

As they made their way out of the hospital, Sarah's phone began to ring. It was Karl but she ended the call, not able to even begin an explanation to him at the moment.

"Thank you for coming, Sarah," Ben said as they got to the main entrance.

"I had to be here. Thanks for calling me. I'm so glad they had your number," she paused, "this is so horrible, god I feel so bloody awful, I just can't believe this is happening."

"Me too, I'll never forgive myself for not taking her the whole way to work, I should've just insisted and then she may not have..."

"Stop it," she interrupted, "Stop," she cried as she raised her hands to his mouth.

No words were spoken, they both knew it had been an accident but blamed themselves for different reasons. He felt bad for not getting her to work safely and she felt bad for not even being there, right then when she needed to be and for the rest of Kate's life which had now ended to short.

"I've spoken with Kate's aunt, she's been so kind, you know her adoptive aunt," he asked, "Sally. She's going to let us know when the funeral is, so I'll let you know yeah?" he said, holding her arm.

"Yes, please do. Maybe I should meet with her?"

"She did actually mention that she would like to meet you, but I didn't know how you would feel. We met a few weeks back and I saw her earlier when I got here. I'll have a chat with her and maybe arrange something in the next week or so?"

"Okay, thanks. Look, I better go, Tom will be worried about me. I left him in such a hurry earlier, and I'm going to have to tell him what's gone on."

"Right, yeah, I'm going to get home and speak to Tina too," he leaned forward to hug her and for a fleeting moment she felt that same connection from all those years back when she just wanted to be in his arms. Leaning toward him, she gently placed her arms around his waist, and they just held each other for a few minutes.

"What the bloody hell is going on here?" came a stern voice from behind them.

As Sarah turned toward the familiar sound, her heart sank as she saw her husband standing there looking at the two of them in an embrace, "Tom," she exclaimed, "what are you doing here?"

"I was worried about you, so I thought I'd come and see if you were okay but clearly, you are," he replied angrily, nodding towards Ben who was standing awkwardly at a slight distance from them now.

"It's not what you think," Sarah exclaimed, glancing from one to the other.

"I think you better go mate," Tom looked at Ben who held his hands up and walked away leaving Sarah stunned and now, nervous, and anxious at the news she had to tell her husband, the lies that she had kept from him.

"Tom, I can explain," she said watching Ben leave and her husband's face looking angry and stunned at the same time.

"I think you need to explain. What's going on Sarah, and why the hell are you cuddling Ben like that?" he said as his eyes grew even more stern looking.

"Can we go and sit down, and I will tell you everything, I'm not feeling so great," Sarah replied, ashen white and feeling weak.

Surprisingly calm, Tom followed her into the gardens opposite. He was always the calm one in the relationship and today, even seeing his wife embraced in another man's arms and not knowing what the hell was going on, he remained the beautiful person she knew he was. She knew that she had to reveal all to him and deep down, she was glad to finally let him know what an awful person he had married.

~

"So, that's everything Tom, that's my sordid secret past," Sarah said as they sat facing each other on the small picnic bench, "I'm so sorry I didn't tell you before you married me and I'll understand if you want a divorce now, I just never in a million years expected this to happen. I never thought I would see Kate again, let alone Ben and then this happens as well," she looked at him staring into thin air trying to comprehend all that she had just revealed to him. "Tom?" she asked softly, "Are you okay?"

He nodded, "Yes, well. I guess so. Just one thing," he paused to look at her, "the other night, when he was in our house...why did you make out you never knew him?"

"I," she stammered, "I don't know. I'm sorry Tom, I'm so sorry."

He sat silent for a few seconds, and she thought to herself that she had completely messed up another relationship. One that for the first time ever, felt incredibly special.

She could almost see his mind working overtime with all the information. "Tom," she whimpered, "I'll understand if I've blown it. I deserve what I get if you wanna leave me and get a divorce."

"Sarah, stop," he interrupted her, finally looking over to meet her eyes. As he faced her now flushed face with tears welling up and about to burst, "Of course I don't want a bloody divorce, come here."

He pulled her in close as they now sat beside each other, her head laid gently on his shoulder.

She felt safe in his arms, warm and protected, and loved all over again. She should've owned up ages ago when Ben first came on the scene, that very night in her house. As a final tear silently dropped from her cheek, she vowed to herself at that very moment, that she would never lie to Tom again, not ever.

Chapter Twenty-Four

When they arrived home, Tom emptied the bath that she had forgotten about earlier and ran a new one for her, lighting some candles on the windowsill too and filling it with the last of the bubble bath.

As Sarah undressed, she remembered the note she had written earlier that was still in her pocket for Tom. Her heart ached for Kate right now and she couldn't think of anything else. This wasn't the time to be celebrating when her first child had just died so she folded it back up and put it in the back of the knicker drawer along with the test that was still in there. Maybe in a few days, when she was feeling better, they could have their special dinner again and tell him then. It just wasn't appropriate right now. She wasn't lying to him about it, she just couldn't face trying to be upbeat and happy when she had just been through that ordeal.

Her phone pinged a message, and she noticed there were five missed calls and two messages from Karl. *Shit*, she thought to herself, she had completely forgotten to call him like she said she would. She decided to send him another text back for now, she couldn't talk about the events of the last few hours, and he would understand.

'Karl I'm so sorry. It's been mad and I can't talk about it right now, forgive me but I'll be in touch soon, don't worry, Tom's looking after me and knows everything, speak soon. S. x' and then she switched it to silent. She needed some space from it all and just wanted nothing or nobody else except Tom right now.

"I spoke to Felicity earlier today, she said it would be fine for Albert to come and stay with us this coming weekend, what do you think? Would you rather leave it a few weeks? I'm sure she will understand," Tom asked as he came into the bathroom. He'd bought a glass of wine as she lay in the tub trying to relax and soak away her grief. She took it from him, took a sip and then immediately felt bad. She shouldn't even be drinking now in her condition, so she placed it on the side of the bath.

"No, it's fine, maybe it will help to take my mind off things, having the little one about, you know?"

"Are you sure? We can leave it for a few weeks. I can just go to theirs instead?"

"No Tom," she replied, "honestly, it's fine. It will be nice to have a little one around the house and you need to bond with him more. You can take him to the park with the dogs, he'd like that."

"Okay, yeah, thanks darling. I'll text her later and arrange times and that. Did they give you any idea how long it will be until the funeral? I can come with you...if you want me to, that is?"

Sarah looked down and noticed her belly just peeping out of the bubbles and she couldn't stop herself from crying. Thinking of how she used to look at her tummy when Kate had been inside of her and now, just hours after meeting her after all those years, she was gone from her life once more in such horrible circumstances. But this new tummy had something in there, something she should've been so excited about. How could she though, she couldn't even be happy about it, not right now anyway. Not while she grieved her first-born, beautiful, caring new-found daughter. They would never have that time back again and she couldn't help but sob.

Tom quickly put down his glass, knelt beside the tub and just held her tightly in his strong arms, "I'm sorry, I shouldn't have brought it up."

He knew the pain of losing someone, no matter how long you had known them, so he just held her until she needed him to, trying his best to make her feel safe and loved, and she adored him for being strong for them both right now.

~

The next few days went by as a bit of a blur. She had taken time off work telling the girls at the salon that she had some sort of a sickness bug. She had made Tom carry on with going to work and the dogs never failed to be by her side especially when the morning sickness hit her during the day.

Tina had texted her a few times asking if she was okay, but she had just texted back that she was fine, feeling terrible that Tina didn't have a clue what had been going on with her and Ben. How was she coping with the news of Kate? She hoped she wouldn't text her about that, she really didn't know how to answer if that came up.

She just had to use these few days to get herself together, deal with the pain and hurt that she was going through and face up to the grim reality that the funeral would be planned soon, and she hated that idea the most. She'd had so much going on, she hadn't even thought about when to tell Tom their baby news. The sickness was beginning to subside a little and luckily it hadn't happened when he was around. She had set herself a date that she would reveal the baby news once Ben was out of the picture. She needed that closure first and deep down she knew that Tom would want her nowhere near Ben once he knew about the baby.

The funeral was planned for two weeks' time and although Sarah and Ben were going to attend, they decided it was best for them to stay in the background at the cremation and didn't take up the invite to go on to the wake afterwards. It didn't seem right, and Sarah felt too distraught to be around strangers who may think harsh of her for not even being a mother to Kate for real.

~

"Ben messaged me earlier," Sarah said as they sat

down to dinner in the kitchen that evening. She had promised Tom that she wouldn't hide his messages.

"Oh," Tom replied, chucking the dogs a slice of sausage from his plate, "What does he want now?"

Nervously, she replied, "he wants to meet up before he goes to Germany, just to say goodbye I guess but I wanted to check you are okay with it before I agreed to it."

"Arsehole," he said gritting his teeth, "sorry but I don't like it or him and I'd rather you never see him again but," he paused, seeing her now, worried face, "I know I can trust you darling even if I wouldn't trust him with a bargepole. And if it's for good this time, then…well, you gotta do it I guess."

"Thanks darling," she replied, relieved, "I know all this craziness must be so hard for you to get your head round, and I'm so sorry for putting you through it, I really am."

"I'm a big boy babe and like I said, I trust you," he stroked her chin, "I love you, it's me that's got the best wife in the world, not him, and plus…he's a big dickhead who will be gone from our lives so you go tell him to do one. I'll be right here waiting for you," he smiled an extra wide grin at her, reassuringly, and his funny sarcasm made her chuckle just a little bit.

"Man, I love you so much Mr. Cooper," she said, smiling back at him. And she really did love this amazing man so much. He was her rock right now, sticking by her through it all and he meant the absolute world to her. They felt stronger than ever before as a couple, and she felt excited about the closure of one chapter and the opening of another for them. This new baby would bring joy to the sadness that they had all encountered over the past few weeks and years, especially for Sarah. A new beginning was coming, and she couldn't wait.

~

Being at this place once again wasn't the best thing for Sarah, but she knew the time had come and she just had to face up to him and get it over with. She had to finally say goodbye to this person who had broken her heart more than once in one way or another. She had to now hope that this broken heart of hers would slowly begin to fix itself.

They had decided to meet at the skatepark where it all began so many years before and since meeting up again just weeks back. It seemed like the most appropriate place to say their final goodbyes, say goodbye to all the horrible memories that were made and the very few happy ones that had been those few hours with their daughter before she was taken away so soon.

Ben arrived ten minutes late and he looked rough. Dressed in overly ripped jeans and a t-shirt which looked like it hadn't been washed for a week. He'd not been the best dressed man at any time but today, he looked a bit worse than usual.

"Hey," he said, puffing away like a chimney on a cigarette as he approached her. He looked nervous, and his voice sounded jittery. As he passed her a small bunch of flowers, she noticed his hands were shaking and his nails were bitten back and sore, "mum said to always bring a girl flowers when there was an apology to be said and I owe you loads."

"Oh," Sarah replied, slightly taken aback by the pretty gesture of a hand tied posy consisting of a few pink roses and striking purple sprig or two of lavender. She took the blooms and tried to put her thoughts to the back of her mind about how he looked and why he looked that way today. Maybe the grief was catching up on him now that he was about to leave the country? She felt sorry for him, and the flowers were a nice touch.

He sat beside her, still chugging away on his smelly cigarette, "Look, I'm sorry I messed you up...again, it really wasn't supposed to turn out like this," he took a deep inhale and immediately exhaled the smoke out again, "I thought, well, I don't know what I thought might happen really, we could have been friends, maybe even a family, you know the three of us, but obviously now…"

"Ben, we would never have been a family. Too much history and pain. The only thing we had in common was Kate and she's…" she gulped back the hard lump in her throat as the dreaded words that she'd gone didn't want to come out. She hadn't meant to reply so harshly, but she couldn't help herself. Her daughter, their daughter was dead, and they had not even had the chance to get to know each other properly. She couldn't believe he would even think that they may have become a family unit.

"Oh Jesus, this is so crappy, it really is. She was so…," he paused, taking another deep inhale of smoke into his lungs, "she was so beautiful, like you were, like you still are

Sarah. I just wish I had taken her straight to her work instead of dropping her off up the road, she might have been here still now. Why am I always such a dickhead?" he raised his voice in anger and puffed the potent smoke, blowing it back out into the air away from her.

Sarah said nothing back, she couldn't bring herself to talk about it anymore with him. They sat on the bench in silence just staring ahead at some youngsters on their scooters while he finished his cigarette.

"I can't stay too long Ben," she said, glancing at her watch and realising they had already sat there for ten minutes. She really didn't want to be there longer than she had to.

"So, Tina left me," he suddenly replied, as he stubbed the cigarette onto the floor with his foot, "I told her everything."

"Everything?" Sarah questioned in the hope that he had left her out of the story.

"Well, not about you. I made some crap up that Kate's real mum didn't want to know, and she was fine with that, but she didn't want to come to Germany with me so I'm going on my own. I'm going to try and start a new life there and get all this out of my mind. I can't love her enough at the minute, I don't even love myself Sarah and to be honest, she's probably best off without me bringing her down. I don't know why I expected her to just up and leave her life that she clearly loves."

"Oh," replied Sarah, shocked that he was leaving his wife behind, that their marriage was now in fact, over.

"She doesn't know about you Sarah, I promise, I never said anything to her about us. I wanted to do the right thing for you, finally and I'm just sorry about everything," he moved closer, but she edged away. Sensing her awkward distancing, he said, "I'm gonna go now and you won't hear from me again, I promise, this is it."

"You're making a lot of promises here Ben, how can I trust you mean it?"

"Well, I guess I am but hey, I'm a dick, always have been, always will be but Kate changed the way I think about stuff. She made me realise that I need to take other people's feelings into consideration a lot more than I have before. I've hurt you too much, especially back when we were young, and I honestly feel terrible about that now. I really do feel bad Sarah, what you must've gone through...and on your own at that age."

She looked towards him as he glanced up and their eyes met, "Ben..." she said calmly.

"Don't say anything, hey," he interrupted, "life's too short, we know that more than most people. Let's just say our goodbyes today, yeah?" he continued, "it was great to see that you've found someone so cool. You look at Tom the way you used to look at me all those years ago. It's nice. It hurts me like hell with what we've now been through but I'm so happy for you, I really am," he gently placed his hand upon hers and she didn't move away this time, as he stroked her fingers and continued, "the funeral was beautiful and I'm glad we could both go, you know together," he paused again to swallow the lump that had now built up in his throat, "you won't see me after today, I promise I'll stay away this time. Just enjoy your life with Tom, he's a great guy and if things had worked out differently, maybe we could have all been friends, who knows."

She looked down at his hand which was still stroking hers affectionately. That vile tattoo she had spotted so many years ago, when they had first met at this park, now looking a lot lighter in colour than it had back then.

"Thanks for bringing Kate into my life," she said quietly, "those few hours we had together were so special and I'll never forget it. I'll never forget her, it meant so much to meet her and see what a beautiful person she became."

"It was my pleasure, it was lovely to watch you both chatting and that and I know how excited she was to have met you too, she didn't stop talking about it on the way to her work that day, I just wish…"

Before he could say what, she knew he was going to say again, she stopped him, "It wasn't your fault Ben, it was an accident, you have to stop blaming yourself okay?"

He looked down at the floor and she noticed a tear slowly falling down his cheek weaving its way through his overgrown stubble. He squeezed her hand, then let go and stood up, lighting up another cigarette, "Right, I'll be seeing you then Miss Roberts," he said trying to portray a brave smile and wiping his face of the tears that had fallen.

"It's Mrs. Cooper remember?" She corrected him and as he began to walk past her, she felt compelled to stop him, grabbing hold of his arm, she said, "our daughter was beautiful Ben, at least we got that bit right, hey?"

He nodded in agreement, "she was, we made a beautiful soul." he smiled back, rubbed her hand, and then made his way out of the skatepark into the main car park where he got in his car leaving her sat alone.

She glanced down at the cute little bouquet of flowers laying on the bench. They were very pretty but she couldn't and wasn't going to take them home, so she picked them up and placed them beside the nearest wall. Standing back up straight, she turned, and captured one last glimpse of him disappearing at the junction in his car.

That was it, that was the last time she would see him, and she knew that for sure this time. They had been through so much in the past weeks and it had been so stressful but with a few happy memories too. It hadn't been like all those years back when it was just horrible thoughts about him, how he'd shrugged her off as a nobody, as a nothing and the pregnancy that led to the adoption trauma she had gone through. New beginnings now for them both, that was the future.

She took her phone out of her pocket and scrolled through her contacts. As she got to Ben's name, she clicked delete contact and with a flash, he was gone from there too. All traces in her phone were erased. Then she scrolled down a bit further until Kate's name appeared. She had saved the details as 'Katie-Jane', that's what she knew her as, that's what she named her and couldn't have logged her by any other name. But now, she wondered, what should she do with these details? It wouldn't be calling her or texting her ever again. It wouldn't be one that she would ring and try to hear that voice and that hurt so badly. Staring at it for a few seconds, she realised that she couldn't delete it, she couldn't erase the only digital thing she had left of her daughter, so she locked her phone, held it close to her chest and looked up at the sky. The clouds were stark white and fluffy with striking sun beams trying to get through. She just whispered up towards them in one last emotional moment, "Goodbye Katie-Jane, goodbye."

Chapter Twenty-Five

"Hey mate, come on in... if you can get through this scatty lot," said Tom as he wrestled to keep the dogs from jumping up with excitement to see Karl.

Karl made his way into the hallway fussing with each dog's head as they licked and panted beside him.

"Sorry mate, they haven't been out in a few days, Sarah's not been up to it, you know and now they're full of energy which just won't burn off in the garden," he laughed, ushering them all up the hallway.

"No worries, mate, how is she doing anyway?"

They finally got to the kitchen and Tom started preparing coffees, "Yeah, she's okay, well, as okay as you can be I suppose after what's gone on, you know," he shrugged his shoulders, "She's out at the minute actually, meeting up with the arsehole that caused all this bloody trouble in the first place."

"Oh really? Why, what does he want from her now?"

"Well, apparently he's shipping himself off to live in Germany, so he wanted to see her one last time and say goodbye. Hopefully that will be the last of his ugly mug, I mean, Jesus, hasn't he done enough damage to the poor girl?"

"Crikey, yeah he certainly has. Did you not want to go with her?" Karl asked as he passed Tom the cream from the fridge.

"No, I did suggest it but, she knows how to handle him and to be honest, I think I may have lumped him one," he said as he made a fist, "I think she knew that too, so probably best I stayed away," he joked, "I trust her to take care of it."

"Yeah, too right, I may have punched him one too if I'd seen him. The cheek of the guy. Anyway, at least she's out. We had a quick chat last night on the phone but I just wanted to come over and see how you both were really, oh and to give her these of course," he pointed to the small bunch of flowers that had made it in with him, "I know she's not a great lover of flowers but, I thought she might prefer them over chocolates in case it made the sickness worse or something,"

"Sickness?" Tom asked, sounding confused, "oh the tummy bug, she's not got a bug really mate, she just told work that, so they didn't ask questions about having some time off. Especially with Tina still working there and that, I'm not sure she knows the whole truth about her husband

and Sarah's past you know?"

Karl looked back with a surprised look on his face and realised Tom didn't know about the morning sickness and obviously that also meant he didn't yet know about the baby. He hoped he hadn't put his foot in it and joked back, "oh, I see, right, got ya, she does think of everything doesn't she?"

Tom didn't notice Karl's awkwardness as he stirred the spoon in each of the coffee mugs, "Yeah, Tina doesn't know about Sarah and that's the way we want it kept really. She can't handle much more stress this year. I'm gonna try and take her away. Get some sun and that," he continued, "she needs some rest and relaxation, just for a week maybe or a long weekend somewhere, any ideas?" he asked, passing a mug to Karl.

"Erm, not sure mate, maybe you'll have to chat with her first. I know she loves it hot; she was in her element in Florida but that may be a bit far to travel at the minute."

"Yeah, I was thinking more Ibiza, Tenerife, just a few hours flight time so we can spend more time together on a beach than on a plane."

"Nice…" Karl replied, sipping his drink, "You know how she loves Norfolk if you wanted to stay local…"

Before Tom could reply, they heard the front door open and then close. The dogs bolted upright and went bounding into the hallway. It was Sarah.

"Hello, hello…come on, where's daddy?" she said playfully fussing each dog's head in turn and eventually making her way to the kitchen.

Tom stood up and kissed her on the cheek, "You okay babe? Did it all go to plan?" She nodded back, rubbing his arm, "talk about it later, yeah?"

"Sure. Do you want a coffee, the kettle is not long boiled?"

"Ooh yes please, make it a strong one... hey Karl," she said as she noticed him sitting at the table, "what are you doing here?" She gave him a peck on the cheek as she sat beside him with Elvis jumping up at her legs wanting to get on her lap.

"Just checking up on you both really and thought these might help cheer you up a bit," he reached for the bouquet of flowers that lay on the table, "I don't know, you know I'm crap at this sort of stuff," he laughed back shyly.

"Oh, thanks darl, they are pretty, Tom, is there any of that cake left?" she asked, taking the blooms, and smelling them. This bunch were more impressive than the ones earlier and she could keep these too.

"Yeah, here you go," Tom replied as he passed her the leftover cake slices that Janice had brought round the day before. "I'm just gonna get this crew outside, throw them a ball for a bit, jeez, they need to get to the park babe. Maybe we can go later when Albert gets here?" Tom ushered all the dogs to the back door, as Sarah nodded back laughing at them all scrambling to the back door. All three of them except Elvis, the little sausage dog who had now snuggled himself up in his blanket in the corner of the kitchen.

Once the dogs and Tom were outside, all that could be

heard was Elvis snoring away in his bed. Sarah smiled down at him with that yellow blanket that was so special but so old and worn out now. That was the blanket that she swore would never leave her no matter what. Especially now after what had happened to Kate, she couldn't even contemplate losing it or chucking it away. It meant even more now so maybe she needed to store it instead of letting Elvis drag it around all day. He did love it so much though and it was nice to see it every day as a reminder.

"Sarah, Tom doesn't know about the baby yet does he?" Karl whispered, quietly, interrupting her thoughts and reaching for a slice of cake.

"Oh err, no. I keep meaning to tell him but then all I think about is Katie and I can't do it, it just breaks my heart Karl," she held her chest, "I want it to be a special moment, you know. All I feel is sadness at the minute and Albert is coming to stay tonight for the weekend so there's not really gonna be a time to tell him until next week now at least," she nibbled on a slice of cake too but didn't want to make herself feel sick, not with Tom here at the moment, "I love seeing him so excited about Albert so..." she glanced down and rubbed her tummy. She wasn't showing at all yet, she knew she wouldn't for a while still being slightly on the plump side, but she loved her 'puppy fat' as she called it and didn't strive to be, what she called 'a skinny minnie'. She'd always been curvy and didn't care.

"Phew, Right, well, just so you know, I nearly slipped

up earlier," he told her, "I said I had brought you flowers instead of chocolates because they might make the sickness worse, he looked well confused," he chuckled, taking a big bite of his cake, "you should've warned me mate."

"Aww, sorry. My mind is all over the place, I thought I had told you. Anyway, yeah so work is fine, you know always busy, but I've enjoyed the past few days off to be fair," she said changing the subject as Tom stammered back in almost getting knocked over by the still very excitable dogs.

"Man, they've worn me out," Tom chuckled, slurping up a big gulp of his coffee which he'd forgotten to take out with him, "do you wanna stay for dinner Karl, meet Albert? I can fetch the kids too while I'm collecting him if you like. It would be great for them all to meet, wouldn't it Sarah, if that's okay with you darling obviously?"

Sarah nodded, "of course it is," smiling back at his flushed cheeks from all the ball playing.

Karl replied, "sounds like a great idea mate but I'll get their nan to drop them off. They went there after school to help with some books or something, cheers."

"Cool, right, I'm gonna change quickly and then go fetch my nephew, oh man, you're gonna love him mate, he's the cutest, isn't he darling," and with that he kissed her head and ran upstairs excitedly with Charlie still bounding along behind him, toy hanging from his drooling mouth.

Karl and Sarah just looked at each other and laughed, "He's so taken with his new nephew, Karl, it's so sweet."

"He'll be so taken with his baby too," Karl replied as he pointed to her belly, "you have to tell him soon Sarah, you don't want him finding out from someone else, we know how that feels don't we?" he said, as he raised his eyebrows to her.

"I know, I know. Monday night I promise. Let him just have his weekend with Albert first, it's the first time he's stayed over with us, he's been decorating the spare room. He just needs this time with him before I laden him with more excitement."

Karl placed his fingers to his lips, "My lips are sealed until you say otherwise. I'll give Janice a ring now and get her to drop the kids round, you sure it's okay for us all to be here, it's not too much for you?"

"Of course it's not, don't be silly, you know how much I adore those kids of yours and you are all welcome in our home anytime."

"I'm really happy for you Sarah, this new baby will bring so much joy into your lives," he said as he stood up, holding her shoulder with assurance, before going outside to make his phone call, throwing a ball for Rufus as he dialled.

Sarah looked down at Elvis again in his bed. She took a deep breath as she knelt beside him stroking the blanket covering his little brown body, "we're okay aren't we Elvis?" she whispered to him, "you looking after our special blanket?" his puppy dog eyes briefly glanced up at her without even moving his head and she smiled down at him, "Good boy."

~

Tom hadn't been wrong about Albert; he really was one of the sweetest little boys they'd known. With his hint of a French accent coming out every now and again in certain words, he was winning everyone over in no time. He loved playing with the dogs and specifically took a liking to Donut who kept jumping up into his lap and making him laugh as his flappy tongue would lick his face.

They ordered takeout pizza for everyone and then Cassie did some chalk drawing outside with him on the patio.

"He's quite artistic, isn't he?" said Sarah as she placed her arms around Tom's shoulders.

"He is, yeah. James used to love painting and drawing, the number of times he got told off for drawing on his bedroom wall was hilarious," he chuckled, watching Albert drawing a big chalk rainbow on the floor, "James would've loved him so much."

Sarah kissed his head and rubbed his shoulders, lovingly. She wished for him that his brother was here to see this too and she could see the love that Tom had already for this little boy. It was adorable to watch, and her mind wandered off for a moment thinking about her own predicament. Their own baby which she could tell him about soon. She had already imagined the pure excitement that he would feel about it and her tummy felt calm for once.

"Right, I suppose we better get off now guys," said Karl as he finished his coffee and placed the mug on the table,

"I've got a bit of paperwork to catch up on, come on Cass, Rob, let's leave these three to get some rest."

"Ohhh," came the reply from Cassie. Having someone to draw with was something she had missed since her mum had died so she was really enjoying the flare of creativity that she now had to share with Albert, "can't I stay a bit longer dad, please…" she pleaded.

"She can stay over if she wants Karl," Sarah said as she watched Cassie trying to work her magic eyes onto her dad, "we've got another pull out camp bed if she wants to stay the night of course, or I can drop her off in a little bit? It's not that late."

"Please dad, can I.?" pleaded Cassie again, smiling cheekily back at Sarah.

Karl looked at Sarah then back at Cassie, knowing this would be an argument he may not win at, "Okay. Only if it's not too much trouble for you guys, it's been a busy day for everyone, especially the little man," Karl said, nodding over to Albert who was now yawning, stretching his arms up.

"Not at all," said Sarah, winking at Cassie, "it's okay with you isn't it babe," she asked Tom with which he nodded as he took a mouthful of coffee, "great, come on Cass, let's grab the extra bed and some blankets for you. Tom can put Albert to bed in the spare room while we do that. Karl, I'll walk her back home tomorrow with the dogs, is that cool?"

"Oh, alright then," he answered reluctantly, "cheers guys, see you tomorrow then. Come on Robbie, we can have a quick game of footy on the PlayStation," answered Karl ruffling Robbie's hair who was head down into his phone playing some new puzzle game.

In just an hour, Albert was fast asleep on one bed in the little spare room after Tom read him one of his new favourite David Walliams books and Sarah had settled down on the sofa with Cassie. Tom made them all a hot chocolate and they watched a film together until ten o'clock when Cassie had also fallen asleep.

"It's like we're being a little family isn't it darling," Tom whispered as he nibbled on the last of the salted peanuts as they cleared up the lounge.

"Sort of I suppose." Sarah whispered back, pulling the sofa throw over Cassie's shoulders.

As they crept quietly out towards the stairs, Tom asked, "Are you okay?"

"Yes, I think so," she answered, yawning, "I've just been thinking about Kate and that, you know," she sighed, "I feel so lucky to have met her but so unlucky too, does that make sense?"

"It does and I'm sorry I never got to meet her. I'm sorry for you darling but you know I'm here for you and you can tell me anything from now on yeah?" he cupped her tired face softly as they reached the top of the stairs, "No more secrets," he said, switching the landing light off behind her.

Sarah paused, almost stopping breathing for a split second, and just looked at him. She knew she did have one last secret that she was keeping from him but again, tonight wasn't the right time. If she blurted it out at that moment, while they were all too tired, it may not be the magical memory that she had imagined it would be after taking the test. She had planned to tell him with her little note and a romantic meal. Not as they crept up the stairs trying to avoid waking Cassie or Albert or even disturbing the dogs for that matter. Her mind was playing the whole scene in her head, with Tom screaming in delight, the dogs barking, the kids waking up wondering what the hell was going on, so, no, it wasn't appropriate right now. They needed to get to bed and rest, finish their family weekend roleplay before that news.

As she lay beside her husband, watching him drift off to sleep, she set the day for it. Monday evening, she had decided on and it would be amazing. She would stage the whole evening with candles, his favourite takeaway, and find the note and the test to confirm the positive result. This was going to be some good news for them after the crazy few months they had been through, and she was now finding it hard to get off to sleep thinking about how excited he was going to be when he found out.

Chapter Twenty-Six

The weekend seemed over so quickly and by Sunday evening, Albert had returned to his mum's house, and everyone felt exhausted. It really had been such a fun weekend for all of them and the dogs had loved having a new playmate to run around with in the garden and at the park.

More than anyone, Tom had enjoyed it the most, meeting and spending quality time with Albert had brought back all the memories that he had had with his brother James when they were younger, and Sarah had watched in awe of her husband at his happy and excited face constantly the whole weekend. All the while thinking about his reaction when she would reveal their news to him, and it made her smile imagining what he would do and what he would say. The thoughts of him diving straight into the decorating of the nursery that he so wanted to do; that only recently they had spoken about but ended up having an argument instead. He would now get his chance to create that beautiful room and she was adamant that she would leave him totally in charge of it. Something so exciting that she couldn't wait to see what he would come up with.

Tom had driven Cassie home to Karl's house and ended up staying for a few hours chatting all things Albert with them. Playing a few rounds of a new football game with Robbie and having a few beers with Karl had given Sarah some time back at the house to feed the dogs and clean up. It had been such a busy few days, she hadn't even thought about housework stuff like running the hoover over or putting washing on ready for the week ahead. It had been her turn to wash the salon towels, so she gathered them all up from the two big bags in the hallway, threw them into the washing machine, then quickly ran the hoover over the downstairs rooms singing along to her favourite tunes that were playing on the radio.

She felt extremely tired tonight though and decided to leave the rest of the hoovering until tomorrow. She had treated herself to a new bottle of her favourite bubble bath and was looking forward to a nice half hour or so relaxing soak in the tub.

Yawning widely, she thought that her new little body addition must have been taking up more energy than she imagined it could, but she loved that fact more than anything right now and gave her belly a gentle rub, grinning like a Cheshire cat to herself, "tomorrow little one, tomorrow we can tell daddy," she whispered.

The decision was final, tomorrow would be the day of revealing this bump news to Tom and then they could announce it to everyone else. A new chapter was about to start for them all and hopefully help her to recover her broken heart just a little bit.

Wrapping the hoover lead over the handle and popping it back into the hallway cupboard, she was done with the housework for tonight, "Right, you lot," she said as she made her way into the kitchen to see the dogs had all finished their dinners, and patiently waiting by the back door, wagging their tails, "Let's get you outside to do your business and then mummy is having a long soak in the bath, come on."

As she approached the back door, and watched the three of them run out, immediately cocking their legs on the short fir trees that they'd had planted last year, Elvis came waddling up in front of her with his special blanket clasped tightly in his jaws, dragging it behind him. That blanket needed a wash so badly, but she just didn't want to take it from him. He seemed to drag it everywhere he could like he knew how special and comforting it was for Sarah. Her heart sank a little bit as the thoughts of Kate appeared in her mind once again. The thoughts of what they could have had together, a mother/daughter relationship had not had a chance to even get off the ground and now never would. Her daughter was gone, and she hated it.

She watched the four dogs sniffing and doing their business in the garden and took a deep breath as a tear escaped down her slightly chilled from the wind face. Would she ever be able to forgive herself fully? Would she ever get over the fact that her first born daughter was gone and would never be able to see or talk to her again? She hoped so much she could get over it in time but also had such angry thoughts to herself that she didn't meet her sooner.

Elvis returned quickly and plonked his butt onto her foot. She looked down towards him, his cute button eyes looking back up at her, like he knew she needed comfort at that very moment, and then he licked her foot making her chuckle and sniff back the tears from her eyes. She bent down and picked him up snuggling him into his blanket which she had managed to salvage from going outside. She would wash it tomorrow while Tom took them on their walk maybe. She could explain to Tom then why she had kept it for so long, to whom it used to belong. For the next hour, she needed time to relax so she locked the back door once the dogs had finished and made her way upstairs.

With the bath running and the bubbles beginning to froth up nicely, she sat on the toilet seat scrolling through her phone and then quickly sent a text to Tom.

'*Just getting in the bath, don't be too long... we are all missing you already.*' she typed adding four dog emojis on the end, and pressed send.

A simple love heart emoji came back and then five seconds later, a short and sweet, '*love all five of you, won't be long. xx*'.

She couldn't wait for him to get back and had even considered bringing tomorrow's news forward to tonight. She quickly went into the bedroom to find the note that she had stored away in the back of the knicker drawer. As she glanced down at it, she smiled to herself again. She felt so happy right now for this to happen but knew the moment had to be special, so she hid it away one more time and made her way back to the bathroom to turn off the taps.

As she started to get undressed, she began to feel a bit sick suddenly. It didn't feel the same as before though and her tummy ached almost like shooting period pains. Looking down at herself, she noticed that her white knickers had some other colour on them. It was red, it was blood, she was bleeding. Immediately, she just knew what that meant. She felt her heart shatter into tiny pieces with the grief of what she was seeing and how she was feeling this time round. Her face drained all its colour, turning ashen white and her head spun with dizziness. She tried desperately to hold onto the sink, her legs turning to jelly as she went down and then blacked out.

The next thing she knew, her blurry eyes opened to see Tom who was cradling her in his arms, on the bathroom floor, "Hey, it's okay darling, I'm here," he whispered softly.

"What...what happened?" she stammered, wiping her brow which felt clammy with sweat.

"You fainted darling. I heard this thud just as I started

coming up the stairs. You've not been out long but, are you hurt anywhere else, did you bang your head at all?" he asked.

Slightly confused about his question, she shook her head slowly, and answered, "I don't think so?" raising her arms and twisting her elbow to look. It did feel a little sore but there was no blood or anything. She hazarded a guess that she probably banged and bruised it on the way down. Then, suddenly, it hit her what she had seen before blacking out. Her underwear, the blood, it all came rushing back to her why she was on the floor, he must have seen it too? She looked down, her lower half was covered with a towel, just her t-shirt and knickers were all she had on underneath. Tom must have put the towel over her when he came in. That's why he asked if she was hurt anywhere else, "I... I…need to get up," she said, trying to sit up.

"Take it easy babe, slowly does it."

She wasn't sure what to say or what to do. She didn't want to look under the towel, but she knew she would have to, and she needed to know if he had seen anything.

"Tom…," she whispered quietly, "did you see the blood?"

His paused silence said it all and he held her a little bit tighter, "yes," was all he could utter.

They sat together for what seemed like an hour before anyone could speak or even move from that point. She cried silently, knowing full well what was going on and how terrible it must be for Tom. Just a few hours before, all she could think of was his excitement at becoming a dad when she told him the news and now that chance had gone. Their chance to be a family, to have their own child together, just how he wanted. She'd already grown to love the bump and the good times that it would have brought them, but it wasn't to be.

"We need to get you to the hospital Sarah," Tom finally managed to say when her gentle sobbing had slowed, "You'll have to be checked over. I'll get you some fresh clothes to put on, are you okay here for a minute or do you want to get into the bedroom?"

She just stared into nothing with a blank expression on her ashen face as he wrapped her dressing gown from the back of the door around her shoulders and left the room. Everything seemed dreamlike, the bath was still full of the bubbles quietly popping away, the steam rising from the heat of the water, the candles flickering peacefully giving the room a warm glow. But it wasn't a dream, she was sitting on the floor in her bathroom losing the baby that Tom hadn't even had the chance to know about or worse than that, have the chance to grow to love. She pressed her palm into her chest to try and suppress the sorrow. This sensation of loss was slicing her up into tiny pieces with every second that passed.

~

The car journey to the hospital was made in a stunned silence. Sarah just stared out of the passenger window the entire time not even realising the route. She was looking at people, trees, signs that they drove past but nothing was sinking in, she felt utterly lost and bewildered. She couldn't even bring herself to look across at Tom driving. She hadn't made eye contact with him since waking up on the bathroom floor. It wasn't his fault this had happened, but her heart was broken for him as well as for her.

"It could be nothing darling," he'd said to her as they'd got in the car back home, but she had little hope that it would be a mistake. Her tummy ache was confirming otherwise, and she was in pain mentally as well as physically now. She had not experienced this type of stomach pain, since the days as a teenager when her periods were at their peak with terrible cramps. Her back hurt too and she knew she was still bleeding.

Laying on the hospital bed, waiting for the doctor to arrive, she couldn't take the silence anymore, "I'm so sorry Tom," she finally said, leaning into his embrace, sobbing into his chest, "I should have told you earlier but with Albert coming, then the business with Katie, and bloody Ben turning up, I just lost my way…" her words were coming out in a blubbering mess but he just held her in his arms and let her cry, let her grieve and talk, "I feel like such a failure, like I've let you down with one of the most important things that could happen in your life…this is something you wanted so badly and now…I've ruined it…you didn't even get the chance to have that moment, the moment I had planned. Honestly, please forgive me," she cried, "I was going to tell you tomorrow over dinner and… I just don't know how to say sorry enough Tom…I'm so sorry Tom, I'm so, so, sorry."

"Sarah, please," he had to stop her, she was getting in such a state, "don't be sorry, it's not your fault," he hated seeing her in pain but more than that, he hated seeing his wife in so much torment for something that wasn't her fault, "It's okay, shh, come on now. You are the most important thing in my life," he wiped her tears from her cheeks, "you coming into my life was...well, it was incredible. I love you so much, no matter what, believe me okay," he leaned back and cupped her face, holding it firmly but lovingly, "we need to get through this hurdle, we need to be strong. It's me and you together. It will be alright, I promise."

She wasn't sure how much more sadness or anguish she could take this year and now she felt as though she was causing all this grief upon her husband. He hadn't signed up for all this craziness and her heart ached for his loss so much now. But there he was one more time, her soulmate and rock of a husband being her strength and pulling her through this ordeal. Never failing to utter the right words or do the right thing and at the exact right time she needed it most.

At that very moment, she realised for the hundredth time, how incredibly lucky she was. She had found and married the most caring and loving person who it seemed was at peace with the world and the terrible things that it can bring to people. Not only had he lost his younger brother to suicide, but he had also now lost his unborn child that could've brought them so much joy for the future. This heartbreaking event would never be something either of them would get over, but deep down, she knew he had nothing to forgive her for. Her inner conscience would just have to work on the ordeal of being able to forgive herself now, for everything. They were a team, and he would be there to build her back up. She felt so safe in that knowledge. She was safe with him beside her.

~

"I'll be back first thing tomorrow morning okay. As soon as they call me and say you are out of surgery, I'll be here," Tom said as he sat on the edge of the hospital bed, holding her hand tightly.

"I don't want to be without you Tom, I don't feel brave enough to cope with this," she replied, her chest suddenly feeling tight again, like it may explode any moment.

"Hey, now come on missus. You are one of the bravest women I have ever known, Sarah. It's just tonight and then we can get you home to recover."

"But they're just going to take it and that's it then isn't it, the end for our baby."

"Darling, I know this is so hard for you but sometimes, nature takes charge and it's out of our control. We can always try again another time but for now, you must have this done and be here. I know the team here and you are in good hands, okay?" He grabbed a tissue from the box nearby on the hospital side table and wiped the tears from her flushed face. She sniffed and just looked up at him. All he knew what to do then was smile, hoping his strength would transfer through to her. He so hoped she could stay strong, and he wouldn't have left her if he hadn't had to.

She lowered her head and replied with nothing, she didn't know what to say anymore, she just wanted to go back a few hours and have that intense feeling of excitement to what could have been.

Just then, a nurse arrived, knocking gently on the door first, "sorry to disturb you. Hello Mrs. Cooper, my name is Valerie, I'll be taking care of you for the evening."

Sarah just looked across at her trying to muster up a little bit of a smile but even that was hurting to do. She had nothing to smile about today, "I've got your gown and slippers for you, the surgery team will be along to collect you soon, within the next half an hour," she placed the items onto the end of the bed as Tom stood up, "I'm sorry to ask but, do you understand the procedure you are going to have?"

Sarah nodded silently and wearily.

"Alright. I'll leave these here for you, ring the bell if you need any help with securing the gown or if you have any questions," she placed her hand on top of Sarah's. It was warm against Sarah's who felt chilly. She couldn't seem to warm up since she left home.

A second later, Sarah and Tom were alone again. Although her crying had stopped, she was numb, so he stayed until they came to collect her, helping her get ready before. With their goodbyes done, she was wheeled off by the hospital porter. Tom stood watching as she disappeared through the double doors at the end of the corridor. He took one deep breath as a tear fell from each eye. He thought about the conversation they had previously had about having children together and immediately felt terrible for putting that pressure on her. He just wanted her, he just wanted them to have their happiness back. The joy that they had found each other in such a strange way and the love that they had found too was overwhelming. As much as he wanted a child of their own, he just wanted Sarah. He wanted his wife back in his arms, happy, free from pain and sadness. He vowed to himself right there that he would take care of her even more than ever now. He would try his hardest to protect her from any more sadness. This was now his mission.

Chapter Twenty-Seven

The next few days dwindled by in a blur for Sarah. Most of the time, she just wanted to rest, sleep, and try to heal her broken heart more than anything. She hadn't been in much pain from the surgery, just sore more than anything. The dogs had even been allowed to sleep in their bedroom with Elvis having pride of place on the end of the bed with her and his special blanket. Seeing that item wrapped up in her favourite dog brought her so much more comfort than she imagined it would at this time. She had explained to Tom about why it was so dear to her heart, and he finally understood why he couldn't convince her to buy a new one. It had started to get a bit dog eared in places from all the dragging around the house it got by Elvis.

"Hey sleepy head," Tom said as he entered the room with her lunch on a tray and a pretty flower from the garden, "I've done you a bit of soup and one of your favourite tiger bread rolls to dunk in it."

She sat up, "Aww, thanks," she replied wearily, "I'm gonna get up today. I think I may even take the dogs for a walk, maybe later this afternoon?"

"Sounds good darling, the fresh air will do you good, I'll come along. I've not got work tonight, Billy is covering for me until Monday now," he said as he placed the tray onto her lap.

"Okay. Oh, this smells lovely Tom, thank you," she inhaled the aroma of the cream of mushroom soup and ripped a bite of the tiger roll to dip in it.

He sat watching her after reaching for his coffee mug off the tray. He thought to himself how much better she looked today and loved seeing her perk up and finally eat something. She hadn't eaten since she came out of hospital, just drinking coffee and water in between sleeping and he had been starting to get worried. Something had clicked inside of her though, something was giving her the strength to finally get going and he wasn't going to complain about that after the traumatic few days they had had together.

"I checked in on the salon when I nipped to the shop earlier, took in the towels and that folder of paperwork that was on the table," he said as he took a sip of coffee, "they are all fine, busy as usual and send their best wishes that you are on the mend soon."

"Oh. Did you tell them what happened then?" she stopped slurping down her soup and looked up at him, worried.

"I just said you'd had a bit of a bad cold," he replied in a nervous voice, "I didn't want to say anything that you didn't want me to and that's all I could come up with, is that cool?" he asked, hoping he hadn't messed up or said the wrong thing.

"Oh, yes, that's fine. I don't really want the girls knowing, especially Tina, just in case, you know…she may still be in contact with you know who."

He gave a curt nod, and a reassuring expression back to her, "we are going to be okay darling," he placed his hand on her leg, "I promise. I'm here to look after you until we are old and grey. Me and this crazy lot it seems," he laughed as he nodded his head towards the three dogs who were sitting beside the bed staring straight up at Sarah eating her roll and soup. It made them both chuckle.

"Don't forget my little Elvis hey?" she turned her head towards the noise of her little sausage dog snoring quietly at the end of the bed.

As Sarah finished her soup, she remembered that she still had that letter to get through from Jane.

"What time do you want to go for that walk babe?" asked Tom as he gathered up the tray and mugs.

"Erm, maybe in about an hour. I think I may have a shower first," she replied, sniffing her armpits in jest.

"Okay, I'll get cleared up downstairs, just have a bit of paperwork to sort out and email over to Andy, do you need anything else before I go down?"

"Actually, could you grab something out of the safe for

me?"

"Sure," he placed the tray on the end of the bed and grabbed the key from his bedside drawer. They each had a key just in case one got lost, "what is it you want out of here darling," he said as he crouched down unlocking it and opening the door.

"The letter in the red envelope with my name on, well it says cheeky minx," she sniggered.

"Here you go," he passed her the envelope and then ushered all the digs to go downstairs, "We will leave you to it, text me when you wanna get up, just in case you feel giddy or anything," he winked at her as he closed the door behind him.

She stared down at the envelope again remembering the last time she had read a block of it. This time, she would finish it, no matter how long it took.

'So, I guess that if you are reading this then I'm gone, no more Jane to moan or nag at you to get a man in your life or stop being such a minx hey? But seriously, I wouldn't have had you any other way and when it's your time to come be with me, we can be together again. I hated being apart from you when you went away for that year to live with your aunt. I know I mentioned it before and now I'm going to tell you the truth...I know Sarah. I know about the baby."

Sarah's jaw dropped and she felt as though her throat was closing with shock at what she had just read. She read the sentence again in her head, *'I know Sarah. I know about your baby.'*

Jane knew about the baby, but how? She sat bolt upright and scoured the letter more, *'I never told you that I knew because, well I hoped you would confide in me with it but it's fine. I know how hard it must have been for you to keep that to yourself through the years and to be honest, it wasn't my business to know why. Do you remember we had a phone call and I said I had gone round to see your grandparents? Well as I left that day, I heard your grandad talking about it. They never knew that I'd overheard them. I was trying to fasten my silly boots; you remember the ones with the six-foot-long laces up to my knees!'*

Sarah cupped her hand to her mouth. Why hadn't she asked her about it over the years? Her best friend knew all about it but was decent enough not to pry, not to bring it up and more importantly, not to make Sarah feel worse than she already did about the whole thing.

'Anyhow, it doesn't matter to me. We can chat about it when you get up here, wherever 'up here' is, I guess. Hopefully heaven.

Sarah, my darling little minx of a best friend, you really are so brave, so beautiful, so courageous. All you have been through and then I put you through this malarkey having to keep my secret and then having to run around and take care of me. I'm sorry but I'm sure you will forgive me. You were, you are, you will always be...my best friend in the whole world. Xxxxx Now please…. go find a man to take care of you for a change…. lol.'

Sarah swallowed a hard lump that had built up in her throat. She was totally shocked that Jane had known all that time but never said anything and she missed her so much. Her chest felt like it would explode with all the emotions she had in there right now and as she glanced over to the wedding photo that was on the windowsill, she whispered, "I done it finally Jane, I found my man," and two big tears rolled down her face. In some way, she felt relieved but also felt guilt too. Her life had been such a roller coaster and she just hoped from now on that it would be a smoother ride.

Things were falling into place and chapters were being closed. She had had to say goodbye to so many dear people in her life but was determined to not let Tom leave anytime soon. She would cherish him and be the ultimate in wife material from this day on. In honour of Jane too, who without doubt, was the bestest friend she could have asked for and she knew this now more than ever before.

Practically jumping out of bed after tucking the letter back into the envelope and kissing it, she put it into her bedside drawer and walked into the shower room with her phone. Texting Tom that she would be ready to go in half an hour and wanted to pass by the cemetery on their walk, she showered as quickly as possible and got dressed.

~

"Hey missus," Sarah whispered quietly as she knelt beside the grave.

Tom had gone across the road to fetch them both a coffee and give her five minutes to herself to be with Jane. The sun was beaming down through the fluffy clouds and although it was cold, Sarah had warmth in her heart today just being there. As she rearranged the flowers that had been refreshed recently, a little robin flew down just feet away and pecked at the grass giving fleeting looks at Sarah.

"Is that you Jane?" she couldn't resist it. She had always heard the saying that 'when robins appear, a loved one is near' but never thought it could be true, "silly me hey," she said to herself shaking her head, but the robin stayed around while she sat thinking about all their memories that they'd made together.

"Here you go darling, a nice americano," Tom appeared and sat beside her, "you know I couldn't resist grabbing a cookie too," he smiled at her winking, revealing the all-important brown paper bag treat in his jacket pocket.

"You devil," she laughed, "look at that," she pointed, "...oh, it's gone. There was a little robin just now. Is it weird to say...I think it was watching me?"

Tom arched his eyebrow as he looked around, "Erm…you losing it love?" he joked.

"Oh, don't Tom," she chuckled at the strange expression on his face and his beautiful, cheeky smile along with it. She playfully nudged him in the ribs.

"Do you remember when we had our first coffee together?" he asked.

Sarah nodded, sipping at her very hot and very strong coffee, "I do indeed," she replied, blowing into the cup to try and cool it down.

"I was so nervous about it you know," he passed her half of the cookie as he bit a large chunk out of his.

"Really?" she replied, sounding slightly puzzled. He'd seemed so confident that day but judging on what she had gone there to do and the confusion and grief she had been feeling at the time, maybe she just hadn't noticed his nerves, "it didn't show," she said, reassuring him.

"Phew, that's okay then," he chuckled, "The first time we met, I don't know, I guess it was love at first sight or something, but no-one has ever had that impression on me,"

"Aww, you're just a big softy hey," she edged her body into his side and winked at him.

"Now you stop, Mrs. Cooper, don't go teasing your old husband."

They sat for a few minutes taking in the fresh air and listening to the birds chirping in the trees above them.

"This is nice Tom, I know it's a bit weird, but I do like to come here. I now understand why Jane did too. She came here so much during that last year. I used to think it wasn't good for her but from her letter and how she coped, I understand it so much more now," she sipped another mouthful of coffee feeling the warmth of it run through her body.

"Yes, I know what you mean. When James went, all I could think of to do was be here with him. I gave him a little fist bump and hello on the way in just now," he glanced across the way where he could see his brother's grave in the distance.

"That's sweet Tom, I forget sometimes that you've dealt with this before, sorry."

"Don't be silly, he knows the score," he replied, this time nudging her arm in jest.

"Jane knew about my past, Tom. About me getting pregnant, about Kate being adopted."

"Really?" he said, as he screwed up the now empty

paper bag and tucked it back into his pocket, "when did you find that out, I thought no-one knew?"

"Me too. You know her letter to me, the one I read this morning in bed? She wrote it in there, I couldn't believe what I was reading at first, I had to go over it twice more."

"Wow. How do you feel about that? The fact that she actually knew all along?"

"Well, to say I am utterly shocked is an understatement but Jane was Jane so I shouldn't be surprised really, I guess. She never said a bad word about anyone, never pried into people's business. I feel a bit, well, I feel quite a lot of guilt for not confiding in her, but she said she understood my reasons and respected them. Man, I miss her and our friendship," she said, her chest suddenly feeling painful with sadness.

Tom moved closer to her and put his arm around her shoulders. He knew she was getting upset and needed that extra reassurance that he always tried to give her.

"Why didn't I just bloody tell her Tom?" she said angrily, "I should have just told her, of all the people I could have shared my sordid secret with, it should have been her."

"Don't beat yourself up about it, like you said, she understood your reasons as do I, you are, and have to be allowed to forgive yourself babe," he rubbed her arm gently up and down, "you need to try and let go of these negative thoughts and stop punishing this beautiful soul that you have, things happened, you made choices, it's the past now, there's no looking back with what ifs and buts. I could say the same about James, if I had just gone over sooner, he might still be here today, but you can't do that okay sweetheart?"

She laid her head on his shoulder, knowing he was right, yet again. She did have to stop being so negative about the choices she had made and what had happened to her over the years. Losing her parents, grandparents, Jane, Katie, and now the baby that she never thought she would even carry had tormented her brain into thinking that she deserved all this sadness and painful chapters. The big thing was that she didn't deserve any of it and he was right, things do happen that are out of your control sometimes and she had to build herself back up. The only way she knew how was to do as Tom suggested, stop thinking negatively and stop punishing herself. All these events had been out of her hands and as much as she hated every single one of them for happening, she had to forgive life and the journey it had so far taken her on. She had Tom, their crazy four dogs and of course Karl and the kids to help build her up and keep her strong. Albert was another positive aspect of their lives too and she was determined that this meant the start of new and exciting times for all of them.

"I love you Mr. Cooper," she looked up to her husband and kissed him gently on his chin.

"Ditto right back at ya, Mrs. Cooper," he replied, kissing her head.

Chapter Twenty-Eight

The following Monday, Sarah decided to return to work. She had neglected the business for weeks it seemed, but the girls had been holding the fort and taking care of it with no problems at all. Although she felt nervous about going back, there was no need and she fell straight back into the swing of things in a matter of minutes. Clients were booked in back-to-back in the busy run up to Christmas. The girls had even learnt more designs in nail art for those clients who wanted Christmas themed nails.

Tina had taken charge of decorating at the beginning of December, and it looked stunning as usual with a few extra fun touches this year of the Elf on the shelf. The girls had had a field day putting him in various predicaments to make the customers laugh. Cards and gifts rolled in each time a client arrived and before long, the pile under their little Christmas tree was huge.

It felt so good to be there doing what she loved with her beauty treatments and seeing her regular customers again after the weeks she had been through was cheering her up no end. She was also loving all the banter with the girls that she'd missed too.

Laila and Shelly had turned twenty-five so had lots of photos to show Sarah of their birthday holiday celebrations in Ibiza. '*Oh, to be that young again*' Sarah thought to herself as she browsed through the snaps on Shelly's phone. Laila had met a guy over there, so she was then excitedly telling her all about him and when they were going to meet up again in London. Shelly's girlfriend of six months had sprung a big surprise. At the top of the London eye, she had proposed on their weekend back after the holiday, so she was already becoming obsessed with wedding plans.

"Wow, I remember planning our wedding. Seems like forever ago though and there's so much more available now isn't there?" Tina said to Shelly as they gazed at beautiful wedding gowns in one of the many bridal magazines that she had just brought from the newsagents next door.

"Yes, it's mind blowing to say the least, but I can't wait, Meg has said I can plan whatever I want, her father is quite well off, works for Apple in New York most of the year. Anyway, he has said he wants to pay for everything," she continued, "I'm not sure whether to accept, you know, being an independent chick and all that," she giggled, nudging Sarah's arm, "Meg really wants it in New York, you know, for the actual ceremony. Imagine that? Married in the big city," she shrieked, excitedly, throwing her arms up as though she could see the big city lights in front of her.

Sarah stood back for a moment watching her fabulous staff all chatting and laughing together. It was so nice to be back in this cheerful atmosphere, just what she needed right now. She had missed these times and with it being Christmas too, the whole environment was a happy one with great people. But for now, she needed to open for the day as clients would soon be knocking at the door to get their dose of beauty, so it was time to crack on.

"Right ladies, I guess we better get to work now," exclaimed Sarah as she finished up her morning coffee and unlocked the front door, "I've missed you lot," she said, turning to face them all but they were running around, busily preparing their stations for their first clients to arrive. Sarah chuckled to herself and smiled. She was back where she belonged and ready to face the new week ahead.

~

"Phew!" she said as she plonked herself on the sofa in the staff room. It was only a tiny room with enough space for a two-seater sofa and a coffee table, but it was a nice little area to chill out and have a quick caffeine boost in between clients.

Tina had just sat down too and was scrolling through her phone, catching up on her social media role and sharing the morning's client treatments. "I can't get to grips with the Tiktok thing, do you know anything about it?"

"God no! I'm useless with it all. I can just about manage to post a few Instagram things and always forget about using the hashtag thing on them," Sarah replied watching Tina getting a growing confused look on her face.

"Urgh...think I'll leave that one for now then, look at these lashes Laila did earlier," Tina passed her phone across, "she's so good at them now, isn't she? That training we sent them on has really paid off."

"Yeah, they're both coming on so well. They'll be wanting the next stages soon, I guess. We will have to see what's available for them. Anyway, how are things with you now Tina?" Sarah asked, dipping a chocolate biscuit into her mug of coffee.

"Oh, you know, same old, same old, nothing much changed in that department sweetie," she replied, sipping on her honey and lemon cup of tea. It smelt so strong, and Sarah often wondered how she drank it.

"Are you dating or anything yet?"

"God no. I think I'm done with men for good after marrying Ben and all his shenanigans. Hell no, the last thing I wanna do right now is start all that dating nonsense and at my age Sarah," she laughed, "Ooh no."

The mention of his name echoed through Sarah's ears, making her unconsciously take a deep breath. But, although she had this reaction, it was different now to before. Her new attitude and view on coping with the past and the memories that they brought, meant that she dealt with the feelings much better these days. She and Ben had made their closure that day. They said their final goodbyes at the skate park, and she felt content with it all. It didn't change the fact that she still had some feelings there, just not hate or regret now, "Sorry, I didn't mean to pry into your personal life," she apologised, "sorry," she repeated, feeling rude for asking.

"It's okay sweetie," Tina replied, playfully rubbing Sarah's leg, "pry all you like honey, but I can assure you, it's going to be boring," she giggled again turning off her phone and placing it on the sofa arm beside her, "as you mention it, talking of my husband, the tyrant that he is. Well, actually, he messaged me at the weekend. He's not been feeling too good, he thinks he may have some depression. To be honest, I think losing the daughter that he didn't know he had, you know, in that way, really hit him hard. He's been drinking like crazy most nights and he's back to smoking that weed stuff too," she pushed her cup further onto the coffee table, "He's a mess basically. I mean, I feel so bad for not going with him to Germany now. We made vows for better or worse and all that jazz, but it just wasn't the same in those last few months, we weren't really clicking for some reason, you know what I mean?" she leant forward, taking a biscuit from the wrapper, dunked it into her tea, and swiftly took a bite before it melted.

Sarah just stayed silent, nodding. Tina obviously needed to unload this information on someone, and she felt it right that she should just listen.

"I sometimes wonder if he'd been seeing someone else in those last few weeks before he left. He had cheated on me in the early days of our relationship, more than once actually. I suppose we could've worked things out, started a new life over there," she mumbled as the biscuit crumbled in her mouth, "but, oh I don't know, life's too short isn't it. To stay with someone just because of the marriage vows you made together, when you both know there's, no love left anymore, no, I couldn't do it. And plus, I blooming love it here. I have my job in this wonderful establishment," she smiled and winked at Sarah, "super-gorgeous friends, and my parents need me here. I guess I'll just mosey along and be a friend for him when I can. That's all I can do with our relationship now Sarah."

"That sounds like the best idea Tina," Sarah watched her and felt sad that her marriage had broken down and she had been part of that secrecy with him. She would hate for her to ever find out that she was in fact the mother to his child. Turning her thoughts to him once more and the fact that he wasn't doing good made her remember that she had deleted him as a contact on her phone. In some weird way, she now wished that she had kept it stored so at least she could message him, knowing now how bad he was suffering with everything that had happened. Maybe it wouldn't be so bad, just one text to say hi from her would help him cope a bit better? No, she couldn't do that, her and Tom were what mattered now, it was their future she had to focus on. Shaking the crazy, random thoughts about her ex out of her head, she replied, "just being there for someone is all they need sometimes, you know, on the end of the phone," she smiled at Tina who was now finished drinking her tea and wiping the crumbs that had fallen onto her lap, "just messaging them every few days to check in on a person, can be all that's needed for some people."

"Yep, exactly and that's what I've been doing, just weekly messages unless he contacts me. I'll always be there for him. I mean I married the guy; we did have some good times over the years," she chuckled, shrugging her shoulders, "anyway, that's enough about my doomed marriage and the woes that it's festered. I've got my next nail client in a few minutes. She wants Christmas trees on them, so I had best get my station ready, I don't want the boss sacking me hey?" she nudged Sarah's arm playfully as she got up and left the room whistling along to the Christmas tune that was playing on the radio.

Tina had been so brave and supportive to Ben throughout everything, trying her hardest to be a good wife and she had succeeded. Sarah thought back to the evening when she had turned up at the house distraught about him having a secret child turn up. She'd been so upset but mastered on and Sarah admired her strength. Unfortunately, it wasn't meant to last for them. Tina was such a kind and forgiving person, but Sarah wasn't going to risk telling her the truth. Some secrets were best kept hidden. She and Ben had agreed to keep that information to themselves, and Sarah was confident after their last conversation that he would keep that promise. She just hoped that over time, he would be okay, just like Tina was moving on, he should too at some point.

She decided to send a quick text to Tom just to say she loved him and stuck three love heart emojis at the end. She felt so lucky to have him, every day seemed to get better even after all that had gone on lately and she couldn't wait to get home later and spend the evening together. But her work claimed her duties for now. Two more clients to create luscious hybrid lashes, one final eyebrow wax and tint, then she would be finished for the day and ready to get home to relax with her man and her gorgeous four dogs. Maybe even grab a few bottles of wine and their favourite chocolate bars on the way home.

~

The next few hours flew by with all the girls busy with clients. Christmas was fast approaching, and everyone wanted to get all their treatments done in time for the festive season. Sarah and Tina had come up with various beauty packages and they were selling out every day.

"Have a lovely Christmas Anni and say hi to Oliver for me," Sarah said as she walked to the front of the salon with her fourth lash and brow client of the day.

"I will Sarah, you too, and thank you so much for fitting me in at short notice."

"No problem at all, here, take a few choccies with you," Sarah passed the glass bowl of sweets that they had filled for the customers. The girls, including Sarah herself kept picking at them each time they came up to the desk and needed them gone before they shut for Christmas, "I'm sure Oliver won't turn them down." she laughed.

"No, he's a bigger chocoholic than I am," Anni chuckled, "see you in the new year, bye girls," she waved as she left.

Just as the door closed, it opened again immediately after, and a lady appeared. Sarah glanced back as she had started to make her way back into the staff room to make a fresh brew for everyone. Within seconds, her heart began to pulsate harder at the sight in the doorway of her salon. Slow motion movements and complete silence seemed to fill the building. Today had been going so smoothly up until this moment and it took a minute for Sarah to move. Swiftly making her way back to the front before any of the other girls noticed, the voice spoke.

"Hello Sarah, how are you?"

Chapter Twenty-Nine

The lady stood there motionless for a few seconds, waiting for a reaction from Sarah who had fallen silent at the sight of her.

"I hope you don't mind me imposing on you like this. You know, turning up at your workplace unannounced. I just needed to see you, just for half an hour or something, if you aren't too busy. I can come another day if it's better for you," she softly asked, almost babbling.

Blankly, Sarah seemed frozen to the spot unable to summon words, "No," she finally mustered up, "not at all. It's lovely to see you again, is everything okay?" suddenly realising who it was standing there in her salon.

"Yes, yes," she replied, shuffling awkwardly on her feet, "it's just, well, could we have a few moments to chat? Is it convenient now for you? It's just, well I was passing, well no that's not true," she paused to take a breath, "Sorry Sarah, I'm not making this clear, am I? I am a bit of a blubbery mess."

"Do you need me to book this lady in Sarah?" asked Shelly who had approached the welcome desk.

"Erm, no. Thanks Shelly, I just need to pop out for a bit, can you cover the desk for me?" Sarah said anxiously. She hadn't mentioned anything to the girls at work about everything that had happened over the past few months, and she wasn't keen for them to start asking questions or getting suspicious. It was just a lady enquiring at the desk so why would they? But she couldn't take the chance, "my next client cancelled so I'm okay for an hour, let Tina know for me please, I think she's nipped to the loo," and she grabbed her bag and ushered the lady outside, "we can go to the little seating area across the way," she pointed, "sorry but it's better to not discuss personal stuff at my work, is that okay?"

"Yes of course, I understand, that's absolutely fine."

Sarah glanced at her face, she seemed quite breathless and weak, "are you okay to walk over there?" she asked, concerned.

"Oh yes, I'll explain when we get to sit down. I'm just a little slow these days."

When they eventually reached the grassed area, and found a bench, there was a brief silence while she got her breath back and then began routing through a large bag, she had with her.

Sarah was feeling worried, her heart thumping wildly

through her chest. She was anxious about what might come out of that bag and wondered what the reason was that she was here at all in the first place. The last time they had seen each other was at Kate's funeral and that was only for a few minutes with both not being in any fit state to sit and chat.

Twiddling her fingers, Sarah noticed a small coffee van, "Do you want a coffee or tea from there?" she asked, pointing to the cute little vintage styled mobile vehicle that was parked up close by. She was really trying to kill some time as she seemed to be taking ages to arrange the things in the bag.

"Erm," she glanced up and across the grass, "maybe a nice hot cup of tea, yes, that's kind of you Sarah, thank you, oh and could you see if they have anything sweet like a biscuit or something, my diabetes is giving me so many issues this morning and I forgot to pack my normal choccy bar."

"No problem," Sarah replied as she stood up and began to walk over to the van. Buzzing thoughts ran through her mind again as to why this was happening and why this lady was here today. What was so important that she needed to turn up at her work too? She didn't think there would be any further contact after the funeral. She had just about managed to come to terms with the fact that Kate was gone and then after her miscarriage, she didn't think she could cope with any more surprises or stress this year. She looked over at the bench while the drinks were being prepared. Trying desperately to remember her name, it finally came to her, and she was so relieved. Her brain was working overtime and it had just drawn a blank when she'd seen her enter the salon, "here you go Sally," she confidently said as she passed the paper cup of tea, "they only had this cake bar though, is that alright for you or I can nip over to that shop and get you something else a bit more chocolaty?"

"No, no, that's fine, thank you," she took the cake and immediately began opening it, "bloody diabetes, I tell you, it's a nightmare sometimes but," she paused as she took a bite, "mmm, that's lovely," she said, slightly mumbling as the food turned to dust in her mouth as she ate it so quickly, "thank you again Sarah, what do I owe you?"

"Oh, don't worry, it's on me, as long as you feel better."

"So," she said in between the final few bites, "you are probably wondering what I'm doing here aren't you?"

Sarah nodded as their eyes met.

Taking a final bite and then slurping on her tea, she replied, "as you know, I was Kate's aunt. After her mum...you know adoptive mum..." she placed her hand on Sarah's knee as if to apologise for saying the word mum. As if it seemed inappropriate in front of Kate's biological mother.

"It's okay, I know what you mean," As much as it hurt, Sarah knew that Fiona had been the one Kate called mum for all those years so it was only fair that she still had that privilege. She only got to be 'mum' for a few hours before the accident. A few hours that were now so extra special and had a place in her heart forever.

"Right, ok, well, Fiona, asked me to take care of some business for her if anything happened to Kate so," she reached across to the small red shoe box that was now placed beside her, "before my sister died, she said that she wanted Kate to find her birth mother when the inevitable happened to her. She knew she didn't have long, god rest her soul," she paused as she took a breath and another sip of her drink, "I know she found you and how awful it was that you only got a day together before Kate," she stopped again, tears welling up in her eyes and her chin began to quiver.

Sarah reached across this time to comfort her with a hand touch to her leg. This poor lady had not only lost her sister suddenly, but she had also lost her niece who she had cared for over so many years, basically bringing her up during her teens and into her twenties, "Are you okay?" Sarah asked.

Blowing out a breath, Sally replied with a shaky voice, "yes, yes. Give me a second," she took a final gulp of tea and placed it to the back of the bench, "right, now here is the reason I needed to see you today," she passed the box placing it into Sarah's lap, "this little box was put together by my sister for Kate when she reached thirty but, as you know, the poor mite didn't quite get there so...I wanted you to have it."

Sarah glanced down at the box.

"You don't have to look in it now if you don't want to, but I have gone through it and it's all the things to do with

Kate's adoption, birth, first photos and things like that. Fiona was adamant that if Kate ever found you, this box should be shared with you."

"I, I don't know what to say Sally, that's, well, that's incredible and so lovely of you to think of me...to do this, I, I seriously don't know what to say," she stammered, emotionally charged with sadness but happiness at the same time, "thank you."

"My pleasure Sarah. I hope it will bring you some comfort in knowing that she really did have a great childhood. My sister loved her so deeply, she was her life, but she always kept little reminders so that one day, Kate would know the truth."

Sarah was still staring at the box, and she placed her hand over the top where Kate's name had been written. It was childlike writing as though she had written it herself.

"Fiona got Kate to decorate the lid before she put anything it so that it was even more personal."

A tear fell from Sarah's eye onto the lid of the box where she quickly wiped it dry. She couldn't quite believe what and why she was being able to have this type of gift. Never thinking she deserved any memories except the few hours that she'd had after she was born. That moment in the hospital when she got to hold her for a while. Those minutes were precious but only in her mind so to have even more now, meant the world and she couldn't help but cry, "I'm sorry," she said as she wiped her eyes with a tissue from her pocket, "This is so nice," she lifted the lid slowly and just smiled at the contents inside, "I will have a proper look when I get home but again, thank you so much, I will treasure this forever."

"That's good to hear. I'm glad you are pleased. I didn't know how you may react but it's good, it's great actually," she smiled at Sarah and held her hand, "You may not know this, but Kate had a bit of a rough time in the few years before she left us," she paused, "she got with someone who turned out to be, well…let's just say," she raised her eyebrows as Sarah looked at her, "he wasn't the right person for her and me and her uncle felt so responsible. It's too long a story to go into but we got it all sorted and that's when we decided she should know the truth and be able to make her own choices as to if and when she wanted to find you and her real father."

"Oh, I didn't know about that, but we didn't really have a chance to talk about all the years that had passed. She did say she hadn't found the one yet after just breaking up with someone, maybe she was referring to that, to him, do you think?"

"Yes, I would imagine that would be it, he really was trouble for her and she had totally fallen for him, like us women do sometimes hey?" she chuckled, nudging Sarah's arm, "Anyway, I really must go now, I have an appointment at the opticians in an hour and it's all the way across town from here, I need to get that bus," she pointed towards the road where the bus stop was, "Sarah, it's been lovely to sit and chat with you. Ben was right when he said what a beautiful person you were."

Sarah's eyes widened at the name and what he must

have said about her to Sally. In her heart, although she was glad he was gone, she still had feelings down there somewhere for him. At the end of the day, their history was part of her life, and they had both lost Kate. Both lost her twice even.

Sally continued, "Please do keep in touch if you'd like to but I understand if it's not appropriate or you'd rather just forget it all. I've put my number on a card here just in case you need to ask me any questions about anything. I mean it Sarah," she stood up slowly, "Kate was a very special part of my life, and we knew each other inside out. So, the offer is there, anytime you want, or need a chat about her and her childhood, or anything else for that matter, it would be nice to stay connected somehow to Kate by knowing you. The number is there whenever you feel like, if ever you want to, obviously."

Sarah placed the special box onto the bench beside her and stood up next to Sally, who was gathering her coat and the remains of her bag together. She felt compelled to hug this wonderful lady so gently wrapped her arms around her. The embrace continued for around ten seconds although it seemed longer and then they said their goodbyes and Sarah watched Sally walk off towards the bus stop on the other side of the grassed area. What a beautiful, kind woman and how hard it must have been to let these cherished items leave her side. She vowed right then to keep in touch with her, it would be lovely to see even more photos of Kate's life before she was sadly taken from them.

She gathered up her box, threw the empty paper cups into the nearby bin and slowly made her way back to the salon, swiftly grabbing one of their paper bags from under the desk to wrap the box in.

"Everything alright boss?" asked Tina, appearing suddenly as Sarah folded the bag back on itself to hide the contents.

Jumping slightly with nervousness more than anything, Sarah replied, "Oh, you made me jump, yes all good here, just a little gift for the hubby, you know," she winked, smiling awkwardly, hoping she wouldn't ask to see what was in the bag, "Do I have any more clients this afternoon? I've lost track of them today. I'm thinking I may pop off early and meet Tom from work."

"Let me just look," Tina replied as she checked the diary on the front desk, "There's a wax and tint appointment at four but I can do it if you like? It's Caroline from the gym I go to so I could have a good old chinwag and catch up with her," she laughed, "You get off, go meet that luscious husband of yours," she joked, nudging Sarah's arm, "you deserve an early one for a change."

"Cheers Tina, you are funny, thanks, see you tomorrow girls," Sarah called, as she got her coat and bags from the office and made her way to meet Tom.

~

"So yeah, she gave me all of this Tom, look at it," Sarah said, sifting through the box of photos and hand drawn pictures, "Such precious memories that I never thought I would experience or witness."

"That's such a thoughtful thing for her to do," Tom replied, taking out a picture of what he thought must have been a dog. He turned it sideways and tilted his head, "this is cute, ha-ha, I think it's a dog or maybe a bear?" he laughed, passing it to Sarah.

She had gone to meet him at his work, and they'd decided to collect the dogs and walk to their favourite spot in the park. Sitting on the bench while the dogs played with the 'bubble lady' as Albert called her, they cherished the time to have these images sink in. All the time, Sarah remembered what a beautiful person Kate had been and with so much love in her heart to forgive Sarah for giving her away. She wished every day that they had been given more time together, more years to form a relationship but she understood that things happen for a reason. Maybe the reason so many people were taken from her life was a lesson to appreciate things and not hold grudges against herself. Her mind wandered time and time again, swaying between the positive and negative but she had this little box now and she was over the moon with it. It would be a constant reminder for her that she made a mistake, but it was okay. She didn't have to punish herself anymore.

Chapter Thirty

So, there you are. My crazy, manic, very sad year was done and dusted. My secret was told, my heart shattered but I've done it. I survived that turmoil.

I'm Sarah Cooper, hi.

As the years rolled by, my life did gradually get back on track, finally. I'm heading slowly towards the grand old age of fifty now and it's been a smoother ride for the past ten years thank goodness. Business is still booming, I'm happily married to my soul mate, and I have had the pleasure of being able to watch my best friends' children grow up and flourish and become beautiful adults.

Cassie and Robbie: What do I say about these two? Jane would've been so proud of them and what they've become. I love them both dearly. Cassie is fighting the fight against cancer with all her charity work and training to become a Macmillan nurse was a major goal for her where her career was concerned. She hates the c-word with a passion and her vitality for helping people at one of the most stressful and delicate times of their lives is incredible. Robbie is married to his college sweetheart and are now five months into their first pregnancy. He has asked me to be the godmother which blew my mind and of course I agreed to, no question. I cannot wait to spoil that baby and be the best godmother possible.

Karl: Mr. Walden, one of the strongest and kindest men I have ever had the privilege to know. I love him so much, he's just like the big brother I never had as a child and our weekends together are awesome. He's always been there for me since Jane left us and I'm glad I could be there to help him through it too. Our friendship grows stronger year on year, and we always celebrate the birthdays and anniversaries that he misses with Jane. My constant moaning and nagging about getting him together with someone have finally paid off and I set him up with one of Tom's work colleagues. She's a nurse at the hospital and there's only a few years age difference between them. They've been seeing each other every week and I'm so happy for him. He keeps promising me that it won't turn into anything serious, but I see the way he looks at her when the four of us have been out for dinner. Maybe he thinks Jane wouldn't approve, maybe he thinks the kids wouldn't allow another woman into their lives. I know that he had the conversation about him moving on and the children are so grown up, they would welcome her in I'm sure of it. I keep a check on him and always reassure him it's okay for him to have these feelings. Hopefully one day, he will realise that.

Albert: This little boy who entered our life out of the blue is still super cute in adulthood and he sees Tom regularly. It has been so lovely to be able to watch Tom and his nephew bonding. As he grew older, they would sit down and look at the many photographs of James and Tom reveled in the process. Telling him all their childhood stories and adventures that they'd had themselves as little boys and Albert loved learning about his dad. He looks the absolute image of James too, it's uncanny.

Ben: I've never heard from him again since that day we said goodbye. Tina mentions him occasionally and I'm happy in the knowledge that he's doing much better than he was early on after leaving for Germany. She has visited him a few times but doesn't say too much on her return. I honestly wish him the best with whatever he decided to do. The hard feelings and regret that I had with him have now all faded into the background. We went through some sad times together, some things that will never leave this little brain of mine but it's the past and that's where he shall stay.

The Salon: My work is so important to me and although I've been reducing my hours there, I still love it so much and the staff I have are amazing. Within a few years after I was back at work full time, we were able to extend the premises too as next-door became available. It's been an amazing time for the business and lovely to have four new members of the team join us over the past year or so. I had a bit of a rebrand two years ago and named it Beauty Angels after a favourite Robbie Williams tune, Angels. Jane would have loved that.

Tom: My darling, adorable, supportive, and rather gorgeous husband, what more can I say about him? I just don't know where to start apart from the fact that he has been my absolute rock throughout everything and I'm grateful each and every day that he continues to be in my life. We decided not to go on the adoption route for a few reasons really. It took me a while to mentally come to terms with all my loss of Kate and our baby that never was. We both felt we were content enough with each other and the dogs. Sometimes I wonder if Tom regrets the choice, we made but he has never said anything to confirm my thoughts. I think having Albert to concentrate on over the years has helped.

Elvis: My beloved Elvis died a good while ago now and after his cremation, we buried him in the garden with his special blanket. He had gone to sleep one evening wrapped up in it as usual and never woke up, so I didn't want to take it from him. He was such a loving, loyal dog, bless him. Tom arrived home a year later with a puppy sausage dog for my birthday, and he looked just like Elvis. I cried like a bloody baby when I saw him, we called him King.

Katie-Jane: I still think of her every day and my heart will never quite heal completely for losing her like we did. I have never been able to fully forgive myself for the early stages of her life. Giving her up and not having any contact with her until she found me. It's just not as easy to forgive myself for that. Her memory box that I was given is something I will always treasure, and I have it wrapped up in the top of our wardrobe. Occasionally, I will look through it and smile, sometimes weep for the girl I lost so suddenly but, it's also a life we celebrate. She was beautiful, kind, and so forgiving and I will always have the fond memory of the very short day we spent together. She was the final piece of the puzzle, my daughter Katie-Jane. And as much as I want to say I'm sorry to her, I know that she would tell me again, just like she did that day we first met properly, to not be sorry and that means the world to me. Even this many years on, I hear her words in my head, telling me not to blame myself for trying to do the right thing by her. What a super special human being she was, and I feel proud to have created her and nurtured her in my tummy even knowing how hard it was going to be.

Jane: This woman, my very best friend, is one I still miss so much. We still have our chats when I visit her grave and there's always some sign that she's with me, albeit a butterfly flapping around nearby or the little robin that seems to get closer each time I go. The pain and agony she went through to try and protect us all was truly amazing, and I respect her fully for it. Over all the years we were friends, she never let on that she knew about my past, my secret and this makes me love her even more, which I never thought possible. She was an inspiration to me and my backbone when I lost my parents and then my grandparents. I will never forget that lady, never in a million years.

Me: So, this was my little story, my roller coaster life that I've managed to come through somehow. At times, I honestly felt like giving up, ending the sadness that I thought I couldn't cope with anymore but, I'm still here to tell the tale. Sometimes I wonder how but I know it's because of the people I still have with me. That's the reason I've become so much stronger rather than it all killing me and I'm thankful every day for them and what they've all done for me individually. I hit some very dark times and they pulled me through, sometimes when they didn't even realise they were doing so. What absolute gems I have, how lucky I feel.

If I've learnt anything during this manic, crazy life of mine, it's that nothing is forever, life is precious and sometimes cut so short so you should appreciate your time here and especially the people you love and have with you. Tell them regularly what they mean to you, love them, cherish them and be there when they need you to be.

Whatever situation arises, whatever life challenges you are set, take them head on, embrace the moments you have and above all, try to stay strong and resilient throughout anything in which you feel you cannot, because you can. You can do it.

We are all put here for a reason, some get longer than others and some are taken too soon. Those special ones can impact your life incredibly so again, cherish them, hug them. You never know when or if that last goodbye will be the end. That one last hug, one last conversation, one last time to hold their hand, make it count.

To all those that were part of my life, for no matter how long you were in it, just know, you have all gained a special piece in my once very fragile heart and I love you all dearly.

My life has been mind-bending at times, full of twists, turns and seriously high-end challenges for one person. I tried to face and cope with it all the best way I could, and I guess still being here means I pulled through.

One piece of the jigsaw which I never imagined could be put back did get its place. Katie-Jane came back into my life. She will always now be the beautiful butterfly who flew in so gracefully and completed the puzzle.

My broken heart will never quite be whole again, but I am thankful for what it's been through, and the best thing is…

I have no more Secrets & Lies.

Enjoyed This Book

If you enjoyed this book, please take a few minutes to review it on Amazon as that will help even more readers find and enjoy Secrets & Lies.

Simply go to Amazon, search for 'Secrets & Lies' and click the number next to the review stars to write your own customer review.

x Thank you so much x

Other Books By Me

Reasonable Lies. Released March 2020.

Jane's Journal. Released August 2021.

About The Author

Traci writes under the pen name T.A. Rosewood, and this is her third book.

Writing her first 'book' at age thirteen, in a school textbook, Traci has always dreamt of having a real book and loved the idea of publishing her own novel one day.

Her dream came true, after meeting and being inspired by best-selling author, Jojo Moyes in their local bookstore. That one evening changed the course of things when she wrote and then released her debut novel in March 2020 called, 'Reasonable Lies'.

After creating her own Instagram virtual book tour, she wrote her second book using the feedback from the readers about Reasonable Lies. This was in the form of a short novella, called, 'Jane's Journal' which was released in August 2021 as a follow-on book.

Traci lives in North Essex with her husband, children and two west highland terriers.

Come Say Hi

I really love hearing from readers,
and seeing posts come up about my books,
so please come and say hello, tag me on
Instagram, Facebook, or Twitter:
@TARosewood
using the hashtags
#tarosewood or #secretsandlies.

Let's keep in touch.
For more bookish news, updates,
book signing events, giveaways, book tours,
and competitions,
please visit my website:
tarosewood.com

Acknowledgments

As always & forever, huge thanks go to my husband, Leonardo. I truly don't know what I'd do without your love and support and above all, your patience. Love you Fifty Hundred Word Files.

My beta readers – you have been so helpful with this project, and I thank each one of you for taking the time out to proofread, advise on the storyline and for giving me such useful feedback to help me produce the final book.

My children – well…just for being blooming amazing.

My Instagram followers – too many to mention in here but you all know who you are, and I thank you from the bottom of my heart for the amazing support you give me over there.

And finally, to you – the person reading this. Thank you so much for taking a chance on this book.

THANK YOU.

Printed in Great Britain
by Amazon